MW00465550

CHRISTMAS TEXAS BRIDE
THE BRIDES OF BLISS TEXAS, BOOK 4

Printed in the USA.

Cover Design and Interior Format

Christmas Texas Bride

The Brides of Bliss Texas—Book 4

KATIE LANE

To my beloved readers,
this book and all my books are written for you

CHAPTER ONE

"I'M NEVER HAVIN' S-E-X."

Cord Evans almost choked to death on his own spit. After he finished coughing, he glanced over at the little blond-headed girl who perched on his brand new fence. Carrie Anne Buchanan's face was serious and her hazel eyes were intense. Since the last thing he wanted to do was get into the can of worms she'd just opened, he kept his mouth shut and went back to spreading the load of coarse sand in his new corral. He hoped she would get the hint and move onto a more appropriate subject. But he was learning that six-year-old little girls rarely did what you hoped they would.

"Do you know what S-E-X is?" she asked.

Cord knew. In his heyday, he'd been quite the ladies' man. Every town he'd traveled to had been filled with women wanting to take a ride with a real-life rodeo cowboy. And he'd always been happy to oblige. He'd been to bed with so many women that he couldn't remember their names or their faces. Or maybe he couldn't remember because he'd always been drunk off his ass. When he'd finally given up the bottle and realized what a shit-fest he'd made of his life, sex was the last thing he worried about.

He continued to smooth out the sand and tried to change the subject. "How was school today, Half Pint?"

"Okay. We got to draw a picture and talk about what we did on Thanksgiving break and I drew a mag-nif-a-cent picture of a wedding and told everyone about Coach Murdoch and Autumn getting married and about how I got to drink Sprite from a champagne glass when we made a toast and how I catched the bouquet and now I gotta get married." She paused for a quick breath. "And my friend Becky asked who I was gonna marry, but I didn't tell her 'cause my grandma—God bless her soul—said that sometimes girls need to have their secrets. But I did tell Becky that it wasn't gonna be a deadbeat like my daddy. 'Cause we Buchanan women are through with deadbeats."

He cringed. According to what he could piece together, Carrie Anne's father had been a rodeo bum like Cord. And like Cord, he'd chosen horses and bulls over his wife and kid. It was a bad choice, one Cord regretted and wished he could fix. Unfortunately, as much as he might want to, he couldn't go back. His first wife had divorced him long ago and was now happily remarried. And his only son was grown, married, and starting his own family. Cord could only hope that he'd be part of that family. Which was exactly why he'd moved here to Bliss, Texas.

"I'm sorry about your daddy, Carrie Anne. Sometimes daddies are just lost and think that running from their responsibilities is the way to be found. But running just makes you tired and even more lost. Hopefully, your daddy will figure that out like I did."

Carrie Anne scrunched her face in thought. "Mama says that once a deadbeat always a deadbeat." Which probably explained why Carrie Anne's mother didn't care for Cord. She was always polite, but more than once he'd caught her looking at him like he was a cockroach she'd like to crush under her boot heel. Thankfully, her daughter didn't feel the same way. She flashed a bright smile. "But now that I know you, I think my mama's wrong."

He winked at her. "Thank you for the vote of confidence, ma'am." He went back to raking. "So what else did you do in school?"

"We had a snack and went to recess where Jonas Murphy chased me on the playground and told me that he'd marry me. That's when he told me about S-E-X. He said that husbands and wives do it at night in the dark when all their kids are sleeping. He found out about it 'cause he woke up one time and heard his mama moaning like she was in pain. And when he woke up his big brother, his brother said, 'They're just havin' S-E-X, stupid. Go back to sleep.' And I figure if something made his mama moan out in pain that it can't be fun, so that's why I ain't doin' it never with my husband." She paused and when he glanced over, she gave him another bright smile. "And I just wanted you to know."

Cord continued raking. On one hand, he was relieved that she didn't know the particulars of sex, but on the other, he was annoyed at Jonas and his big brother for tarnishing her innocence even as much as they had. Carrie Anne was a sweet little thing whom Cord had gotten quite attached to since her mother had started working for him. She followed him around like a little lost lamb, and damned if he didn't feel protective of her.

"Jonas Murphy, huh?" he said. "And he's in your class at school?"

"He's six like me, but he's not in Mrs. Trammel's class. He's in Miss Jules. I wish I had Miss Jules 'cause she's nice. Mrs. Trammel is a meanie. She talked with Mama and told her that I need to get better at reading because I don't sound out words I just make them up. I don't make them up. I look at the pictures and tell a story, and that's exactly what reading is. But now mama feels all bad 'cause she drugged me all over the countryside this summer and didn't teach me enough phone-tics."

He had to bite back his laughter. "Your mama shouldn't feel bad. I'm sure you'll figure out phonics soon enough. It's pretty easy. Every letter has a sound. Once you remember each letter's sound, you can sound out a word. C-A-T spells cat." He said the word slower, enunciating each sound. "Do you hear the three different sounds that come together to form the word?"

"CCC-aaa-ttt," she mimicked.

As he continued to rake, he gave her a few more examples of three-letter words and sounded them out for her. After she finished sounding out the word bat, there was a long pause. "So what does S-E-X spell?"

Cord mentally cussed himself for walking right into that trap. Thankfully, before he had to figure a way out of it, her mama showed up.

Christie Buchanan was a good-looking woman. She had pretty hazel eyes that were greener than her daughter's and wheat-colored hair that she kept in a braid that hung all the way down to her butt. She was petite and couldn't weigh much more than a hundred-pound sack of feed. But he'd come to realize that inside the small package was the heart of a tiger. And he had to confess that he was a little scared of her. Which was complete nonsense seeing how she was closer to his son's age than his.

"What are you two up to?" She asked as she rested her arms on the fence next to Carrie Anne.

Before he could say a word, Carrie Anne jumped in. "Me and Cord was just talkin' about S-E-X."

He cringed. Oh boy. This wasn't going to be good.

Christie's eyes flashed fire, and he watched her hands grip the fence railing as if she was about to vault over it and rip him to shreds. Before she could, he held up a hand.

"Now, Christie, it's not how it sounds." He looked at Carrie Anne. "Why don't you run into the barn and give Maple a treat? When I was talking with her this morning, she told me how much she was looking forward to seeing you after school."

Carrie Anne sprang down from the fence, her tattered tennis shoes sinking into the thick sand. "See, Mama, I told you that horses can talk. They talk to Cord all the time. And he said when I become better at listening, they'll talk to me too." She looked at Cord as if he were the best thing since Cracker Jacks.

It had been a long time since he'd gotten that kind of adoration from a kid, and damned if it didn't make him feel ten feet tall. He reached out and ruffled her hair. "Horses do like listeners, but they don't mind talkers either. Just keep your voice low and soothing. And stay away from Raise-a-Ruckus. He's not ready for polite company just yet."

"Will do, Cord." She raced out of the corral.

When she was gone, Christie gave Cord the same look she always gave him. A look that knocked him down from ten feet to about two . . . inches. "Well, explain."

He leaned on the rake handle. "I was not talking about sex with Carrie Anne. In fact, I was trying my darnedest to avoid talking about it. But Carrie Anne isn't the type of little girl who lets you avoid anything. She's as headstrong as her mama."

"I'm not headstrong." Christie's brow crinkled. "If she didn't learn the word from you, where did she learn it?"

"From a little boy at her school."

Christie's eyes widened. "Oh my God."

Cord held up a hand. "Now before you go postal. All he told her is it's something a husband and wife do at night in the dark." He figured he could leave out the moaning part. This conversation was uncomfortable enough as is. "His older brother was the one who spelled the word out for him. I figure he's the one who needs a good talking to."

"Talking? He needs his ears boxed. And I plan to go up to the school first thing tomorrow morning and make sure the principal does something about it."

He leaned the rake against the fence. "Now I don't know if I'd do that. I think that might be pretty embarrassing for the parents to be called in front of the principal. I think it would be better if you talked with Jonas Murphy's mother yourself. I'm sure she'll handle it from there."

He thought his solution was a pretty damned good one, but Christie didn't agree. "Thank you for the advice, but Carrie Anne is my child and I'll deal with the situation as I see fit."

He wasn't surprised by the prickly response. He was learning that Christie Buchanan was one prickly woman. She reminded him of the abused filly he'd helped train when he was working at a ranch outside of Amarillo. The horse hadn't trusted any human to get too close. If you did, you got bit, kicked, or bucked off on your ass. It had taken Cord months of soothing talk and gentle handling to get the horse's trust. But it had been worth it. Best damned horse he'd ever worked with.

He handled Christie the same way he'd handled the horse. He kept his distance and his voice low and calm. "Of course she's your daughter. I was just trying to help."

"I don't need any help raising Carrie Anne. I can do it just fine on my own. I appreciate all you've done for me in the last couple months. I appreciate the job you gave me and I appreciate the loan to fix my car. But your kindness doesn't give you any rights to my daughter."

"Neither the job or the loan was a kindness," he said. "It was purely selfishness. I desperately needed someone to help me with my website and social media, and I didn't want to have to go pick her up if I needed her to come out here and take pictures of an old rodeo cowboy's"—he held up his hands and did quotation marks—"'ranch life.'" He lowered his hands. "So I didn't do you a favor. You did me one. But you're right. I don't have any business butting my nose into things that don't concern me. Especially where Carrie Anne is concerned. As everyone knows, I'm the worst father this side of the Pecos."

Her shoulders visibly relaxed and most of the fire left her eyes. "Believe me, you aren't the worst. You and Ryker seem to have a good relationship."

"I don't know if I'd call it good."

His son still hadn't completely forgiven him for deserting him. And Cord hadn't forgiven himself. Late at night, when he was lying on his blow-up mattress in the big ole empty ranch house he'd built, he thought about all those years he'd missed with his son. All the time he and Ryker could've shared as father and son. He wasn't a crying man, but he'd shed more than a few tears for those lost years. And what broke his heart even more was that he knew his son had too.

"I should've been there for Ryker when he was growing up," he said. "I should've been there to take him fishing and play catch . . . and just to talk to about important things like S-E-X."

A smile broke out on Christie's face. The only word that came to mind was *dazzling*. Christie had the kind of smile that lit up the world. It was a shame she didn't use it more often.

"S-E-X." She shook her head. "Good Lord. What's that child going to come up with next?" She paused and looked at Cord with those big hazel eyes. "I'm sorry for assuming the worst. I should've known better."

"Don't ever apologize for watching out for your daughter. Carrie Anne is lucky to have a mama like you."

"I don't know about that. Sometimes I feel like all I do is get after her. In case you haven't noticed, she's been quite a handful lately. I realize that her acting out has to do with starting a new school in a new town, but it doesn't make it any easier to deal with. And now that my babysitter, Mrs. Miller, has gone to spend the holidays with her kids and grandkids, I have to bring Carrie Anne to the bakery with me. I'm sure Summer isn't happy about having a six-year-old around."

When Christie wasn't helping him with social media, she worked at the Blissful Bakery in town. He thought she worked way too much, but he wasn't about to tell her that.

"Summer would tell you if she had a problem with you bringing Carrie Anne to the bakery. My daughter-in-law isn't the type to beat around the bush. But if you want, Carrie Anne could always hang out here. Besides the occasionally uncomfortable conversation topic, she doesn't cause me any problems."

She shook her head. "Thank you, but you've done enough for us. I'm sure I'll figure something out." She pulled a cellphone out of the back pocket of her jeans. "Right now, I need to get a couple pictures of you working on your corral for today's posts."

"You want to post a picture of me raking dirt?"

"Yes. The picture I took of you shoveling horse

manure got over twenty thousand likes on Instagram and even more on Facebook." When he looked shocked, she laughed. "I know. I don't get it either. For some reason, people like to see you getting dirty. Or maybe they just like to see that famous folks work just as hard as they do. Of course, you being shirtless in the last picture probably helped. Women love a hot cowboy with a nice, hard bod—" She cut off, and her cheeks flushed pink.

He felt a little flushed himself. Christie thought he was a hot cowboy with a nice body? Before he could even digest that piece of information, she quickly hurried through the gate of the corral. "Well, we better get that picture. Just go back to raking and act like I'm not—" The high heels of her city boots sank into the deep sand, and she stumbled. Her cellphone flew out of her hands and hit the ground, but before she could, Cord reached out and caught her.

It had been a long time since he'd held a woman. Too long. The libido he'd put into hibernation woke up like a hungry bear ready to feast. And what it wanted to feast on was the woman in his arms. She smelled like a mixture of ripe strawberries and fresh baked bread right out of the oven. Which didn't help his hunger. Nor did the soft breasts that pressed into his chest or the trim waist his hands could almost span. And when she lifted her head, he got lost in twin pastures of brilliant green and earthy brown that brought up thoughts of springtime and picnics . . . and rolling naked with a woman in fresh-cut grass.

"You were right, Cord!" Carrie Anne's voice

broke through his misbehaving thoughts. "Maple missed me." He quickly released Christie and stepped back just as Carrie Anne came tearing into the corral.

"And Raise-a-Ruckus missed me too," she crowed as she stopped between him and Christie. "When I went by his stall, he stuck out his head and grinned at me. Just like this." She bared her teeth. When neither Cord or her mother said anything, she looked between them. "What's wrong? Why are you both all red in the face? Are you still talking about S-E-X?"

They hadn't been talking about it.

But now Cord sure as hell was thinking about it.

CHAPTER TWO

"WHY DID WE HAVE TO leave Cord's so fast? I didn't even get to say goodbye to Maple and Raise-a-Ruckus." Carrie Anne kicked the back of Christie's seat. Usually, Christie got after her daughter for kicking the seat. Today, she had something else on her mind.

Like her own stupidity.

How could she have let Cord Evans know she thought he had a nice, hard body? Geez Louise! He probably thought she had been scoping him out for the last two months waiting to pounce on him. Or throw herself at him like she'd done in the corral. Damn her clumsiness. And damn her weakness for rodeo cowboys.

The moment his strong hands had closed around her waist and he'd pulled her flush against him, she'd been lost. Lost in the scent of fresh hay and wide-open countryside. Lost in the feel of a body honed by hours spent riding horses. There wasn't an ounce of fat on the man. Not one ounce. His arms had felt like coiled steel and his chest like a solid block of granite. And when all those hard spots had pressed against all her soft spots, she had been rodeo toast.

Which is exactly how she'd ended up in bed with Danny Ray. She just couldn't resist a rodeo cowboy. She loved the way tight Wranglers hugged toned butts. She loved the way belts with big buckles cinched trim waists. And she loved the way sexy Stetsons shadowed handsome faces.

There was no doubt that Danny Ray and Cord were handsome. Just in different ways. Danny Ray was a pretty boy. Almost too pretty. Cord's features weren't pretty so much as ruggedly attractive. His face was a collage of beautiful angles—from his chiseled cheekbones to his square jaw that almost always had a sprinkling of dark stubble. His eyes were the only things that weren't totally male. They were long lashed and a soft, velvety sable brown that reflected whatever they were looking at.

Today, they had reflected a sex-starved woman. She hadn't been with a man since Danny Ray had left six years ago. She'd been too busy raising a daughter to worry about sex. So when Cord had touched her, all her pent-up desires had flooded to the surface and there had been no holding them back.

"And why do I have to sit in a stupid booster seat?" Carrie Anne cut into her thoughts. "I'm not a baby. I'm in first grade."

Christie heaved a sigh of exasperation. Something she'd been doing a lot lately. She loved her daughter more than life itself, but there were times she didn't much like her. "Because it's the law, Baby Girl. You have to sit in a booster until you turn eight or weigh more than eighty pounds."

Of course, kids didn't care about laws. Carrie Anne continued to complain about the booster seat while Christie went back to thinking about her reaction to Cord.

That was all it was—a reaction. After being without a man for so long, her body had reacted to being held in a handsome cowboy's arms. But her mind knew better. Both her grandma and mama had spent their lives pining for the no-good cowboys who had left them. Christie refused to do the same. She was through with cowboys. She was through with men altogether. She didn't need a man screwing up her life or Carrie Anne's. They could make it just fine on their own.

"Damn straight," she said under her breath. Of course, Carrie Anne heard.

"Ahh, you cussed, Mama. You told me never to cuss and you just cussed. And if you can break the laws, I don't see why I have to sit in a booster."

Christie sighed.

She should've taken Carrie Anne back to the trailer that they rented from Spring Kendall and worked on the phonics homework Carrie's teacher had sent home with her. But the trailer was small and she couldn't stand the thought of being cooped up in it with her argumentative daughter. So instead, she headed into town.

Bliss, Texas, was the definition of a small town. There were no chain department stores, fast food restaurants, or designer coffee shops. The businesses that lined Main Street were owned by the residents of the town and the owners treated their customers like family. It was one of the things Christie loved about Bliss. It had been just her and her mama growing up. While she had felt loved and secure, she'd envied her friends who had siblings and big families. In Bliss, everyone was family.

Of course, Christie really did have family in the town. They just didn't know it yet.

"Doesn't the town look Christmasy, Mama?" Carrie Anne asked.

She was right. All the businesses were spruced up for the holidays with wreaths on their doors and colorful lights around their windows. Twinkle lights draped every tree along the sidewalk and greenery and red bows entwined every old-fashioned lamppost. The holiday decorations should've made Christie feel happy, but instead they made her anxious.

She wanted this Christmas to be special for Carrie Anne. Her daughter had been through a lot in the last year with her asthma getting worse, her grandmother dying, and moving away from the only home she'd ever known. Thankfully, the new medication the doctor had prescribed for Carrie Anne's asthma was working. She hadn't had any attacks for months. But there was no medicine that could bring back a grandmother.

Christie's mom had always made Christmas the best day of the year, and Christie wanted to do the same for her daughter. She wanted to get a tree and decorate it with beautiful ornaments. She wanted to get some lights and string them up outside the little trailer they were renting. And she wanted to get her daughter a new bike to replace the one she'd had to leave behind.

But in order to do those things she needed money, and her finances were already stretched to the limit. Even with two jobs, she was struggling to pay their living expenses and pay off the credit card debt she'd gotten into when she'd spent the summer searching for her father.

Searching for her daddy had ranked right up there with falling for Danny Ray in stupidity. But after her mother died, she'd felt lost and needy. Her father was the only family she and Carrie Anne had left and she'd wanted desperately to give her daughter a grandpa. So once Carrie Anne finished kindergarten, Christie had sold all their belongings and headed to Texas to find her daddy.

She'd found him. And it turned out that he was just another male disappointment in her life. But he had given her one thing. He'd led her to Bliss. She was starting to believe that this was a place where she could forget her past screw-ups and start over. A place that she and Carrie Anne could call home.

"Yippee! We're stopping at the bakery," Carrie Anne said when Christie pulled their beat-up Chevy Malibu next to the curb. Before she could even open her door, Carrie Anne had her seatbelt off and was out of the car. By the time Christie got into the bakery, her daughter was chattering away to Ms. Marble.

Ms. Marble was a sweet woman in her late seventies who had been the town baker before Summer took over the job. She had planned to retire completely. But after only a few weeks of retirement, she'd gone a little stir crazy. Now she worked at the bakery on Christie and Summer's days off. Not only did she make the best cinnamon-swirl muffins that Christie had ever tasted, but she was also a retired schoolteacher and great with kids. She listened intently as Carrie Anne jabbered.

". . . and Maple told me she loved me by nuzzling her head right next to mine. And Cord says that once I get me some proper boots and a riding helmet, he'll teach me how to ride her."

"You're not riding Maple," Christie said. "She's too big of a horse for you."

Carrie Anne opened her mouth to no doubt start arguing, but Ms. Marble intervened before she could. "How would you like an oatmeal cookie? I baked them fresh this morning. Of course, you'll need to ask your mother first."

"Can I, Mama?"

"Yes, and be sure to say thank you."

Ms. Marble opened the bakery case and let Carrie Anne choose a cookie. When she was munching away, Ms. Marble looked at Christie and smiled. "What brings you to the bakery on your day off?"

"I thought I'd check in and see if Summer needed any help finishing the wedding cake for Tina Foster."

"That's sweet of you, dear. The baby hasn't given Summer morning sickness yet, but it's certainly made her tired. I tried to send her home, but she stubbornly refused to go."

"When babies are in your tummy, they make you sick in the morning and tired?" Carrie Anne shook her head. "Now I'm not having S-E-X or babies."

Ms. Marble's almost invisible eyebrows hiked up beneath her soft white bangs, and for the second time that day, Christie wanted to crawl under a rock and hide.

Instead, she smiled weakly. "It seems that a little

boy at school has been talking about inappropriate things." She sent Carrie Anne a warning look. "And because it's inappropriate, if you spell that word again, missy, you're going to be in big trouble."

Carrie Anne scowled. "Why would I get in trouble? I'm not the one who spelled it. Jonas Murphy's brother was."

"And I'm going to have a talk with Jonas's parents about that." She hated to admit it, but Cord did have a good point about talking with the parents instead of the principal. "Now, I want you to sit right down there at that table and do your phonics homework." She held out the backpack she'd carried in. Her daughter didn't look happy to see it. She stubbornly crossed her arms.

"I don't want to do my homework. I hate phonetics!"

Christie's exasperation must've shown because Ms. Marble walked from behind the counter and took the backpack. "Hate phonics? Why phonics are the building blocks to new and exciting worlds."

Carrie Anne stared at her. "What kinda worlds?"

Ms. Marble smiled. "Worlds filled with awkward princesses, silly monsters, magic wizards . . . and beautiful horses. Horses that talk and dance and fly. And regular horses that just become little girls' beloved pets. I'd love to show you these worlds, but first you have to learn the sounds of all the letters and how they fit together to form words."

Carrie Anne scrunched up her face in thought for a second before she nodded and took a chair. "Okay, but Cord already taught me some. C-A-T spells cat."

Ms. Marble joined her at the table. "Then you already have a head start." She looked at Christie and winked. "I've got this. Why don't you go see if Summer needs help?"

The bakery kitchen smelled like Christie's mama's kitchen used to smell. The air was filled with the scent of vanilla, spices, and love. Her heart tightened with sadness before she noticed Summer sound asleep and slumped over the prep counter with a frosting knife in one hand and a piping bag in the other. In front of her was Tina's half-decorated wedding cake.

Christie stored her purse under the counter before donning an apron. She washed her hands, and then took both the knife and piping bag from Summer and sat down to finish decorating the cake.

Her mother had been a wonderful seamstress and baker. Christie had never gotten the knack of sewing, but she loved to bake. In high school, she had worked at a Walmart bakery where she had learned how to decorate cakes. So it didn't take her any time at all to finish applying the pretty white scrolls of icing to the rest of the cake. When she was done, Summer woke up and blinked.

"Did I fall asleep again?"

Summer was the oldest Hadley sister—not that most people would count seconds and minutes as being older. Summer had been born only seconds before Autumn and minutes before Spring. But even being a triplet, she'd taken on the oldest child's persona. She was controlling, strong-willed, and assertive. But she was also nice. She'd given

Christie a job and treated her like a friend.

"Just a little catnap," Christie said.

Summer looked at the finished cake. "Liar."

Christie laughed. "Okay, maybe you slept a little longer, but it comes with being pregnant. I used to want to sleep all the time when I was first pregnant with Carrie Anne. You're lucky you own your own business. I got fired from my job when Mr. Nash found me sound asleep in the back room of his western wear store."

"You sold western wear?"

Christie turned the cake on the decorating wheel to make sure she hadn't missed a spot. "That was where I met Danny Ray. He came in looking for some new Wranglers. I took one look at his nice bee-hind in those jeans and lost my morals and my wits."

Summer laughed. "Nice-fitting jeans can do that to a woman. I never noticed Ryker's butt until he switched from suit pants to jeans. Now all he has to do is walk by and flash those sweet buns at me and I heat up like a toaster oven. Which is exactly how I ended up in the same predicament as you."

Christie wanted to tell her that she wasn't close to being in the same predicament as she had been in. Summer had a husband who loved and cared for her, not a no-good rodeo bum who would skip out on her right after her child was born. But instead of being a Debbie Downer, Christie kept that information to herself and smiled.

"The exhaustion will go away soon. Now I better get this cake into the refrigerator before my handiwork melts in the heat of this kitchen."

After Summer helped her put the cake in the

refrigerator, Christie whipped up a batch of cupcakes that she planned to decorate to look like reindeers and santas. While she was creaming the butter and sugar, Summer's sister Spring walked into the kitchen. While Summer was controlling and assertive, Spring was easy-going and carefree.

"Hey, y'all! Isn't it a gorgeous day?"

Summer rolled her eyes and spoke close to Christie's ear. "I feel like I've run a marathon and my little sister, who's also pregnant, comes bouncing in here like Tigger."

Christie held back a laugh and shut off the mixer. "Hey, Spring. How was work?"

"Busy, but that's how I like it."

Spring was an office assistant for her husband, Sheriff Waylon Kendall. She was also the town fixer. If you had a problem, Spring was the one to call. She had rented Christie her vintage trailer when Christie didn't have a place to live. She'd also helped her get the assistant job with Cord. Spring had the ability to see a need and take care of it. This was proven when she set an opened magazine down on the counter. The "Win $5,000" in the title of the article immediately drew Christie's attention.

"What's this?" she asked.

Spring smiled brightly. "'The Best Gingerbread House in Texas Contest' that's being put on by the Regal Hotel in Austin. I found it in an Austin magazine and I think you should enter."

Summer glared at her sister. "What about me? I'm a baker—" Some unspoken message must've passed between the two sisters because Summer quickly changed her tune. "You're right. I can't even finish a cake without falling asleep. This would be much too big a project for me to take on right now." She looked at Christie. "So it's all up to you to represent Blissful Bakery."

"Me?" Christie appreciated the vote of confidence, but she didn't agree. "I'm not close to being as talented as you are at decorating. And I'm certainly not as talented as the experienced pastry chefs who will more than likely be vying for that five thousand dollars."

Summer shrugged. "Chef is just a fancy title. You're a baker. And a damned good one." She waved a hand around the room. "Not to mention that you have access to everything a hoity-toity chef has access to."

"She's right," Spring said. "Of course, if you can't use the money . . ." She started to pick up the magazine, but Christie grabbed it. Five thousand dollars would pay off all her debt with plenty left over to give Carrie Anne the kind of Christmas she deserved.

"I'll enter, but there's no way I'm going to win."

Summer sent her a stern look. "Of course you won't win with that kind of attitude. You're going to need to be all in if you want to show people what you're made of. Now do you want to build the biggest, best gingerbread house Texas has ever seen and win that contest hands down, or not, Christie Buchanan?"

Christie wanted to win the contest. She wanted to win it in a bad way. And Summer was right. If she was going to get that prize money, she needed to quit being an insecure wimp and start acting like the talented baker she was. She might not have graduated from some fancy pastry school, but she had graduated from the school of hard knocks. She could do this. She had to do this.

For Carrie Anne . . . and herself.

She straightened her shoulders and pumped a fist in the air. "Damn straight, I'm gonna win!"

CHAPTER THREE

"CAN I HELP YOU?"

Cord turned from the antique bed he'd been looking at to the blond bombshell with the pretty blue eyes. Although they weren't near as pretty as a pair of hazel ones that he couldn't seem to get out of his mind.

He took off his cowboy hat. "Yes, ma'am. I need a bed."

She flashed a friendly smile. "Why, Cord Evans. I didn't recognize you with the hat on. I'm Savannah Arrington. We met at my cousin's wedding to your son Ryker."

"I remember. You're Raff Arrington's wife. And congratulations on your new son."

Her eyes lit up and she started chattering like Carrie Anne. "Thank you. Dax is about the cutest thing this side of the Mississippi, if I do say so myself. Although Carly Arrington's newborn son is pretty darned cute too. Have you seen Zane Junior? ZJ is a carbon copy of his daddy. I can't wait for him and Dax to start playing together. Dax usually comes to the store with me—Raff helped me make the sweetest little ole nursery for him in the back room—but today he's home with his daddy doing daddy and son things."

As always, when Cord thought of all the years he'd missed being a daddy to his own son, his gut tightened with guilt, sadness, and a strong need for a stiff drink. He took a few slow breaths and rolled the beads of his hatband between his fingers. Ryker had made him the hatband for Father's Day when he was five—right before Jenn had taken Ryker and left for good. The plastic beads had become Cord's talisman. A reminder of what he had lost to alcohol . . . and could still lose.

"And that's how it should be," he said before he changed the subject. "Now about that bed. Is this the only one you've got? Because it doesn't look quite big enough."

Savannah laughed. "Which is exactly why Raff wouldn't let me put it in our new master suite in the cabin. He said he didn't care if it was over a hundred years old, he wanted a bed with plenty of space for rolling around with his woman." An image of rolling around in a big bed with a woman with miles of hair the color of an autumn wheat field popped into his head, but he pushed it right back out again.

"As long as it's big enough for me, I'll be good," he said.

Savannah glanced around. "Unfortunately, my inventory is mostly antiques that are full-sized. What about ordering one online?"

"I'm not real good at ordering online. The air mattress I ordered is a perfect example. Besides being uncomfortable as heck, it got a small leak last night and is now flatter than a pancake."

"Well, I certainly can't let Ryker's father sleep on the floor." She walked over to the counter where a computer sat and started clicking away. "I have an account with a wholesaler who carries great beds. I'm thinking a masculine frame with a cushioned headboard and a California King mattress with a nice pillow top and extra support."

"That sounds like heaven to me."

In about fifteen minutes, Savannah had a bed and mattress ordered for him, along with all the bedding to go with it. "I got express delivery, but it still won't be here for a few days."

"I think I can manage until then. I sure appreciate the help. What do I owe you?"

"You can pay me when everything gets here. And I'm giving you the wholesale price because Ryker gave me a great deal on setting up my new website. Your son is a computer genius."

He couldn't help feeling proud. Before Ryker had moved to Bliss, he'd owned an online job search company that he'd helped turn into a billion-dollar business. He was now trying to do the same thing for Cord's cowboy boot company. Cord didn't need to make a lot of money. He just wanted his son back.

"Well, he sure doesn't get his genius from his father," he said. "I can barely turn on my computer. Which is why I hired an assistant."

"I heard that Christie Buchanan is working for you. I haven't gotten a chance to talk with her much, but she seems sweet as apple pie. And her daughter is quite the little pistol."

Cord grinned at just the thought of Carrie Anne.

"That she is."

Savannah moved out from behind the counter. "Is there anything else I can do for you?"

"As a matter of fact, there is. I heard that you helped my son and daughter-in-law decorate their house and I was wondering if you would do the same for my ranch house."

Savannah's face lit up. "I was hoping you'd ask, honey." She grabbed a pad and pencil. "Now what would you say your style is so I can start looking for furniture and décor that would suit you?"

"Actually, I don't want you decorating the house in my style. I'd like you to decorate it in Ryker and Summer's." Savannah looked confused, and he figured she had a right to be. But he didn't want his Christmas surprise ruined so he told a little white lie. "I love the way you decorated their house and want mine to look similar. I'd also like you to turn a room into a nursery for my grandchild."

Savannah's eyes welled with tears. "That's so sweet. I wish Raff's parents lived closer so they could spend more time with Dax. Sweet babies should get to be around their grandparents." She leaned in and gave him a hug. "I'll make it just as adorable as Dax's nursery—unless that baby turns out to be girl. Then I'm going to make it a princess nursery to beat all princess nurseries."

He laughed. "I'll leave that up to you."

They were deciding what day would be best for her to come out to the ranch and measure the rooms when the door opened and Raff came walking in. He was carrying a dark-headed bundle the size of a football in the crook of his arm. The sight was like being kicked in the head by a brahma bull.

Cord remembered holding Ryker in the crook of his arm. He remembered how small and perfect Ryker had been. He also remembered how quickly he'd wanted to hand his son back to his mama. At the time, Ryker had felt like a burden to Cord—a weight that was holding him back from making something of himself. He'd been so young and stupid. So damned stupid.

A sharp hunger for a drink slammed into him. It grew even stronger when Savannah hurried over and kissed her husband. Cord could've had this. He could've spent his life with a loving wife and a perfect son . . . and maybe a pretty little girl as feisty as Carrie Anne. He could've had twenty years of memories with a warm and loving family. Instead, he had vague memories of drunken nights spent in cheap hotel rooms.

"Hey, Cord," Raff said with a proud smile. "You want to meet my son?"

Cord didn't want to. He wanted to get the hell out of there so he could get a handle on the addiction that gnawed at his belly. But he'd tried running before, and he knew it only made things worse. He had to face his demons. No matter how painful.

He forced a smile as he rolled the beads of his hatband through his fingers. "Yes, sir. I sure do." He briefly made a fuss over the chubby sleeping baby before he turned the conversation to cattle and Raff's ranch, which was not far from Cord's. After what felt like an eternity, he put on his hat and excused himself. Once outside, he released his breath and tried to block out the images sweet baby Dax had conjured up. But he couldn't. He couldn't stop the flood of memories of Ryker at the same age and all those precious moments he'd wasted.

His gaze wandered over to the only bar in town. *Just one drink. Just one shot of tequila to take the edge off the sharp pain of regret.* But before he could step off the curb to cross the street, someone called his name.

"Cord!"

He turned to see Christie hurrying toward him. She had on a down jacket, skinny jeans, and the high heeled boots that had caused her to fall the day before. The memory of holding her soft body against his replaced the need for a drink with his newfound need for sex. He didn't know which was worse. Either could screw up everything he'd worked so hard to reclaim. And he wasn't about to let that happen. He wasn't going to lose himself in a bottle again. And he certainly wasn't going to lose himself in Christie Buchanan's arms. Not only was she his assistant, she was also much too young for him.

"Hey, Christie," he greeted her.

She stopped in front of him. The wind blew a strand of her pretty wheat-colored hair out of her braid and she tucked it back behind her ear. "There's something I wanted to talk to you about." She paused. "Actually there are two things I wanted to talk to you about."

"Shoot."

Before she could, another gust of wind had Cord's cowboy hat tumbling down the street. He ran after it. Regardless of the pledge he'd just made to keep his thoughts about Christie purely platonic, he couldn't help being conscious of his limp. It wasn't that noticeable when he walked, but running was a different story. Of course, maybe it was a good thing she saw him as the beat-up old cowboy he was. He scooped up his hat and walked back to her.

"What say we continue this conversation at Lucy's Place Diner?" he said. "No one can talk in this wind, and I haven't had lunch and I'm starving."

They were given the corner booth at the diner. Once they were seated, Cord waited for Christie to start talking. When she didn't, he decided to fill the awkward silence with a little Bliss trivia. "Did you know that this is the very booth where the famous writer, Lucy Arrington, used to sit and plot all the books in her Tender Heart series?"

She looked impressed. "No, I didn't."

"Did you read the series?" He pulled out two menus from behind the sugar container and handed her one.

"As a matter of fact, I did. Did you?"

He shook his head as he opened his menu. "I wasn't much of a reader. I wanted to spend all my time with horses."

"Did you grow up on a ranch?"

"Not until I was in my teens. Before that, I lived in Lubbock. After my dad died, my mom remarried a man with kids of his own. I was a little resentful and became a handful so I was sent off to a boys' ranch for troubled teens."

She lowered her menu and looked at him. "I'm sorry."

"Nothing to be sorry about. I loved being at the

Double Diamond Ranch. The two guys who ran it were these gruff old rodeo cowboys who loved horses and helping delinquent kids as much as they loved to argue and chew tobacco."

"So that's where you got your love for the sport."

He nodded. "And you? What was your childhood like in Wyoming?"

She smiled sadly. "Perfect. My mama was the best mother in the entire world. She was a seamstress and could make wedding dresses as beautiful as any big city designer. She loved to bake and sing country songs at the top of her lungs—even though she couldn't carry a tune to save her soul. She was a horrible singer, but a wonderful mother and grandmother. I think some of Carrie Anne's acting out is because she misses her Mimi so much."

He set down his menu, even though he didn't have clue what he was going to order. "It sounds like you miss her too."

For a moment, he didn't think she was going to answer. Then she released her breath in a puff of air. "So much that I uprooted my daughter from a home she loved and went on a wild goose chase looking for a father to replace her."

"And did you find him?"

"Yes." She closed her menu like she closed the conversation. "I wanted to ask you if your offer to watch Carrie Anne still stands."

He really wanted to ask more questions about her father, but he had a gut feeling that he wasn't going to get any more answers so he let it go. "I'd love to."

"Thank you. It will just be for a couple weeks. I'm working on a new project at the bakery that's going to need my full attention."

"Must be some wedding cake."

"Actually, it's a gingerbread house. I'm entering a contest. And I don't expect you to watch Carrie for free. You can take it out of my pay just like you're taking out the cost of fixing my car."

He shook his head. "Now I took out the money to fix your car because you got pretty wired up about it. But I refuse to take money for watching Carrie Anne when I enjoy her company so much."

"She talks your ear off."

"And that's what I enjoy. Listening to her talk, keeps my mind off other things." Like being a bad father . . . and a bottle of Patrón.

She hesitated for only a second before she nodded. "Fine. But if she should start to drive you crazy, just let me know. And you won't have to watch her today because Ms. Marble offered to tutor her in phonics a couple times a week."

He grinned. "You mean phone-tics."

She laughed. "My daughter."

The waitress walked up to take their orders. Christie just ordered water. He was really getting tired of his assistant's refusal to take anything from anyone. He ordered the Sander sisters' chicken fried chicken. He had ordered it before and had no trouble eating the two pieces of crispy chicken and mountain of mashed potatoes covered in gravy. But when the waitress set the plate on the table, he acted surprised by the huge portion.

"There is no way I can eat all this. You better bring another plate." When Christie started to argue, he held up a hand. "If you don't eat it, you can take it back to Summer. Of course chicken fried chicken just doesn't taste the same when it's heated up."

Christie ended up eating her portion, but she was smart enough to figure out his ploy. "I'm not a starving homeless person you need to feed, Cord. I work at a bakery where Summer lets me cook anything I want for lunch."

"But can you make chicken fried chicken as good as this?" He took a big bite and winked.

She laughed and shook her head as she went back to eating.

"So what was the other thing you wanted to talk to me about?" he asked.

She paused with the fork of chicken half way to her mouth. She set it down on the plate and lowered her gaze. "I just wanted to make sure that you didn't misunderstand what I said the other day about . . ." She swallowed. "About you having a nice body." She lifted her gaze. "It was just an observation. I don't want you thinking that I'm interested in you."

There was a part of him that was relieved. He didn't need any distractions from his goal of mending his relationship with Ryker. But there was also a part of him that felt a little deflated. It had been ego boosting to have a pretty young thing find him attractive. But his ego was what had turned him into a dumbass drunk. It was best to leave his ego out of things.

"I didn't think you'd be interested in an old rodeo bum like me."

She seemed surprised by his reply. "You're not that old."

"At forty-five, I'm a lot older than you. I figure

you're around Ryker's age. Twenty-four? Twenty-five?"

She smiled. "Thank you for the compliment, but I'll be thirty-one on December 25th."

He was surprised. She looked much younger. "You're a Christmas baby. Let me guess, your full name is Christmas Buchanan."

He meant it as a joke, but she didn't laugh. Her smile faded as she grabbed her coat and scarf. "I really need to get going. Thanks for lunch. And thank you for watching Carrie Anne for me." She slid out of the booth and left the diner before Cord could get over his confusion.

Why would she get so upset? The only thing he could come up with was that Christmas was her name and she didn't like it. His eyes narrowed as he watched her cross the street.

Or maybe she just didn't want anyone knowing it.

CHAPTER FOUR

IT WAS FUNNY THAT PEOPLE couldn't see what was right in front of their eyes. Or maybe they just didn't want to see it. The truth, more times than not, was painful. And it was better to hide from it, then face it.

Maybelline Marble could attest to this fact. When she was younger, she had hidden from the truth and chosen not to see what was right in front of her eyes. And it *had* been painful to finally come to terms with the fact that Justin Bonner, who she'd loved with all her heart, hadn't felt the same way. He had married her and given her months of happiness before he died, but he had never loved her like he'd loved Lucy Arrington.

Having gone through that pain, Maybelline had sworn to be more observant. Studying people had become one of her favorite past times. Over the years, she became extremely good at reading people and discovering their truths.

Although figuring out Christie Buchanan's truth hadn't been all that difficult.

All you had to do was look closely at her daughter.

"Did you know I'm gettin' married, Ms. Marble?" Carrie Anne licked the frosting off one of the Santa sugar cookies Maybelline had given her as an afternoon snack.

"And who is the lucky man?" Maybelline asked as she continued to frost the rest of the cookies. She had plans to take the cookies to church on Sunday for the children in her Sunday school class. The promise of a sugary snack made children much better listeners during the bible lesson.

"Oh, I can't tell you," Carrie Anne said. "If my mama found out, she'd have a fit." She licked off the rest of the frosting before she bit off Santa's head in one big bite. "If there's one thing my mama hates, it's a—"

Maybelline held up her frosting knife and stopped her. "Finish eating before you speak. Ladies do not talk with their mouths full."

"Oh, I ain't a lady. I'm a kid."

Maybelline bit back a smile. "You're a kid who also happens to be a young lady. Now finish that bite."

Carrie Anne chewed rapidly, then took a big gulp from her glass of milk, leaving a white mustache above her top lip. Yes, if anyone in town took the time to look, they would recognize those lips and the stubborn chin and the sparkle of mischief in the hazel eyes.

"What is it that your mother dislikes?" she asked.

"Rodeo cowboys. And she doesn't just dislike them. She hates them as much as she hates hairy spiders and slimy snakes and me saying 'shut up.' My daddy is a rodeo bum who left me and my mama without so much as a goodbye or a wedding ring. It all has to do with the Buchanan Curse. My grandma—God bless her soul—told me all about it. Her mama fell for a rodeo bum. Mimi fell for one. And so did my mama. Before she went to heaven, Mimi said that I'm the only spark of hope left to break the curse. I can't fall for a no-good rodeo bum. I have to marry a prince among men."

"And this man you're going to marry is a prince?"

"Yep." Carrie Anne bit off a Santa leg and would've started talking if Maybelline hadn't lifted an eyebrow. The little girl chewed and swallowed. "'Cept he don't got a castle."

"Doesn't have a castle."

"That's right. He don't. But he's got a big ole ranch house with plenty of room and lots of horses. And he's going to teach me how to ride those horses as soon as I get me a pair of boots and a helmet. And he's not going to make the same mistakes my grandpas and my daddy did because he already made those mistakes with his last wife and his kid. And he's sorry. Real sorry. 'Cause I've seen big tears in his eyes some times when he's looking at his son and I figure he's learned his lesson. Just like I learned my lesson when I didn't listen to Mama and ate that hot slice of pizza before it cooled. And let me tell you, a blister on the roof of your mouth will make a believer out of you in a hurry."

It didn't take a genius to figure out who Carrie Anne's prince was. And Maybelline wasn't surprised. She had known Cord Evans was a prince as soon as he came into town. He had worked so hard to get back in his son's good graces, and he'd achieved that goal. Ryker had forgiven his father.

Now all Cord had to do was forgive himself.

Carrie Anne wiped her mouth with the napkin Maybelline handed her. "And once me and Cord get married—" She realized her slip and stared at Maybelline with wide hazel eyes.

Maybelline alleviated her fear. "Your secret is safe with me."

Carrie Anne looked suspicious. "Promise on your grandma's grave? Because if word gets back to Mama, she'll put a stop to me and Cord getting married in a heartbeat. She's pretty much against marriage and men."

"But your mother will have to find out eventually. Or are you planning on eloping?"

"No, I'm getting married in the little white chapel just like Autumn and Coach Murdoch. But I'm inviting my entire school and the town. Except for Stuart and Race. I'm not inviting those poop heads because they call me Brat and won't let me follow them around. And I'm gonna tell Mama eventually, but I want her to get to know Cord a little better. I figure once she sees what a nice man he is, she won't keep me from marrying him. Then maybe she'll be able to forgive my daddy. And maybe he'll come back. And just like Cord, maybe he'll be real sorry for leaving and won't be a deadbeat no more."

It suddenly dawned on Maybelline why Carrie Anne had chosen Cord as her prince. It wasn't just his big ranch house or his horses. It was the hope that if Cord had turned into a good father, then maybe her father could too. The longing in the little girl's eyes made Maybelline's heart break. Not just for Carrie Anne, but also for a father who didn't realize what he was missing. She wished she could tell the precious little girl that her father would come back, but only God knew if that was true.

She reached out and patted Carrie Anne's arm. "There's nothing wrong with hoping that your father will recognize his mistake and start acting like a daddy. But even if he never does, you are blessed to have a mother who loves you with all her heart. Now finish your cookies so we can start on your phonics homework and make your mama proud."

As Carrie Anne polished off her other sugar cookie, Maybelline continued to frost the rest of the cookies. While she worked, she thought about how sad it was that Carrie Anne didn't have a father to love her. And that Christie had lost her faith in men. And that Cord was struggling to forgive himself. They were certainly three broken hearts that needed some mending. And love was the best way to mend a broken heart.

As the town matchmaker, Maybelline was experienced at getting couples to the little white chapel. She had helped fix up all the Arrington cousins and most of the Hadleys. But Cord and Christie weren't going to be easy to get together. She didn't know of two people less ready for love. Christie didn't trust men, and Cord didn't trust himself. It would take a miracle to get them to love again.

Maybelline glanced down at the Christmas cookie she was frosting and smiled.

Luckily, this was the season of miracles.

CHAPTER FIVE

CHRISTIE SAT AT THE DESK in Cord Evans's office and tried to concentrate on the post she was writing for his blog announcing his new line of cowboy boots. But her attention kept getting distracted by the cowboy working in the corral right outside the window.

Cord was training Raise-A-Ruckus. He had the beautiful sorrel stallion on a long rope and was using a lunge whip to get Ruckus to walk, trot, and run in a circle around him. Christie had been appalled when she'd first seen Cord using the whip until she'd realized that he never touched the horse with it. He just lowered, raised, or cracked it to get Ruckus to do what he wanted. It was fascinating to watch.

It was also erotic.

There was something so sensual about the way Cord handled the horse. The way he used the rope and the whip to get the animal to bend to his will. Even though it was a chilly first of December, Cord didn't wear a jacket, and she could see his muscles flex beneath the thin cotton of his worn western shirt. Muscles she had touched when he'd caught her . . . and wanted to touch again.

She'd thought that after Danny Ray, she'd be immune to cowboys. Which is why she had taken the job from Cord. She'd figured that she had more than outgrown her infatuation. But falling into Cord's arms had completely obliterated that theory. In the last week, she couldn't stop her gaze from wandering to his large hands that had spanned her waist or his defined chest that had pressed against her breasts. Her preoccupation was damned annoying. She didn't have time for sexual thoughts or fantasies. She had a child to raise, two jobs to hold down, and a gingerbread contest to win. And the latter wasn't coming along so well.

In the last few days, she and Summer had drawn out numerous ideas for gingerbread houses. But not one of them seemed original enough to win. With only weeks before the judging, she needed to come up with a plan soon so she could start building it. Which meant she needed to stop ogling Cord and finished his blog so she could get to the bakery.

She turned away from the window and back to Cord's laptop. She was almost finished with the blog when a tap had her glancing at the doorway. Cord's son stood there with a friendly smile on his face.

Ryker was a carbon copy of his father—from the deep chestnut hair that had a tendency to curl over his forehead to the soft chocolate eyes that held a wealth of emotion.

"Sorry to interrupt you while you're working," he said. "But there's a publicity idea that I wanted to run by you."

"Of course," she said. "Although I'm not really an expert on the subject."

"You've been doing a pretty expert job. Since you took over Cord's social media, you've upped his engagements by forty-eight percent." He laughed. "I tried to tell him that no one cared what he was having for breakfast."

"Breakfast is the most important meal of the day." Cord appeared in the doorway next to his son, confirming Christie's earlier thoughts on Ryker being his carbon copy. The only difference between the two men was that Ryker had the smooth skin of a younger man who spent most of his time inside, while Cord's skin was bronzer and there were squint lines at the corners of his eyes. But, for some reason, that made him even more attractive.

"I'm glad you're here," Ryker said. "I wanted to run something by you and Christie."

"Let's hear it." Cord held out a hand for Ryker to take one of the chairs in front of the desk before he sat down in the other. Which left Christie sitting behind the desk feeling awkward.

She quickly got up. "You sit here, Cord."

He shook his head. "I'm fine. I never was a desk type of guy. The only reason I got it was because Ryker said I needed one." He winked at her. "And it's worked out great for my new assistant."

"You need more than a desk," Ryker said as Christie sat back down. "When are you going to buy some furniture for this monstrosity of a ranch house?"

Ryker had a point. As far as Christie could tell,

the only room in the house with furniture seemed to be the office. The huge great room with the stone fireplace had nothing in it. The chef's kitchen with the mile-long marble island only had a coffeemaker. And the guest bathroom she and Carrie Anne used when they were there didn't even have towels. She'd had to bring a roll of paper towels and hand soap for them to wash their hands.

"Savannah Arrington is working on that," Cord said. "My new mattress and bedroom furniture was delivered yesterday. And today, she's coming out to measure the other rooms." He paused and sent his son a hopeful look. "Before she gets here, I was thinking that maybe you and I could go fishing."

"Sorry, but I have to check on the electrician that's working at my house. When Summer and I bought the house down the street from Waylon and Spring's, we thought it would be fun living in a hundred-year-old Victorian. We didn't realize that old meant falling down around your ears. After we moved in, I had to put on a new roof and now it looks like the wiring needs to be redone."

"Sounds like you bought a bit of a money pit," Cord said.

"You can say that again. If anything else breaks, I'm going to start looking for another place to live. Although Summer loves the old house. She thinks it has character."

Cord smiled. "Believe me, she'll like a brand new house even better." Since Ryker hadn't been talking about building a brand new house, the comment was a little odd. Ryker must've thought so too.

He stared at his father with confusion. "I'm not

planning on building a house. It wouldn't be finished before the baby got here."

"Of course. My mistake." Cord quickly changed the subject. "So what did you want to talk to me and Christie about?"

"With your new line of cowboy boots coming out, I thought we should do some extra promotion. I placed ads in a few ranching and western living magazines, but we still need to do something for social media. And I was thinking about a holiday giveaway. People love winning things. Your followers would especially love winning a pair of your new boots." He glanced at Christie. "What do you think?"

"I think a giveaway is a great idea," she said. "How would you want to set it up?"

"I was hoping you'd have some ideas. You've been doing a great job of posting pictures that Cord's followers seem to really respond to. The picture of him cleaning out the horse stalls got thousands of likes. So I say we go with something that has to do with his life here on the ranch."

She thought for a moment before an idea popped into her head. "What about 'Christmas on the Ranch?' or 'A Cord Evans Christmas'?"

"Or 'A Big Boot-iful Texas Christmas.'" When both Christie and Ryker looked at Cord, he shrugged. "It was a joke. Obviously, not a good one."

Ryker laughed. "A little too corny, Cord. I love Christmas on the Ranch. It has a nice ring to it and will appeal to your demographic. We can post pictures of you decorating for the holidays to coincide with the giveaway posts."

Cord didn't look all that excited. "I think we need more than just pictures of me stringing lights and hanging ornaments on a tree. That doesn't say Christmas on the ranch as much as lonely old cowboy. It would be better if we posted pictures of me and my son."

Ryker's hesitation was brutally obvious. The hurt look on Cord's face said it all. Christie shouldn't feel sympathy for him. All her sympathy should be with Ryker. She had been on his side of the fence and knew what it was like to be deserted by your father—what it was like to hope that your daddy would come back at Christmas and do all the things with you that other kids' dads did with them. And she knew the resentment you felt when your father never showed up. She saw that resentment on Ryker's face and could read his thoughts—*if you didn't want to spend Christmas with me as a kid, why do you want to spend it with me now?*

And yet, even knowing how he felt, she couldn't help feeling sorry for Cord. His face was etched with such pain and regret. Maybe that's why she had sympathy for him. He felt regret for what he'd done. Some fathers never did.

She sent Ryker a beseeching look. "I think people would love seeing pictures of Cord and his son and daughter-in-law."

A long moment ticked by before Ryker nodded. "Sure. I guess Summer and I could help decorate a tree and string some lights." He glanced at his watch. "I better get going." He got up. "I'll call you later, Christie, and we'll go over all the details." He lifted his hand. "See ya, Cord."

Cord nodded. "See ya, son."

Once he was gone, Cord's shoulders slumped. "Cord. I'm starting to hate the name." He blew out his breath and stared down at his boots. "He used to call me Daddy. Whenever I came home after weeks on the rodeo circuit, he'd come running with his little arms wide open, yelling "Dad-dy! Dad-dy!" He slapped his knee with his hat. "And I screwed it up. I damn well screwed it up."

Christie couldn't help the tears that sprang to her eyes. She didn't know if the tears were for Cord, Ryker, or herself. Maybe they were for every dad who screwed up and every kid who had to deal with it.

"What he calls you doesn't matter as much as how he feels about you," she said. "And it's obvious that he cares about you. But becoming a father he can trust will take some time. It's not something that's going to happen overnight."

Cord ran a hand through his wind-tousled hair. "I know. And I know I get pushy at times and try to force things. If I'm not careful, I'll force him completely away."

"Loving him won't force him away, Cord. Everyone wants to be loved by their parents. He's just resentful that you didn't show him that love sooner. But he'll get over it."

Cord lifted his gaze and studied her with soft brown eyes. "When you mentioned your father the other day, it didn't sound like you were over your resentment for him."

"My resentment is still there because my father never did love me. And judging from how our first and only meeting went, he never will."

"Is he the one who named you Christmas?"

She had hoped that Cord hadn't made anything out of her rushed departure from the diner the other day. She should've known better. She'd acted like a complete idiot when he'd only been teasing her. If she had kept her cool and laughed, no one would know her real name and her secret would be safe. Of course, if she kept her cool now, maybe it still would be.

"No," she said. "My mama did. But I really hate the name. So if you would keep it under your hat, I'd appreciate it."

"I don't know why. Christmas is a beautiful name." He studied her intently. "Just as beautiful as Spring, Summer, and Autumn."

So much for keeping her secret.

She sat back in her chair. "How did you figure it out?"

"It wasn't all that hard once I knew your name. It never made sense to me why a single mom from Wyoming would suddenly show up in Bliss, Texas, and want to put down roots. I would think that a single mom would want to live close to family so they could help her." He smiled. "Of course, that's exactly why you want to live here, isn't it? You want to be close to your family."

She shook her head. "It's not about me. I've survived with only a mama for over thirty years. I figure I could survive with just me and my daughter for the rest of my life. But I want more for Carrie Anne. I want her to have what I didn't. I want her to have cousins to play with and aunts and uncles to spoil her rotten."

"So what are you waiting for? Why haven't you told the Hadleys that Holt is your daddy?"

She shrugged. "I was going to, but then I figured I'd wait until they got to know me and Carrie Anne. It will be easier for them to accept a friend as family than a stranger."

"From what I can tell, you *are* friends with them."

He had a good point. She had become friends with the Hadleys. She got along with all three of the triplets and she talked with Dirk every morning when he came into the bakery before he started his day as mayor. She'd even babysat for his triplet girls a few times while his wife Gracie volunteered at the Tender Heart Museum or worked on the book she was writing. So what was she waiting for? Why hadn't she told them about being their half-sister? There was only one answer.

"I guess I'm scared. What if they hate me after they find out? What if they hate Carrie Anne?"

"I can't see that happening."

"But it's possible. They believe that their mama was the only woman Holt ever loved enough to have children with. I'll blow that theory completely out of the water. Not to mention screwing up the entire Hadley birth order. Summer is quite proud of being the oldest Hadley. I can't see her taking kindly to being bumped out of that position."

Cord laughed. "You do have a point there. My daughter-in-law loves ordering her siblings around. But I doubt you being older will change that. So where did Holt meet your mama?"

"In Wyoming. He was working on his uncle's ranch and entered a county rodeo and won the bull-riding contest. My mama was the one who awarded him the trophy. And that was all it took.

The women in my family have always been suckers for cowboys." Her cheeks heated when she realized what she'd said. "Not me . . . I mean, not me anymore. Now I hate rodeo cowboys." She cringed. "Present company excluded, of course."

He sent her a skeptical look. "Of course. So I gather your father didn't stick around once he found out your mama was pregnant."

"She didn't know she was pregnant until after he was gone. When I was born, she got his address from his uncle and sent Holt a letter telling him about me, but he never replied. I wanted to believe that he never got the letter." She paused. "But it turns out he did get it." She looked at him. "I know it seems silly that I would go in search of a father I'd never even met. But after my mother died, I had this huge hole inside me that I just needed to fill. So I got Holt's last address from his uncle and came to Texas. I had this dream that he'd be excited to see me. Instead, he couldn't have cared less. He didn't even shed a tear for my mama passing away."

Cord studied her, his eyes sad. "I'm sorry."

"What for? You aren't responsible for all the sins of all the deadbeat dads in the world."

He tapped his hat on his knee. "No, I guess not. My sins are heavy enough a burden."

"Are you going to tell Summer about me?" she asked.

"It's not my secret to tell. But I do think that you need to. I know you're scared, but I don't think the Hadleys are the type to shut out a good woman and a sweet little kid." He got up and pulled on his hat. "You can trust me to keep your secret."

"Thank you," she said. "Thank you for giving me

a job and being so nice to me and Carrie Anne. Ryker should be happy to call you his dad. Hopefully, one day he will."

He didn't say anything. He just stood there for a moment with his heart in his eyes before he nodded and walked out of the room.

When he was gone, Christie thought about their conversation. He was right. She shouldn't be scared of telling the truth. The Hadleys weren't the type to hold a grudge against her for something she'd had no control over. She would tell them the truth . . . but after the holidays.

Just in case she and Cord were wrong, she refused to ruin Carrie Anne's Christmas.

CHAPTER SIX

SAVANNAH ARRINGTON WAS A GO-GETTER. Once she'd measured Cord's house and made sketches of the layout, she went right to work on filling it with furniture. Furniture trucks from Austin arrived daily loaded down with couches, tables, chairs, and more beds. And packages were delivered at all hours from online stores filled with things Cord hadn't even known he needed. Like colorful throw pillows, a bright turquoise kitchen mixer, a Trojan horse doorstop, and all kinds of gewgaws and knickknacks.

By the end of the week, the ranch house had started to resemble a home . . . just not a home that looked anything like Summer and Ryker's. And since they were the ones he'd built the house for, he wasn't too happy. Once it was all decorated, he planned to ask Ryker and Summer to come live on the ranch. He had missed most of his son's first twenty-four years, and he didn't want to miss a second of his next twenty-four. This was a chance to give his son a home. This was his chance for redemption.

Of course, he'd always tried to steer clear of saying things to women that might upset them, especially one who had been working so hard to help him. But his dream of having a family came before a woman's hurt feelings. So on Friday morning, he broached the subject with Savannah as soon as she arrived.

"The house sure looks nice, but it's not quite what I had in mind." He waited for her to either get mad or burst into tears, but Savannah Arrington didn't seem the least bit upset. She just flashed that brilliant smile of hers.

"Yes, I know that you wanted your décor to look similar to Summer and Ryker's. But after coming out here and seeing the house, I knew it was all wrong. Summer and Ryker's home is an old Victorian. This is a new ranch-style home. Putting nineteen-century antique furniture in it would be like serving mint juleps with Mexican food. They just don't go, honey." She lifted a hand to the great room, careful not to wake up Dax who slept in a baby backpack that hung in front of her. "Your décor needs to be western and rugged." She winked at him. "Just like its owner. If you wouldn't be comfortable in that little bitty ol' antique bed I had in my shop, you certainly wouldn't be comfortable on a little ol' antique loveseat or a spindly-legged chair."

"But I want my son and his wife to feel comfortable here."

She patted his arm. "I promise they will be comfortable, honey. Just look at those big cushioned couches I ordered for you. Who wouldn't be comfortable sitting on those?"

She did have a point. The couches were damned comfortable. And the leather massage chair she'd order for the master bedroom was like sitting on a cloud with magic muscle-relaxing fingers. Once Ryker and Summer moved in, Cord planned to give them the master suite. He was keeping the chair.

"But, of course, if you really hate the way I've decorated," Savannah said. "I'll be happy to send things back and redo it to your liking."

He looked around the room. He didn't hate the way she'd decorated. In fact, he pretty much loved it. He loved the painting of the running horses above the mantel and the Native American pottery she'd strategically placed on the bookcases with the hardcover books about horses and the old west. He loved the rustic bedroom furniture she'd ordered for him and the soft, fluffy comforter that covered his king-sized mattress. And he loved the sturdy dishes she'd placed in the cupboards with coffee mugs that fit nicely in his hand. Even the wooden rockers on the front porch seemed to fit his butt perfectly.

He hadn't thought he had a style, but obviously Savannah had found one. She had turned his house into a home that he felt comfortable in. All it needed was his family. And maybe once Ryker saw it, he'd like it too. After all, he was his father's son.

"No, don't change it," he said. "Let's leave it as it is."

She smiled brightly. "You won't be sorry. You're going to love living here. Now follow me and I'll show you what I've done in the nursery."

They walked down the hall to the room closest to the master suite. Cord figured Summer and Ryker would want their baby's room nearby. Savannah opened the door to the room, and Cord was struck speechless.

Three of the walls were painted the soft blue of a Texas sky at dawn and the other wall behind the white crib was covered in gray barn wood. There was a spotted cow skin rocking chair in one corner, a wooly white throw rug in front of the crib, framed pictures of cute cows, sheep, and ponies, a bookcase filled with books and stuffed ranch animals, a dresser and changing table with little horseshoe knobs, and a rocking horse with big brown eyes and a yarn mane and tall.

"I kept everything gender neutral since we don't know if the baby is going to be a boy or a girl," Savannah said. "I think it will be perfect for either." When Cord didn't say anything, she turned to look at him. Her eyes instantly grew concerned. "You don't like it."

He shook his head. "No, it's perfect." It was perfect. The kind of perfect nursery a father should give his child. Cord couldn't even remember what Ryker's nursery had looked like. That was the kind of crappy father he'd been. The sharp hunger for a drink hit him hard in the gut.

"Are you okay?" Savannah asked.

"Yeah," he said. But he wasn't. He wouldn't be until he got his son back. The doorbell rang, and he went to answer it. It was another delivery—this time, the furniture for the other bedrooms.

Savannah told the delivery guys where she wanted it placed. After the beds were set up, Cord tipped the guys and helped Savannah start putting on the clean sheets and bedding. They had only done two rooms when Dax woke up and started to fuss. Savannah headed to the kitchen and returned only moments later with Dax out of his backpack and a bottle. She handed both to Cord.

"Would you mind feeding him while I finish up? I've never met a man yet who knows how to make a bed properly or arrange throw pillows."

"I'm not really good with babies either." Cord tried to hand the baby and the bottle back to her, but she completely ignored him and picked up the comforter.

"That's nonsense. If you wrangled wild horses, you can wrangle one little ol' precious baby."

Cord didn't agree. But when Dax started really crying, he tucked him into the crook of his arm and carried him into the great room. He sat down in the cushioned rocker in front of the huge picture window and held the bottle to Dax's mouth. The baby immediately latched on like a calf to his mama's tit.

Cord looked out at the window at the pasture where Maple and Ruckus were grazing and tried to ignore the baby and the pain the tiny, warm body made him feel. But finally he couldn't help but look down. Big bluebonnet eyes the color of his mother's stared back at him. Eyes that held curiosity . . . and trust.

It was the trust that made Cord realize what an idiot he was being. It wasn't this little guy's fault that he had some major issues. He smiled. "Hey, little one, what do you think of this old cowboy?" Dax studied him intently as he drank his milk. "Yeah, I know," he said in a low voice. "I'm pretty screwed up. But I'm working on it."

Dax flashed a milky smile around the nipple of the bottle. But before Cord could take that as encouragement, the baby let out a big fart.

Cord laughed. "Just gas." He cuddled the baby closer and rocked. "I happen to know a song about that." He started singing. "Beans, beans, the musical fruit . . ."

By the time Savannah came out to retrieve her son, Cord and Dax had formed a manly alliance. Cord even burped him—following Savannah's instructions—then carried him out to the car and buckled him into his car seat.

"You're a natural," Savannah said once he'd closed the back door of her SUV.

"I'm learning." He just wished he had learned a little faster.

Once they were gone, he headed out to the pasture. An afternoon storm was forecast, and with the drop of temperature, he figured the forecast was right. He wanted to make sure Maple and Ruckus were bedded down in their stalls before he had to go pick up Carrie Anne from school.

The storm hit on his way into town. Central Texas rarely got snow, but damned if it didn't look like snow flurries mixed in with the drizzle of rain. Of course, a few minutes later those flurries turned to sleet. Thankfully, the elementary school had a covered walkway in front that the kids could wait under for their rides. But when it was Cord's turn to pull up, he still jumped out and held his sheepskin coat above Carrie's head as she got into the backseat of his truck.

"It's snowing," she crowed when he got back in

the car.

He laughed as he pulled away from the curb. "I wouldn't call this snow. It's more like ice. Now buckle yourself into your car seat."

"It's not a car seat. It's a booster seat. Car seats are for babies."

"Whatever it is, your mama wants you buckled in it. Otherwise she wouldn't have spent the money on another one for me to have in my truck when I pick you up."

"She didn't spent money. She charged it. And she was real worried that our card was all full up and that little machine at Walmart was going to beep real loud and reject it. But, lucky for us, it didn't."

It bothered him to no end that Christie was struggling to make ends meet and refused to accept help. And he had tried. He paid her a good hourly wage for doing his social media and blog. But she flat refused to take money from him until she'd paid him back for fixing her car. Now she flat refused money because he was watching Carrie Anne after school. And he didn't even want to get started on her refusing to tell the Hadleys that she was their kin. The Hadleys would be happy to help her until she got on her feet. Of course, he doubted that she would take their help either. Cord hoped like hell Christie won the gingerbread contest. Then maybe she could relax and enjoy the holidays with her daughter.

"Can I ride Maple today?" Carrie Anne asked.

"I'm afraid not, Half Pint. It's too cold. Besides, we need to get you some boots and a safety helmet before you start riding." He had already bought both, but he wasn't about to give Christie another reason to work for free. He planned on giving the boots and helmet to Carrie as Christmas presents.

"Other kids ride without boots and helmets," Carrie Anne grumbled. "My friend, Sue Lee, rides barefoot."

"I don't care what Sue Lee does with her horses. With mine, you're going to wear proper boots."

"You're just saying that 'cause you sell boots."

"Yep. Now how was your day at school?"

"Good. I had a race with Douglas Jeffrey on the playground and won by a mile and a half."

After Christie had told him about Carrie Anne's asthma, he couldn't help but worry about her running. "You probably shouldn't run too fast. Do you take your inhaler to school?"

"Yeah. I have one in my backpack and the nurse keeps one in her office, but I don't need it anymore because of my new medicine. And you know what else I did today? I got to draw a picture of what I want for Christmas. It was the bestest picture in the whole entire class 'cause I'm a real good drawer and use lots of different colors. You want to see it?" Cord heard a zipper being pulled open before a piece of paper hit him in the back of the head.

He reached back and took it. He waited until they were stopped at a stop sign before he looked at the picture. It was of a big Christmas tree with lopsided branches, round colorful circles for ornaments, and a bright yellow star on top. Under the tree was a bicycle and purple cowboy boots. Next to the tree were four stick figures. He could pick out Christie because she had long yellow hair and an oven mitt on one hand. And he could pick out Carrie Anne because she was smaller and had shorter yellow hair, but he didn't know who the other two stick figures were.

"Who's standing around the tree?" he asked.

"Mama, me, you," she paused. "And my daddy."

Cord felt honored to be included. He also felt sad. Had Ryker drawn pictures like this in school? Had he included a stick figure of Cord with hopes that his father would some day show up on Christmas?

He handed the picture back. "That's a beautiful picture."

"Cord?"

"Yep."

"Are you crying?"

"Nope." He swallowed hard. "You want to stop off at the bakery for a cupcake?"

The squeal almost broke his eardrum. "Yes!"

But when they got to the bakery, the door was locked and the lights were out. Cord knocked on the door, and only a second later, Christie came running to unlock it. He ushered Carrie Anne inside and lowered the coat he'd been holding over their heads to protect them from the sleet.

"What's going on?" he asked.

"The storm knocked out the power so we had to close. I'm glad you stopped by. I was just going to call you and tell you to take Carrie Anne to the trailer and I'd meet you there." Christie smoothed Carrie Anne's hair off her forehead. "You okay, Baby Girl?"

"Yeah. There's no lights? Can we light candles? Can I have a cupcake?" Carrie bounced with excitement. "And can I see the gingerbread house?" Before her mother could answer, she raced back to the kitchen.

Christie quickly followed after her. "Be careful and don't fall. And don't you dare touch the gingerbread house. The royal icing isn't dry."

When they got into the kitchen, Cord expected to find a gingerbread house with a candy roof and little gingerbread people. Instead, there was a huge gingerbread cowboy boot sitting on the counter with a door above the heel and windows on the shaft.

"It's a boot," Carrie Anne said with obvious disappointment.

"No, it's not." Christie smiled at her daughter. "It's a house. Just like the story of a little old woman who lived in a shoe and had so many children she didn't know what to do. But this is a boot where a happy Texas gingerbread family is going to live—as soon as I get them made."

"Make a girl like me, Mama!"

"Of course. You're the first one I'm going to make."

Cord walked around the counter and examined the boot from all sides. It wasn't close to being finished, but it had all the details of a well-made boot—from the looped pull straps to the stacked cookie heel and smooth rounded toe. "You've done a fine job."

There wasn't much light coming in from the high windows, but there was enough to see the pride on Christie's face. "Thank you." A teasing smile tipped the corners of her mouth. "I thought I'd call it 'A Big Boot-iful Texas Christmas.'"

She had used his idea, and he couldn't help feeling a little happy about that. He winked at her.

"I think you've got a winner. Now let's get home before this storm gets any worse."

The storm *did* get worse as they headed home. Concerned for their safety, Cord followed Christie and Carrie Anne all the way back to their trailer. When they got there, he became even more concerned. The little vintage trailer they lived in was rocking back and forth in the strong wind like a fishing bobber. He hopped out of his truck and stopped Christie from getting out of her car.

"You can't stay here in this kind of weather," he yelled above the howling wind and the sleet pelting the roof of her car.

"We'll be fine," she yelled back. "Now will you move out of the way so I can get out?"

Stubborn woman, he thought as he stepped back. He held his coat over their heads as she helped Carrie out of the backseat. But before Carrie could climb out of her booster chair, the sleet worsened, pinging off the hood of the car and the aluminum siding of the trailer like a spray of gunshots. Carrie Anne let out a scream and jumped back in the car.

Christie hesitated for only a second before she closed the back door. "Fine. We'll stay at the motor lodge in town."

"No, you won't," he said. "I'm not going to let you drive back to town on slick roads. You'll stay the night with me."

She glanced up at him beneath the shelter of his sheepskin coat, and he could read the consternation in her pretty hazel eyes. He quickly revised his words. "In the guestroom. I'd never think otherwise."

But as he breathed in her gingerbread scent and

lost himself in twin pastures of earthy green, Cord wondered who he was lying to the most: Christie . . . or himself.

CHAPTER SEVEN

"A FIRE? WE'RE GONNA HAVE A fire?" Carrie Anne hopped around like a jumping bean. "Can we roast hot dogs and marshmallows? Can we, Cord? Can we?"

Worried that her daughter was going to knock over the expensive-looking lamp sitting on the end table, Christie tried to corral her. "Settle down, please. You're going to break something."

"There's nothing she can break that's not replaceable." Cord lowered the load of firewood he'd brought in from outside into the tinderbox on the huge stone hearth. "But I'm afraid a weenie roast is out. I don't have any hot dogs. Since I eat breakfast and dinner at the diner, all I buy at the grocery store are sandwich items." He knelt in front of the fireplace and strategically placed the wood inside. "I think I have the makings for ham or peanut butter sandwiches."

"With jelly?" Carrie continued to bounce.

The side of Cord's mouth tipped up as he stuffed some crumbled newspaper under the wood he'd stacked. "With the ham or the peanut butter?"

"With the peanut butter." Carrie Anne scrunched up her face. "Ham doesn't go with jelly, silly."

Cord laughed. "Then PB and J it is."

Christie wanted to decline dinner and head back to her trailer. She felt uncomfortable staying the night with Cord. But the thick layer of sleet on his cowboy hat and the shoulders of his coat told her that the storm had not abated.

"Thank you," she said.

He glanced at her. "That's about the fifth 'thank you' you've given me since we arrived. And I think that's more than enough. I'm not just doing you a favor. You're also doing me one. I hate rattling around in this big ole house by myself. Now why don't you take off your coat and relax?"

She hadn't even realized she was still wearing her coat. Her cheeks flushed with heat as she took it off and walked over to the hall tree to hang it next to Carrie Anne's. Spying her daughter's backpack, she lifted it off its hook and carried it to the dining room table.

"Before you eat dinner, you need to get your phonics homework done, Carrie Anne."

That set off whining theatrics. "But I have the whole weekend to do my homework, and I want to watch Cord start a fire."

Cord picked up a long butane lighter and lit the newspaper under the stack of wood. "There you go."

Carrie Anne watched with disappointment at the flames that were already licking the stacked wood. "That's it?"

"That's it. Now go do your homework like your mama says."

Christie waited to hear more whining, but Carrie Anne surprised her by skipping over and sitting down at the table. Christie didn't know why that annoyed her. Maybe because Carrie Anne listened to Cord better than she did her own mother.

Carrie finished her phonics homework in record time. She knew most of her sounds and was starting to read simple words. Christie figured Ms. Marble's tutoring had helped. Although Cord had been working with her too. Her daughter was always spelling some word that Cord had taught her while she helped him in the barn.

He disappeared during the homework session, but reappeared after it was over with three plates of peanut butter and jelly sandwiches and potato chips. They ate at the end of the long dining room table while Carrie Anne regaled them with stories about school. Thankfully, there were no more stories about S-E-X. Christie had taken Cord's advice and talked to Jonas Murphy's mom. Mrs. Murphy had blushed profusely and said she intended to have a long talk with her oldest son. She'd also thanked Christie for coming to her rather than going to the principal. The principal happened to be a family friend, and if he'd found out, she would've never been able to look the man in the eyes again.

After they ate, Carrie Anne wanted to play a game. Since Cord didn't have any board games, Christie suggested charades. When it was Cord's turn, she worried that he might feel awkward acting things out. But he proved to be a natural at the game. His performance as a simpering Cinderella at the ball had Carrie Anne and Christie laughing until they cried.

Around nine o'clock, Christie brought an end to the fun. "Time for bed."

Carrie Anne started to argue, but Cord rose from the couch and cut her off. "It's my bedtime too. I have to get up early to feed the horses."

"Can I help?" Carrie asked.

"If you wake up in time."

She jumped off the couch. "I'm going to bed right now so I'll get up extra early."

Cord winked at her. "Good idea, Half Pint."

He showed them to one of the spare rooms. Savannah had given Christie the full tour of the newly decorated house the day before, but the guestrooms had still needed furniture. The room Cord showed them to now held an oak dresser and a queen-sized bed with a white comforter and a multitude of colorful throw pillows. The bed looked like a huge heavenly cloud compared to the hard, little mattress she shared with her daughter in the trailer. Carrie Anne must've thought so too because she made a beeline for the bed as soon as Cord left, and Christie had to intercept her before she reached it.

"Oh, no you don't. You are not hopping on a white comforter with your sneakers. Get your pajamas on and brush your teeth, then you can dive in."

For once, Carrie Anne listened. Within minutes, her teeth were brushed and her pajamas on and she was snuggled down in the bed with her tattered Raggedy Ann doll that Christie's mother had made her. Christie usually told her a story before they went to sleep. But the soft bed proved too much for her daughter, and by the time Christie had changed into her flannel pajamas and brushed her teeth, Carrie was sound asleep.

Christie sat on the edge of the bed and smoothed back the hair of her sleeping daughter. A wave of love washed over her, and right behind it came a wave of guilt. Guilt about taking her from the only home she'd ever known and not being able to give her a big soft bed in a nice warm house. Christie wallowed in guilt for a few moments before she turned off the light and climbed into bed. But sleep eluded her. Her mind was too filled with the kind of Christmas Carrie Anne would have if she could only win the gingerbread house contest.

She finally got up and decided to sketch out some ideas of how to decorate the huge boot. She had a pen in her purse, but no paper, so she headed to Cord's office to get some. On the way, she had to walk through the living room. The lights were all off, but the fire was still blazing. There was something hypnotic about the flickering flames. They drew her like a moth, and she walked over to stand in front of the warm fire.

"Trouble sleeping?"

She jumped and whirled to see Cord stretched out on the couch. His boots were off and his stocking feet were crossed. He had his hands behind his head, and the snaps of his western shirt were unsnapped to reveal the center of his hard chest. She had seen him without a shirt when she'd taken a picture of him cleaning out the stalls. But there was a difference in seeing a bare back in a shadowy barn and seeing a bare chest in the glow of a fire. The flickering firelight reflected off the hard swells of his pectoral muscles and the sprinkling of dark hair between.

Danny Ray's chest had been as smooth and hairless as a baby's butt. When she'd first met him, she'd thought it was sexy. But she didn't know what sexy was until now. The sprinkling of hair on Cord's chest sent a deep, sensual longing through her . . . a longing that grew as she followed the trail of manly hair down his flat stomach to where it disappeared in the waistband of his Wranglers.

"Christie?"

Her gaze lifted to Cord's bemused expression. It was obvious that he'd asked her something, but she didn't have a clue what it was. "Umm . . . excuse me?"

He sat up, and his shirt closed enough to get her mind out of the gutter. Or out of Cord's jeans. "I asked if you had trouble sleeping? Is the bed okay?"

"It's fine. I just don't sleep much these days. I have a lot to think about. What happened to you going to bed early?"

He smiled. "Just a ploy to get Carrie there. Like you, I have trouble sleeping." He picked up a mug that was sitting on the end table. "You want a cup of coffee? It's decaf."

"No, thank you. I should probably go to bed. I don't want Carrie Anne waking up and getting scared."

"I don't think that kid of yours is scared of much." He paused. "Please stay. I don't often have company at night. It would be nice to talk to someone . . . other than myself."

She shouldn't give in. She had no business chatting with Cord in her pajamas. Especially when she couldn't wait for his shirt to open back up.

But how could she ignore his plea when he'd done so much for them—including offering them his home. And it wasn't his fault that she had a major weakness for hot rodeo cowboys.

A weakness she needed to get over.

She took a seat on the opposite couch, as far from him as she could get without being obvious. "Just for a few minutes." He settled back with his cup of coffee and his shirt fell open again. She looked away and searched for a conversation starter. "If you don't like rattling around in this house, why did you make it so big?" She planned to keep her eyes on the fire instead of Cord, but when it took so long for him to answer, she glanced over.

He was staring at the flickering flames, his eyes gold and red reflections. "Because I'm not planning on living here by myself."

She didn't know why his answer surprised her. She should've known that a man as good looking as Cord would have a girlfriend somewhere. Or maybe even a fiancé.

"Oh," she said. "That's . . . nice. When does she get here?"

"What?" He glanced over at her, then laughed. "No. I wasn't talking about a woman." She didn't know why she felt relieved, but that was the only way to explain the tension that left her body.

"Then who did you build this big house for?"

He hesitated before he answered. "For my son and his family."

She was confused. "But I thought they have a house in town. You're going to give them this one?"

"I wasn't planning on giving it to them—although eventually everything I own will go to

Ryker. But for now, I'm hoping they'll just come live with me. The house they're living in now is a money pit. This house is brand new and much bigger with a barn and horses and plenty of room to raise a son."

"They're having a son?"

Cord seemed taken back by the question. "Did I say son? I meant their child. What girl or boy wouldn't love growing up on a big ranch? They could ride horses with their dad. Or go fishing. Or just sit around a big fire and shoot the breeze like we are."

Since it would be a long time before Ryker and Summer's child could ride, or fish, or shoot the breeze, she was even more baffled . . . until she finally figured out what Cord was saying. He didn't want Ryker to move here to raise his son. He wanted Ryker to move here so Cord could get another chance at raising his. The realization was tragic. She knew from experience that there were no do-overs with parenting. You were either there when your children were growing up or you weren't. But she couldn't tell Cord that. She couldn't break his heart.

"I'm sure they'll be . . . overwhelmed by your offer. When are you planning on asking them to move in?"

"I was waiting until the house was decorated and the baby's room finished." He leaned up, cradling the coffee mug in his hand. "Did you see it?"

Christie had seen it. She'd thought it was so sweet that Cord had thought to decorate a room for his grandchild to visit. Now that she realized it was for a more permanent arrangement, it wasn't sweet as much as bittersweet. "It's adorable," she said.

"Savannah did a great job. I figure it's my ace in the hole for getting Ryker to move in."

She wished there was a chance that Ryker and Summer would move in with Cord, but she knew there wasn't. Everyday at the bakery, Summer talked about how much she loved her little Victorian. She also talked about how much she liked walking to work and her plans to turn the attic into the perfect playroom. She wouldn't want to move. And there was no way Ryker was going to move without his family.

"Maybe you should wait to ask them," Christie said. When Cord flashed her a curious look, she scrambled for a reason. "I mean the holidays are coming up. And no one wants to move around the holidays. Besides, the bakery is really busy this time of year and you wouldn't want Summer driving back and forth during a storm like we're having right now. In fact, maybe you should wait until spring."

She thought that she'd come up with some pretty sound reasoning, but it didn't work. Cord seemed dead set on his son living with him.

"Nope. I can't wait that long. If I have to drive Summer to and from the bakery, so be it. It might be silly, but I have a vision of the perfect Christmas morning. And it includes having my family around a big tree with plenty of presents and love." He paused and looked at her. "Very similar to the picture Carrie Anne drew in class today."

"What picture?"

"A picture of her ideal Christmas. I think it's in her backpack."

Christie got up and walked to the hall tree where Carrie Anne's backpack hung. She found the picture in the side pocket and brought it back to the couch to look at it.

"I should've known cowboy boots and a bicycle would be in it," she said. "And there's me . . . and Carrie . . . and by the size of the belt buckle, I'd say that was you." She studied the last stick figure. "Who's that?"

"Her daddy."

All the energy drained right out of Christie at just the mention of Danny Ray. She set the picture on the nearby end table and grabbed the throw blanket that hung over the corner of the couch. She snuggled under it and stared at the fire. She expected Cord to have questions about her ex. She just didn't expect the question he asked.

"Do you still love him?"

She didn't have to think too hard to answer. "Yes. I think a part of me will always love Danny Ray Corbett. He's a hard man not to love. He's handsome, charming, and funny. He was my first real boyfriend. The only man I ever had sex with. The father of my child. How could I not love him? It's too bad he wasn't ready to be a father. Or a husband." She sighed. "Damned rodeo."

Cord set his coffee mug on the end table and rested his head back on the couch. "It's not the rodeo. I've known lots of rodeo cowboys who were great husbands and daddies. Unlike Danny Ray and me, they didn't get sucked into their own egos. They didn't let a few good rides and a few star-struck buckle bunnies make them think that they were more than they were. We were just stupid. Like Redford in the *Electric Horseman*, we lost the better part of ourselves."

She leaned her head back on the cushions and watched the firelight flicker across the high ceiling with its huge oak beams. "My mama loved that movie. Every damn time it comes on, I can't help watching it—or crying like a baby when Redford says goodbye to Fonda and starts hitchhiking on that lonely highway as Willie sings 'My Heroes have Always Been Cowboys.'"

"'Hands on the Wheel.'"

She glanced over at him. "What?"

"Willie doesn't sing 'My Heroes Have Always been Cowboys' at the end. He sings 'Hands on the Wheel.'"

He started singing in a low, raspy voice that was sexy and soothing at the same time. Christie hadn't paid that much attention to the lyrics when she'd watched the movie. She did so now, and the poignant story of a man who was lost until he found himself in a woman's eyes made her own eyes sting with tears. One fell down her cheek when that cowboy finally found his way home.

Cord finished singing, and they both just sat there—all the emotions the song had evoked left no room for words. Once the flames finally flickered down to glowing embers, he got to his feet.

"Well, I guess I'll call it a night."

Christie rose. "Me too."

But once they were standing, neither one of them made a move to leave. They just stood there facing each other. Christie's gaze locked with Cord's. In his eyes, she saw the same hungry need that was inside her. A need she could no longer ignore. She knew it was crazy. She knew she would regret it come sun up, but that didn't stop her from lifting a hand and cradling his scruff-roughened jaw.

His eyes slid closed and her name came out in rush of warm breath. "Christie." When he opened his eyes there was nothing but glowing heat that sent any reservations she might still have had up in smoke.

His callused fingers closed around her wrist, holding her hand in place as he turned his head and pressed his lips to her palm. It was the most romantic kiss she'd ever gotten in her life, and she struggled to catch her breath as his hot lips scorched her skin. He kept them there for a long moment, as if savoring the taste of her, before he lifted his head. He hesitated as if waiting for her denial, but, at that moment, she couldn't deny him anything. She held her breath as his mouth lowered to hers.

There were no soft kisses or playful nips. He kissed her like a man kisses a woman—with everything he's got and then some. He didn't just taste her. He consumed her with skillful lips and a wet heat that made her knees weak. She might've slipped down to his feet if he hadn't released her wrist and placed his large hand on her back, pressing her to the hard length of his body.

And he was hard. Hard chest. Hard stomach. Hard bulge beneath faded denim. He flexed his hips, and desire ricocheted through her. She wanted. She wanted like she had never wanted before. She slid one hand in the back pocket of his Wranglers and squeezed his firm butt cheek as she rubbed against his ridged fly, trying desperately to feed that aching need.

He moaned into her mouth, the sound vibrating through her body like a plucked string. With their lips still locked, he two-stepped her back until her legs hit the couch and they tumbled down. As she shifted to accommodate Cord's big body, Christie bumped her head on the end table. It wasn't a hard bump, but it was enough to have Cord pulling away from the kiss.

He opened his eyes, and it was like he'd just woken up from a dream. He stared at her in confusion for a moment before he quickly got to his feet. He stood over her looking like a man who had just committed the worst crime imaginable. His face held a heap of regret, followed by firm determination.

"I'm sorry, Christie, but I can't. I can't make any more mistakes. I've made enough."

He turned and walked away.

CHAPTER EIGHT

CORD WAS A CHICKEN SHIT. There were no two ways about it. He snuck out of the house before the sun was even up, fed the horses, and then hightailed it to town. He got to Lucy's Place Diner just as it was opening and sat at the counter by himself, staring into his coffee and trying to figure out what the hell was wrong with him. Christie was much younger than he was. She was his assistant. And Carrie Anne's mama. For all of these reasons, he had no business messing with her. No business whatsoever.

The last thing Christie needed was another screwed-up cowboy. And there was little doubt that Cord was still screwed up. He had thought he had control over his body's needs and desires, but last night proved otherwise. All it had taken was a Willie song and one caress from her soft hand for him to lose it. If he hadn't pulled away to see if she was okay after bumping her head, he would've had his way with her right there on the couch. It was the way she'd kissed him—like he was a bowl of fresh cream and she was a starving barn cat. She hadn't just wanted him. She'd needed him. And it had been so damned long since he'd been needed that it went straight to his head.

Both heads.

"You're up awfully early."

He turned to see Ms. Marble standing by the door in a knit red hat and matching coat that made her look like Mrs. Claus. And if anyone would make a good Mrs. Claus it was Ms. Marble. She had a way with children, because she'd been a first grade teacher for almost forty years, and she could bake like nobody's business. Everyone in town loved and respected her. Dirk Hadley might be the mayor of Bliss, but Ms. Marble was the Queen Bee. The one who made sure that everyone in her hive was thriving and happy. And in her book, part of being happy was being married.

Which was why Cord avoided her like the plague.

"Good mornin', Ms. Marble," he said. "I was just having a quick cup of coffee before I head back to the ranch." Or over to Summer and Ryker's. There was no way he was going back to the ranch until he had given Christie plenty of time to leave. He *was* a chicken shit.

He started to reach for his hat that was sitting on the counter when Ms. Marble stopped him. "You're not on my list."

He looked at her. "Excuse me, ma'am?"

"My matchmaking list. You're not on it. So you can stop running from me every time you see me."

Before he could get his mouth closed, she walked to the coat rack and hung up her hat and coat. She tugged off her gloves and folded them neatly before tucking them in her coat pocket, then she walked over to the counter and sat down on the barstool next to him.

He couldn't help it. He had to ask. "So why am I not on your list?"

"Because your mind is preoccupied at the moment with Ryker. And until you can get that figured out, you aren't husband material."

Damn, the woman knew more about him than he'd thought.

"Good mornin', Ms. Marble." Bella Sanders came out of the kitchen. She worked at the diner with her sister Stella. She was a nice woman and a major flirt. She winked at him. "Now don't you be tryin' to put the moves on Ms. Marble. You're all mine, cowboy."

Cord wouldn't have joined in on the flirting if he hadn't known that she was happily married with two kids. "You know my heart belongs to you, darlin'. Just so long as you keep my coffee black and my bacon crispy."

"You are such a tease, Rodeo Man." She poured some hot water in a cup and added a tea bag, then carried it over to Ms. Marble. "Here's your regular, Ms. Marble."

"Thank you, Bella." Ms. Marble took the cup. "I guess Carly is still staying home with Zane Junior." Carly Arrington was the owner of the diner, and until she'd had her son, she'd worked there most days.

"She sure is," Bella said. "And I'd stay home too if I had a sweet baby like that to cuddle. My babies are all grown up. Rob's playing high school basketball and Jeff is doing what all freshman college boys do—drinking too much and not studying enough." She wiped off the counter with a wet towel. "So who are you fixing up now that all the Hadley girls are married off? It sure would be nice to have a Christmas wedding in the little white chapel. What about Granny Bon? I heard she was on your list."

"She is, but I haven't yet found the right man for her."

Bella looked at Cord. "What about this cute cowboy? Of course, he's a bit younger than Granny Bon."

"Love is blind to physical looks and age," Ms. Marble said. "But I'm not concerned with my friend Bonnie Blue at the moment. Right now, there's another woman who needs to find a good man. Do you know Christie Buchanan?"

Cord choked on the sip of coffee he'd just taken. Ms. Marble patted him on the back until he stopped coughing. He cleared his throat. "Sorry. It must've gone down wrong." He didn't know why he was so surprised that Christie was on Ms. Marble's list. Christie was single and pretty as a bouquet of spring flowers. And she deserved to find a good man. A young man who wasn't haunted by his past.

"Of course I know Christie," Bella said. "She's the sweetest little thing this side of the Pecos. And from what I hear, she's had some bad luck with men. It sure would be nice if she got herself a man like my Ronny. And Carrie Anne could certainly use a loving father. One with a firm hand who can handle a sassy little girl."

Cord's brow knotted. He didn't much care for the thought of a daddy using a firm hand with

Carrie Anne. "I wouldn't say that Carrie needs a firm hand."

Ms. Marble glanced over at him. Her intense blue-eyed stare made him feel like a kid who needed to explain why he didn't have his homework.

"I realize that Carrie Anne can be a handful," he said. "But I happen to like a little spunk. And I would hate to see her with a strict daddy who would discipline the sparkle right out of her."

A smile lit Ms. Marble's face. "I couldn't agree more. I've been tutoring Carrie Anne twice a week and I've grown quite fond of her. I want her to get the kind of father who would love her as his own."

"Christie needs that kind of caring love too," Cord said. "She's been hurt. And hurt people—just like hurt horses—need careful handling." Not that he had been careful with her the night before. He cringed at the thought of the way he'd manhandled her.

Ms. Marble patted his hand. "You are absolutely right."

Bella leaned on the counter. "But how are you going to be sure the man you try to fix Christie up with will be a perfect daddy and husband? Some men are quite good at putting up a false front just to get into a woman's panties."

Cord had to agree. He had done his share of manipulating women just to get into their panties. And he didn't want some jackass doing the same thing to Christie.

"I think I'm a pretty good judge of character," Ms. Marble said as she got up. "I have the perfect man picked out for her. Now if you'll excuse me, I have some Christmas baking to get done."

"But you didn't finish your tea," Bella said. "You want me to put it in a to-go cup for you?"

"No, thank you, dear. And could you put it on my tab?"

"No need for that. I've got it." Cord stood and pulled out his wallet from his back pocket. "You already have this man picked out? Who is he?"

"Oh, I never divulge who I'm matchmaking until we're at the little white chapel." Ms. Marble smiled and patted his cheek. "But I'm sure you'll be invited to the wedding and we can have us a nice little chat then."

Cord watched as she pulled on her coat, hat, and gloves and disappeared out the door in a swirl of cold air. When she was gone, Bella headed back to the kitchen while Cord sat there and puzzled over who the man could be. He went through all the young men he knew in town, but none seemed like the right fit for Christie and Carrie Anne. And he started to worry that Ms. Marble wasn't as good a matchmaker as she claimed. She hadn't known Christie for longer than a couple months. How could she make a good choice for someone after only knowing them for that short a time?

Of course, just because Ms. Marble tried to match Christie with someone didn't mean that Christie would go along with it. She was one prickly woman when it came to men. Although she hadn't been all that prickly last night. Of course, the holidays did crazy things to women. It made them get all sentimental and hungry for holiday romance. Cord just wanted to make sure she had that romance with the right man. He certainly wasn't the right man, but he was starting to have his doubts that Ms. Marble had found the right one either. The thought of Christie being stuck with the wrong one did not sit well.

The door of the diner opened and Ryker stepped in. Cord was surprised to see his son. Ryker wasn't an early riser. Especially on a Saturday morning.

"Hey there, son. What are you doing up so early?"

Ryker took off his cowboy hat. His jaw was unshaven and his eyes still held the last dregs of sleep. "Summer had a craving for a breakfast burrito." He cringed. "With pickles and lots of green chiles."

Cord chuckled. "Your mama used to want potato chips and mint chocolate chip ice cream. I thought that was weird, but Summer might have that beat. How's she feeling?"

"A little temperamental." Ryker grinned. "But she wouldn't be Summer if she didn't show that phenomenal temper every now and again." He sat down on the stool next to Cord. For just a second, Cord thought he was going to lean in and hug him. But of course he didn't. "So what are you doing here so early? You usually don't get into town for breakfast until after you take care of the horses."

"I had trouble sleeping last night." It wasn't a lie. After the kiss, he hadn't gotten a wink of sleep.

Ryker nodded. "I guess it's hard getting used to sleeping on a real mattress. Savannah did a great job on the house by the way."

Cord was relieved to hear that Ryker liked it. "Savannah did do a fine job. And now that's it done, I was thinking about having a little family dinner party. Maybe get some pictures of us trimming a tree for social media."

"Yeah, sure. Just tell me when so I can give Summer the heads up. We should probably invite Christie too so she can take pictures."

Cord didn't want to invite Christie. He wanted to stay away from her as much as possible. He wasn't about to fire her when she needed the money, but he didn't want to socialize with her either. "Doesn't your newfangled phone have a timer for taking pictures?"

"Yes, but it's a pain in the butt. It would be much easier if Christie just took them." Ryker studied him. "Do you have a problem with that? I thought you liked her."

"I do." A little more than he wanted to. "I just thought it would be nice to have just the family."

Ryker looked like he wanted to say something, but instead he picked up a menu and started studying it. As he did, Cord couldn't help studying him.

It was like looking at himself when he was twenty years younger. Except Ryker was a much better man than he'd ever been. And Cord was so proud. So damned proud. But he couldn't take a speck of responsibility for the way his son had turned out. He hadn't been there to raise him into the man he was.

Bella came back out of the kitchen to refill Cord's coffee cup and take Ryker's order. When she left, Ryker's phone pinged. He pulled it out of his pocket and frowned.

"What's wrong?" Cord asked.

"Summer just texted that the toilet in the master bathroom is stopped up."

"You want me to come home with you and help you fix it?"

Ryker shook his head. "No, thanks." He went back to texting, and by the smile on his face, it wasn't about the plumbing anymore. Cord didn't mind being ignored. He was fine just getting to be in his son's company.

After he'd gotten off the booze and sobered up, he'd worried that he wouldn't have any kind of emotional attachment to his son. Close to twenty years had passed, and he'd been concerned that not only would his son not be able to love him, but he wouldn't be able to love his son. His worry was for nothing. As soon as he'd set eyes on Ryker, he'd almost wept with the strong emotions that had punched him in the chest. And those emotions had nothing to do with his son looking like him. It was a deeper connection—something that was felt, not seen. Cord figured that all parents had that invisible umbilical cord to their kids. Even bad parents like him and Carrie Anne's father.

Danny Ray.

Cord knew the man's name now. He also knew that Christie still loved him. It was too bad that Danny Ray couldn't be the good husband and father Christie and Carrie Anne needed. That would solve everyone's problems. Christie would have a husband she loved. Carrie Anne would have her actual daddy. And Cord would have temptation removed. But Danny Ray sounded as screwed up as Cord had once been. Without someone to knock some sense into him and show him what he was missing out on, he'd probably continue to be.

Cord froze with his coffee cup inches from his

mouth.

Wait a minute. Danny Ray did have someone to knock some sense into him. Someone who knew exactly what he was missing out on and exactly what the ramifications of being a bad father would be.

The waitress brought out Summer's burrito, and Ryker got up and took the bag before pulling out his wallet. "I better go before my wife comes charging down Main Street in her pajamas to get it. Let me know what day you want to have dinner."

Cord stood. "Will do." He couldn't help it. He grabbed Ryker and gave him a tight hug. Ryker didn't exactly hug him back, but he didn't pull away either. He just stood there until Cord finally let him go. After an uncomfortable moment, he pulled on his hat and headed out the door.

Once he was gone, Cord sat back down and took out his phone. It was still early, but Jasper Wheeler was a good friend who wouldn't mind being woken up . . . at least not too much.

"Whoever is calling me this early better have a damned good reason," Jasper snapped in a gruff voice.

Cord grinned. "I'm callin' about a horse."

There was a pause before Jasper laughed. "Why, Cord Evans, you sonofagun. How the hell have you been?"

"Fair to middling, which is better than any of us old bronc busters can expect. How have you been?"

"About the same. My broke back gives me fits when it rains, but I have a pretty little señorita to rub me down when it does."

"Liar," he said.

"You're right, but I keep looking for one. So what has you callin' so bright and early on a Saturday mornin'?" Jasper paused. "You aren't on the juice again, are you?"

"No. I've had enough juice to last me a lifetime. I'm staying sober and living in Texas in a little town called Bliss. If you're ever in the neighborhood, you should stop by. Its name is pretty accurate."

"I might just do that. I could use a little bliss in my life."

Jasper had had a life as hard as Cord—just not of his own making. He'd lost his wife a few years back to breast cancer and didn't have any kids to ease his grief. He had been Cord's mentor when Cord had first started rodeoing . . . until Cord had become too damned big for his own britches and they'd had a falling out. They had hooked back up as part of Cord's Alcoholics Anonymous twelve-step program. Jasper was one of the reasons Cord was still sober. The ornery old cuss had refused to let him give up. And he felt bad that he hadn't kept in closer touch with his friend.

"I'm going to hold you to that," he said. "There's more than enough room in the new ranch house I built."

"You always did enjoy blowing money. Of course, you've got enough of it. Every cowboy I run into is sporting Cord Evans boots. I prefer Tony Lama myself. Only wear yours 'cause you sent me a pair."

Cord smiled and shook his head before he got to the reason for his call. "Do you still have a connection at the rodeo association?"

"Do ticks love hound dogs? What did you need?"

"I need a phone number and address of one of the rodeo cowboys."

"I could probably manage that. Whose?"

"Danny Ray Corbett."

CHAPTER NINE

IT WAS HAPPENING AGAIN. SHE was losing her wits over another rodeo cowboy. All because of one sizzling, mind-blowing kiss that had rekindled the flame of desire she'd thought Danny Ray had permanently doused.

Thankfully, Cord was smarter than she was and had pulled away when he had. He'd called it a mistake. And he was right. Getting involved with Cord would be a huge mistake. Christie had way too many irons in the fire to add sex with a man who had proven he wasn't relationship material. But even knowing that, she was having a hard time forgetting what it had felt like to be pressed against his hard body and kissed like there was no tomorrow.

"Are you hot?"

She jumped and glanced over at Summer, who was taking molasses cookies out of the oven. "Excuse me?"

"I asked if you were as hot as I am." Summer set the cookie sheet on top of the oven and took off her oven mitt. "I swear Ryker turns up the heat every time he stops by."

Relieved that Summer hadn't read her mind, Christie relaxed. "He just wants to make sure that his wife and baby aren't getting cold."

Summer rolled her eyes, but there was a content smile on her face. "Crazy man." She picked up a spatula and started placing the cookies on a cooling rack. "So if you're not hot, explain those flushed cheeks. Autumn used to blush whenever she was embarrassed. Now she blushes whenever she's thinking dirty thoughts about her husband, Maverick. So what man in Bliss has you thinking dirty thoughts?"

Christie's eyes widened. Damn, her half-sister *had* read her mind. "Uhh . . . I wasn't . . . I mean I didn't—"

Summer turned and looked at her with surprise. "I was only kidding, but it looks like I've hit the nail on the head." She laughed. "Ms. Marble strikes again. That woman just put you on her list a week ago and already she found you a perfect match."

"What list?" Christie set down the piping bag of royal icing she'd been using to attach chocolate shutters to the gingerbread boot.

"Her matchmaking list. Don't tell me you haven't heard about Ms. Marble's matchmaking. She's helped almost every couple in town get together."

"Including me and Waylon." Spring breezed into the kitchen. She had shown up that morning and offered to take over for Christie at the front counter, stating that Waylon had gone out to the Tender Heart Ranch to help Raff and she was bored silly. But Christie thought it had more to do with Spring wanting to give her time to work on the gingerbread house.

The sweet gesture was just more proof that Cord was right. The Hadleys were good people who wouldn't hold a grudge against Christie. But there was no way they wouldn't be a little upset when they found out she'd lied to them. Which probably explained why she kept postponing telling the truth. She had finally gotten the siblings she had dreamed about, and she couldn't stand the thought of them being mad at her. She would tell them. She wanted to tell them. But after the first of the year. The holidays were chaotic enough without adding any more drama.

She picked up the piping bag and continued attaching the shutters on either side of the melted butterscotch candy windows. "I find it hard to believe that one woman can play matchmaker to an entire town."

Spring helped herself to a molasses cookie from the cooling rack and took a bite. "Then you don't know Ms. Marble. She is an extremely perceptive person. She knew that Waylon and I were a perfect match from day one. Without her forcing me to stay with Waylon when he was sick, I might not have ever found out what a great kisser he was and wanted more."

Christie knew all about great kissers and wanting more. She had wanted a lot more from Cord. She still did, but she refused to give into that want. "Well, I don't need to be on Ms. Marble's list. Carrie Anne and I are doing just fine without a man screwing things up."

"If that's the case, then who were you just daydreaming about?" Summer asked. "Or sex-dreaming if your heated cheeks were any indication?"

"You were sex-dreaming?" Spring's eyes sparked with excitement as she sat down on a stool next to Christie. "About who?" She held up a hand. "Wait, don't tell me. Cord Evans." Holy Cow! Sisters really could get into your head. "I swear if my heart didn't belong to Waylon," Spring continued, "I'd go after that hot cowboy in a New York second." She flashed a smug smile at Summer. "Then I'd be both your sister and your step-mommy."

Summer stared at her in horror. "That's just creepy, Spring Leigh." She pointed the spatula at them. "But you're right about Cord. Which explains why I fell so hard for Ryker. Hot is in their DNA." She looked at Christie. "Although I'm not sure Cord is ready for a relationship—serious or otherwise. He's still pretty screwed up over the mistakes he's made in the past."

Christie couldn't agree more. His belief that Ryker was going to move in with him was a perfect example. Adult children moved out. They didn't move back in. She wondered if she should tell Summer about Cord's plans, but then decided against it. She didn't like Cord sticking his nose into her business. She didn't need to stick her nose into his. He was a big boy. He could handle his life. She had all she could do to handle hers. And part of handing it was keeping her relationship with Cord on a boss/employee level. No more using him as a babysitter for Carrie Anne. And no more staying at his house . . . or late night kisses that knocked her socks off.

"I'm not interested in Cord Evans," she said. "Seriously or otherwise." It was only a half lie. She wasn't interested in him for a serious relationship, but her body was definitely interested in a physical one. She just chose to ignore her physical urgings.

"Then if it wasn't Cord," Spring said. "You must've been fantasizing about your ex." When Christie looked surprised, Spring reached out and squeezed her hand. "It's okay. If anyone gets it, we do. No matter what our daddy did, our mama was still crazy about him. But Mama didn't have as much willpower as you do, Christie. She welcomed our deadbeat daddy back every time he showed up."

Holt hadn't ever come to see Christie's mother . . . or her. And she didn't know what was worse—a father who showed up rarely or one who didn't show up at all.

"I don't have a speck of willpower," she said. "Which is one of the reasons I left Wyoming and Danny Ray far behind me. Not that he was beating down my mama's door to see me or Carrie Anne. The last time I talked to him was right after my mama died. I called to give him the news." She paused as pain tightened her heart. "Deep down, I think I was hoping that he'd show me some kind of love and sympathy. Instead, he thought I was calling for child support and gave me a list of reasons why he just couldn't spare a dime. When I heard a woman giggle, I hung up without ever telling him about my mama."

Spring squeezed her hand again and sent her a sympathetic look while Summer was a little more vocal.

"Asshole. You're lucky to be rid of him."

"His loss is our gain." Spring winked at Christie.

Summer set down her spatula and picked up a

cookie scoop. "She's right. If you hadn't shown up, Audie would've burned down the bakery by now. And speaking of the bakery, why are you back here instead of waiting on customers, Spring? And aren't you supposed to be keeping an eye on Carrie Anne?"

"The only customers are Stuart and Race, and Carrie Anne can handle herself with our two hometown football heroes. When I came back here to give y'all the good news, she was beating Stuart badly at some game on his phone."

"Well," Summer prompted. "What's the good news?"

Spring's blue eyes sparkled with excitement. "Autumn called and she and Maverick are coming home."

Summer went back to scooping dough onto the cookie sheets. "That's not news. Everyone already knows they're coming home for the holidays."

"But they aren't just coming home for the holidays. They're coming home for good."

Summer spun around. "What? But Maverick has been playing so well I thought the Miami Dolphins would sign him on for next year."

"They wanted to, but he turned them down." Spring smiled brightly. "It seems our brother-in-law would rather be a high school football coach than a professional football player."

Summer let out a loud whoop before she pulled Spring off her barstool and hugged her close, completely unaware of the cookie dough that fell out of the scoop and plopped onto the floor.

The sisters' joy warmed Christie's heart. It also made her a little jealous. The triplets had a bond that Christie would never share. She got up to get a paper towel to clean up the cookie dough and was completely shocked when Summer reached out and pulled her into the hug.

Summer was the tough Hadley sister. The one who never got too sentimental. So it was surprising to find out she was a bear hugger. Christie was pulled into a tight hug that squeezed all the air out of her. And since her mother had passed, Christie had needed a good tight hug.

"Hey, what's going on?"

They drew apart, and Christie turned to see Carrie Anne standing in the doorway. She was about to explain why they were celebrating when Spring spoke.

"We're celebrating girl power." She held out an arm. "Come join us, Sweet Pea." Carrie Anne raced over and was immediately enfolded in the group hug. It was one of the most poignant moments in Christie's life and she couldn't keep tears from filling her eyes. She tried to brush them away without anyone seeing, but of course Carrie Anne saw and brought everyone's attention to them.

"Why are you crying, Mama?"

Christie smiled down at her daughter. "Because Girl Power is a thing of beauty, Baby Girl."

"Damn straight it is." Summer quickly brushed at her eyes before she waved the cookie scoop. "Now everyone get back to work. We've got a business to run and a gingerbread house contest to win."

"And a sister to get ready for." Spring held out her hand to Carrie Anne. "Let's go find some good Christmas music to play, Sweet Pea. I'm starting to get in the holiday mood."

A few minutes later, "It's Beginning to Look a Lot Like Christmas" came out of the overhead speakers in the kitchen. Summer and Christie looked at each other and smiled before they started to sing along as they worked. Neither one had a good voice, but it didn't seem to matter. They sang along with three more Christmas songs before Ryker called and Summer left to meet him for lunch at the diner. Christie continued to work on the gingerbread house.

Once the shutters were done, she made more gingerbread dough for her gingerbread people. She wanted them to be unique, so after she rolled out the dough, she cut each figure out by hand. She made a family of four because that seemed like a nice even number. She made a father, a mother, a little girl, and a littler boy. Because this was Texas, she put a cowboy hat on the father and boots on the entire family. She also cut out some horses.

While she worked, she tried to keep her mind on anything but Cord. But the more she tried not to think about him, the more he snuck into her thoughts. Or not him as much as the kiss and how much she wanted a repeat. Which was crazy. If she couldn't stop thinking about repeating the kiss when she was away from him, what would she do when she was with him? Attack him in the barn if he took off his shirt? Dive on him in the corral if he bent over in those snug-fitting Wranglers? Waylay him in the office and shove him down on the desk?

There seemed to be only one way to keep from making a fool of herself: she needed to quit working for Cord. She didn't doubt for a second that

Cord would be relieved. Last night, he'd looked horrified after the kiss. And this morning, he'd left before they'd even gotten up. Carrie Anne had been extremely disappointed that she hadn't gotten to help him feed the horses. Something she brought up as soon as she walked into the kitchen and saw the gingerbread horses.

"Is that Maple and Raise-a-Ruckus, Mama? I wish Cord hadn't gotten up so early so I could've helped him feed them. And I wish he hadn't left so I could've stayed with him instead of come to the bakery. Where do you think he went?"

"I don't know," she said as she carefully placed the horses on the cookie sheet. "But I do know that getting to hang out in a bakery is much more fun than feeding old horses."

"No, it's not. I like horses better than dumb baking." She sat down and spun around on the stool. "And when I marry Cord Evans, I'm going to be around horses every single—" She stopped spinning and stared at Christie with wide eyes. "Oops."

Christie studied her daughter. "You want to marry Cord?"

Carrie Anne slowly nodded. "But it's okay, Mama, 'cause he's not a deadbeat. And now that I caught the bouquet, I gotta marry someone. And the best someone in the entire town is Cord Evans. He's nice, and loves animals, and he's gonna teach me how to ride a horse. And you don't have to worry about me falling off 'cause Cord said he'll be right there to catch me. And I believe him 'cause he has big muscles."

Christie could attest to the fact that Cord had big muscles that were strong enough to catch you if you should stumble in a corral or if an amazing kiss left your knees as weak as water. But she wasn't concerned with his muscles at the moment. She was concerned about how close her daughter had gotten to Cord. And how devastated she would be when she no longer got to see him.

This was confirmed only a second later when Carrie Anne's eyes lit up. "Cord!"

Christie turned to see Cord standing there. In his Stetson and big sheepskin jacket, he seemed to fill the entire doorway with hot cowboy. Her entire body flushed with heat, including her cheeks, and she was glad Carrie Anne was there to distract Cord from noticing.

Carrie Anne jumped off the stool and raced over to give him a hug. "How come you got up so early this morning? And how come you left without saying goodbye? Can I go out to the ranch with you now and see Maple and Ruckus? And can I ride Maple today?" She pulled back from the hug and looked back at Christie. "Please, Mama. I promise I won't go real fast."

"Hold on there, Half Pint," Cord said. "I told you that we needed to wait until you get the proper equipment." He ruffled her hair. "And you can't go back to the ranch with me because I'm getting ready to head out of town for a few days."

"Out of town?" The words didn't pop out of Carrie Anne's mouth. They popped out of Christie's.

He took off his hat and looked at her. He hadn't shaven that morning—probably because he'd been in such a hurry to leave—and the thicker beard should've made him look scruffy. Instead, it made him look even more masculine and sexy. He cleared his throat. "I was wondering if I could talk with you for a second."

"Of course." She looked at Carrie Anne. "Go out front and help Spring."

Carrie Anne looked like she was about to argue, but Cord stepped in before she could. "If you do a good job of helping, I'll take you over to the diner for a strawberry shake and hamburger before I leave." He glanced at Christie. "That's if it's okay with your mama."

She nodded, and Carrie Anne raced out of the kitchen yelling the news to Summer and Spring. When she was gone, Christie looked at Cord. "You shouldn't bribe her to do what I tell her to do."

"Sorry, but we need to talk in private." He glanced behind him. "In fact, it might be best if we stepped out back."

She didn't want to talk in private. She didn't want to be alone with Cord in case she did something really stupid—like throw her arms around his neck and beg for another kiss. But since she couldn't come up with a reason for not stepping outside with him, she got up and led him to the back door. Once they were standing in the alley, she wished she had stopped to get her coat. The cold December breeze blew down the alleyway like a wind tunnel, and she immediately rubbed her arms to warm them.

"Here." Cord slipped out of his jacket and held it out for her.

She shook her head. "No, thank you. I'm fine." All she needed was to be surrounded in Cord's scent and heat. But of course, he didn't listen and slipped it over her shoulders anyway. She tried not to shiver from the delicious warmth that surrounded her. She waited for him to say something and when he didn't, she brought up the elephant in the room. "You don't need to apologize for what happened last night," she said. "I think we both were a little tired and not thinking straight."

His soft brown eyes studied her for a moment before he nodded. "I still owe you an apology. You were a guest in my home. I should've shown you more respect."

"I touched you first."

He looked down at his boots. Was he blushing? Of course, she was blushing too so she had no room to talk. But her blush had more to do with desire than embarrassment. The man was standing way too close.

"You did touch me." He swallowed hard. "And then I touched you. So I guess we're even. Let's forget about it and move on."

She wished it were that easy. But the melty feeling in her panties said it wasn't going to be. She took a breath and said what needed to be said. "I think it would be a good idea if I stopped working for you."

His head came up. "What? You can't do that. I need you." It was pathetic how the words made her tummy take a tumble. Of course, he wasn't talking about the same kind of need as she was. "As Ryker says, I suck at social media and keeping my website updated. You can't leave me to post pictures of the scrambled eggs and bacon I eat for breakfast. And you can't take Carrie Anne away. She and I have become buddies." He held up his hands as if trying to calm a frightened horse. "You have my word that I won't touch you again. I'm going to be out of town for a few days, so I won't even be around. And when I get back, things will be different. If they're not, then you can quit."

She should've remained strong and refused him. But there was something in his pleading brown eyes she couldn't say no to.

"Fine. I'll wait until you get back," she said. But she didn't see how a few days away from Cord was going to change anything.

She knew for a fact that once you caught rodeo cowboy fever, it was hard to get rid of.

CHAPTER TEN

THE CHEYENNE BAR WHERE CORD finally tracked down Danny Ray Corbett was like all the other bars Cord had spent half his life in. It was too dark, the music too loud, and the smell of alcohol too strong. As soon as he stepped in the door, his stomach tightened with the unrelenting need for a stiff shot of Patrón. Or the entire bottle.

He ignored the craving and shrugged out of his jacket, hanging it next to the other snow-dampened coats that hung on the row of hooks. He left his cowboy hat on and tugged it lower. He didn't want anyone recognizing him and making a scene. He spotted an empty barstool at the bar and headed to it. His butt had barely settled before the bartender showed up to take his order. She was a tough looking gal with bleach blond hair and a mean scowl.

"What do you want?"

"A Coke, please."

"With a shot of what?"

"No shot, ma'am. Just the soda."

She shook her head before she left to get his

drink. When she returned, she set his glass of Coke on the bar. "Since you aren't here to get drunk, you must be here for women. You got the wrong night. Ladies' Night is Tuesday. Monday is dollar beer night. Which explains all the drunk cowboys roaming around."

He took the straw out of the Coke and took a sip. "Actually, I'm looking for a friend of mine. Danny Ray Corbett. You know him?"

She snorted. "Every bar owner in town knows Danny Ray. If he's not getting into fights, he's getting so loaded that he needs a ride home—or to the house of whichever woman he's mooching off of at the time."

The fact that Danny Ray was drinking and carousing while Christie was working two jobs to make ends meet pissed Cord off. He'd done his fair share of drinking and carousing, but he'd always made sure that his family was financially taken care of. He'd sent Jenn a check every month like clockwork right up until Ryker was out of college and Jenn had remarried. Of course, given the choice of money or a father, most kids would choose a father. So in that respect, he was no better than Danny Ray.

"Is he here tonight?" he asked.

She leaned closer and her eyes narrowed. "What do you want with him? If you're looking to cause trouble, I've got a double barrel under the bar that I ain't afraid to use."

He didn't doubt it for a second. The woman's hard look said she'd spent most of her life handling rowdy drunks in her bar. "No trouble. I just wanted to offer him a job in the rodeo off-season."

When Cord first decided to come looking for Danny Ray, he had planned to give him a stern lecture on fatherhood. But on the way to Wyoming, he'd realized what a stupid plan that was. At thirty, Cord had been too full of himself to listen to some old cowboy's lecture on being a father, and he figured that Danny Ray would be the same way. Danny didn't need to be told what he was doing wrong. He needed to be shown. He needed to see what a great kid Carrie Anne was and what a beautiful, intelligent woman Christie was. And he needed to see what a fool he was if he let either one of them go. The only way Cord could figure out how to get Danny Ray to Bliss was to offer him a job.

"A job?" The woman shook her head. "Good luck getting that lazy bum to work. He doesn't even work at rodeoing, which is why he sucks so—" Her eyes widened, and she snapped her fingers. "That's it! I've been racking my brain trying to figure out where I know you from and it just hit me. You're Cord Evans."

He glanced around. "I'd sure appreciate it if you kept that to yourself."

For a second, he thought she might ignore his request. She looked like she was busting at the seams to scream out his name. Instead, she nodded and leaned closer. "Okay, but could you take a selfie with me later? And maybe give me your autograph."

"Sure thing. Now where is—"

She cut him off. "And would you talk to my cousin in Muskogee, Oklahoma, who thinks she's so damned hot because she saw Blake Shelton at a diner and he called her 'Sis.' That's all she brags about at every family reunion." She flapped a hand and fluttered her eyelashes. "'Did you know that Blake eats hamburgers?' I mean who the hell don't eat hamburgers?"

Cord shrugged. "You got me there. Now about Danny Ray . . ."

She jabbed a finger over his shoulder. "He's in the back playing pool with one of his floozies. I could show you where he is if you want. I mean if anyone recognizes you, you might need a bodyguard." She held out her hand. "Sherry McDonald, but people just call me Sherry Mac."

He shook her hand and got up from the barstool. "That's real sweet of you, Sherry Mac, but I think I can find it."

"You're not gonna forget about the picture, right? And the phone call to Oklahoma. Missy will piss her pants when I put you on the phone."

"No, ma'am. I won't forget." He placed a twenty on the bar. "Keep the change."

Sherry Mac jerked up the money and stuffed it down the front of her t-shirt. "Are you kiddin' me? I'm framing this."

Since he never knew how to respond to things like that, he just smiled and nodded before heading to the back room. The room held two pool tables and enough cigarette smoke to cure an entire smokehouse of hams. Games were being played on both tables, and there were people crowded around waiting for their turn.

It didn't take Cord long to find Danny Ray. He had studied Internet pictures of him for hours the night before. He wished he could say he just wanted to make sure he would recognize him, but deep down he knew he'd been looking for defects. Something that would boost his ego. But after looking at the pictures, his ego was pretty deflated.

Danny Ray was young and handsome with the kind of athletic body that Cord once had. And Cord couldn't help feeling jealous as hell. Truth be told, he wasn't just jealous of Danny Ray's looks. He was jealous of the man who had gotten to do more than just kiss Christie Buchanan. Which was pure craziness. He had no business lusting after Christie. And yet, he couldn't seem to help it. Ever since the kiss, his body was one big lump of desire. When he'd been talking to her in the alleyway behind the bakery, he'd almost given into that desire and pulled her straight into his arms and kissed the hell out of her.

He couldn't do that. He couldn't let a woman distract him from getting his son back. Ryker's love was more important. Even if the woman had a golden rope of hair that could wrap around your body twice. Hazel eyes that made you think of lush summer pastures. And sweet kisses that made you forget everything but being deep inside her.

He shook his head. *Stay focused, Cord. All you have to do is get Danny Ray back in the picture, and Christie will forget all about the stupid kiss.* The problem was . . . could he?

He stepped closer to the pool table where Danny Ray was playing. Of course, he wasn't playing pool as much as showing a dark-haired woman how to use a pool cue.

"That's it, honey," Danny Ray adjusted the cue in her hands, rubbing his hips against her butt as he did. "You are getting the hang of this now."

The woman took the shot and completely missed the cue ball all together. Of course, Cord couldn't blame her. It was hard to shoot pool with a cowboy on your ass.

The woman stood and stuck out her bottom lip. "I missed."

"Try again, honey. Practice makes perfect."

Before Danny Ray could cop another feel, Cord interrupted. "Excuse me. I hate to bother—"

Danny Ray cut him off. "Then don't. I paid for the table and I'm not finished with my game yet." He waved a dismissive hand without even looking at Cord. "So adios, amigo." When Cord didn't make a move to leave, he straightened and looked at him. "Did you hear me, old man? Vamoose. Get lost. Go doctor your hemorrhoids or count the remaining hairs on your head—or your balls. Whatever suits you. Just get the hell out of here before I—"

Sherry Mac appeared in the doorway, toting her double-barrel shotgun. She pointed it straight at Danny Ray without the slightest hesitation. "Don't you dare talk to Cord Evans like that, you little piece of rodeo shit. With your PRCA standing, you ain't fit to lick horse poop off this man's boots." She waved the shotgun at Cord. "This here is a legend."

There was a moment of stunned silence before everyone in the room surrounded Cord asking for autographs and selfies. Even Danny Ray and his floozy.

"I'm so sorry, Mr. Evans," Danny Ray said as he jostled for a place closer to Cord. "I didn't know it was you. I thought it was just some old cowboy trying to horn in on my game of pool—not that you're old or anything."

"Of course he's not old, Danny Ray." The floozy pressed her huge boobs against his arm and smiled seductively. "You're the perfect age." She bit her bottom lip and brushed a long red nail over her abundant cleavage. "Will you sign me?"

Sherry Mac moved next to him and shoved her away. "No one is signing your fake boobs, Lizzie. Now everyone just back off. If Cord Evans wants to walk into my bar and be an ordinary person, then I'm gonna make sure he gets to do that. There will be no autographs and no selfies. Unless you want me to charge regular price for those beers you've been guzzling."

The threat of paying more for beer seemed to do the trick. The crowd around him dispersed . . . although everyone still stared at him like he was the main attraction at a freak show. It reminded him of how much he loved living in Bliss. There, people didn't stare or ask for autographs. There, he was just member of the community. And he wanted to get back to his town as soon as he could.

He flashed a smile. "Thanks, y'all. I'll be happy to sign autographs after I attend to some business." He looked at Sherry Mac. "Is there somewhere I could have a private word with Danny Ray?"

"Sure. You can use my office." She pointed to a door at the back.

"Me?" Danny Ray looked befuddled. "Why do you want to talk to me?"

Sherry Mac prodded him with the shotgun. "Just shut up and get your ass back there, Danny Ray."

Sherry Mac's office wasn't much more than a

closet with a small desk and two chairs. Danny took one of the chairs, but Cord remained standing.

Danny Ray eyed him warily. "If this has something to do with what I said about you to Vern Mason at the rodeo in Tulsa, I didn't mean anything. You know how it is when you get all hopped up right before a ride and start talkin' shit."

Cord did know how it was. Lots of cowboys flung shit about their competitors before a ride. And those cowboys were usually inexperienced braggarts with nothing to back up their words. Cord had preferred to fling his shit in the arena by beating his competitors' times. And he had to wonder how Christie had fallen in love with this arrogant man. Of course, love was blind. He didn't know how Ryker's mama had fallen in love with him.

He tossed his hat to the desk. "I'm not here because you talked crap about me in Tulsa. I'm here to offer you a job."

Danny Ray looked even more confused. "A job? But I already have a job. I'm a rodeo star."

The man was too cocky for his own good. Cord had been cocky too, but it was understandable to be cocky when you were on the top of the heap. It was a different story when you were on the very bottom.

"This job is only for a few weeks. I have a horse that needs to be saddle broke and I'm willing to pay you ten thousand for the job."

Danny Ray squinted at him. "Let me get this straight. Cord Evans, a six-time world champion rodeo bronco and bull rider, wants to pay me ten thousand dollars to saddle break his horse?"

The job hadn't sounded so damned stupid in his head. When repeated out loud, it sounded ridiculous. But he couldn't back out now. "That's right."

A second later, Danny Ray let out a whoop and slapped his cowboy hat on his thigh. "I told Vern Mason I was a better cowboy than you!"

CHAPTER ELEVEN

CHRISTIE SPENT THE NEXT FEW days feverishly working on the gingerbread house. She had to have the house in Austin for judging by Saturday and she and Summer planned to drive it up on Friday morning. It was turning out much better than Christie had expected. She had put lights inside the boot before putting on the roof and they shone through the butterscotch windows with a warm, soft glow. She'd added a chimney of red licorice squares on one side and mortared them with gray frosting, then planned to put Santa's legs with cowboy boots sticking out of the top of the chimney.

The gingerbread family was finished. Since she'd decorated the little girl to look like Carrie Anne, she decorated the mother to look like herself. Not wanting an entire family of blonds, she put brown royal icing hair on the man and little boy. Except once she was finished, she realized that with the dark brown hair, cowboy boots, and hat, the gingerbread man looked a lot like Cord Evans. Which made sense given that she spent most of her time daydreaming about the man.

Even with him being out of town, she couldn't seem to get him off her mind. When she wasn't thinking about the kiss, she was wondering where he had gone in such a hurry. Summer seemed to think he'd gone to check on his boot factory in El Paso. But if that were the case, why had he asked Christie to wait a few days before quitting? What difference would going to his factory make? Was he planning on bribing her to keep working for him with a pair of new boots?

She paused in the process of attaching the string of colorful Christmas lights she'd shaped out of melted sugar. Or maybe he wasn't going to bring back boots. Maybe he was going to bring back a girlfriend. Some woman he had in one of the many towns he'd traveled to while on the rodeo circuit. That would certainly solve the problem of their mutual attraction.

For some reason, that solution didn't set well with Christie. In fact, she suddenly felt extremely annoyed at the thought of Cord bringing home some rodeo buckle bunny.

Of course, wasn't that what she was? She hadn't attended rodeos to flirt with all the cowboys, but she'd certainly done her fair share of drooling over them. First with Danny Ray and now with Cord. And she needed to pull her head out of her butt and concentrate on what was important: Giving Carrie Anne a wonderful Christmas.

The thought of her daughter had her glancing at the clock. She quickly got up to wash her hands. "I'll be back in a minute. I need to get Carrie Anne from school."

"No hurry," Summer said as she continued to pipe letters on a birthday cake. "After this morning's rush, things have slowed down."

"I still can't dillydally if I want to have the gingerbread boot ready on time." Christie grabbed her coat before heading out the back door.

The cold snap had run its course, but the wind was still sharp as she made her way down Main Street. She had told Summer she wouldn't dillydally, but she couldn't help stopping to admire the beautifully decorated tree in the window of Home Sweet Home. With only two and half weeks until Christmas, it was a reminder that she needed to get a tree for Carrie Anne. It would have to be a small tree to fit in the trailer, but Carrie Anne would still enjoy decorating it.

When she got to the elementary school, she was surprised to see Ms. Marble waiting out front in her red coat and knit hat. "What are you doing here, Ms. Marble?" she asked.

Ms. Marble seemed surprised by the question. "Why I'm picking up Carrie Anne."

"But this is Wednesday. You only tutor her on Tuesdays and Thursdays."

Ms. Marble smiled. "I guess Summer didn't give you my message. I saw her this morning on her way to the bakery and told her to tell you that I'd pick up Carrie Anne today since Cord is still out of town."

"Summer must've forgotten to tell me. We had to fill a big order for the city council's monthly meeting and this morning was unusually hectic."

Ms. Marble nodded. "I was at the meeting and everyone raved about the delicious pastries and donuts. I even slipped two in my tote for Carrie Anne. Although I have so many baked goods at my house, I don't know why I did. I'm still baking as if I'm in business. Thankfully, it's the holidays so I can give most of my goodies away. I was going to have Carrie Anne help me put them in gift tins today. That's if you don't mind."

Christie was grateful for the offer. It would be a relief to not have to worry about keeping an eye on Carrie Anne. She might even get the gingerbread house finished that much sooner. "She'd love that. But are you sure she won't be too much trouble?"

"She's no trouble at all. I enjoy the company. And I'll be happy to watch her the rest of the week until Cord gets back." Ms. Mable's eyes squinted in thought. "I wonder where that man ran off to. I was going to ask Ryker at the council meeting, but he was busy talking to Sam the plumber. I guess their plumbing is acting up now. It's a shame. They have enough to worry about with their businesses and a new baby on the way."

"Maybe Cord's right. Maybe they should just move in with him." Christie hadn't meant to voice her thoughts, and she could've kicked herself when Ms. Marble intense eyes pinned her.

"Cord wants Ryker and Summer to move in with him?"

She tried to backpedal. "I should've have said anything. Cord told me his plans in confidence."

"It's nice that he trusts you," Ms. Marble said. "And I certainly won't repeat a word about his plans. Of course, they're pure nonsense. A grown man shouldn't be living with his father. But I understand why Cord wants him to. He wants to go back and fix the past. Unfortunately, that's an impossibility—something Cord will figure out soon enough." She smiled at Christie. "Once he figures out that living in the present is much more fun than living in the past."

Christie didn't know why she got the feeling that Ms. Marble was including her in Cord's present. Maybe it was the twinkle in the older woman's eyes. Or maybe it was Summer telling her about Ms. Marble's matchmaking list. Either way, she was about to dissuade the woman from any thoughts of trying to get her and Cord together when the school bell rang.

Children came running out the doors, and Christie worried she and Ms. Marble would be trampled in the stampede. Her concern was unnecessary. The children slowed to a walk as soon as they saw Ms. Marble. Except for Carrie Anne who raced over and almost knocked the older woman down with an exuberant hug.

"Ms. Marble! I didn't know you were getting me today." She finally noticed Christie. "Hey, Mama!" She hugged her. When she pulled back, her eyes were confused. "How come both of you came to get me today? Am I in trouble? Am I doing bad on my reading?"

"You are doing a wonderful job at reading," Ms. Marble said. "I just stopped by to see if you wanted to come to my house and help me make up Christmas goodie tins."

"What's a goodie tin?"

"It's a metal container that you put cookies or candy in as gifts."

"Do I get one?"

"Carrie Anne Buchanan," Christie scolded.

Ms. Marble laughed. "I can't say as I blame her for negotiating payment before she starts working. That's smart business sense." She smiled at Carrie Anne. "Yes, you get one. And I also plan to pay you actual money for helping me."

"You don't need to do that, Ms. Marble," Christie said. "You have helped so much with Carrie Anne's tutoring, she'll be glad to do it for free." She sent a warning look at Carrie Anne to make sure she wasn't going to disagree.

Ms. Marble winked at Carrie Anne. "Nonsense. I've enjoyed helping her open the world of reading. Now we better get going. I have a lot of tins to fill. And when we're finished, you can help me sew the costumes for the church Christmas pageant."

Carrie Anne's eyes lit up. "A Christmas pageant? Is that like a beauty pageant?"

Ms. Marble smiled. "No. It's a play about Jesus's birth that the Sunday school children put on every year."

Guilt consumed Christie for not taking Carrie Anne to Sunday school. But Sunday was the only day she had off and she had about a million other things to do. Still, a good mother would've figured out a way.

"Could I be in it?" Carrie Anne asked, which made Christie feel even worse.

"I'm sure all the parts are taken by now, Baby Girl," she said. "But I promise I'll take you to see it."

"Actually," Ms. Marble said. "The Angel of the Lord's family decided to go skiing in Aspen on the night of the performance so we have an opening."

"I can be an angel!" Carrie Anne jumped up and down, her backpack bouncing. "My Mimi always said that I was her little angel and I would look mag-nif-i-cent in a halo and wings." She stopped jumping and sent a pleading look at Christie. "Please, Mama. Can I? Can I?"

She wanted to say no, but she'd really be a terrible mother if she kept her daughter from being an angel. She'd just have to figure out how to squeeze in rehearsals to her already full schedule.

She smiled. "Of course you can."

Since Ms. Marble lived on the other side of town, they headed back toward Main Street together. Carrie Anne chattered non-stop about what a great angel she was going to be. When they reached the corner, Christie gave Carrie Anne a big hug.

"Try not to talk Ms. Marble's ear off. I'll come pick you up as soon as I—" She cut off when she saw Cord's truck pull up to the curb in front of the feed store across the street. Her heart started beating like a big bass drum, and she couldn't keep from staring as he got out of the truck.

Was it her imagination or had he gotten even sexier while he'd been away? He wore a faded jean jacket over a nice-fitting western shirt and Wranglers. The jeans hugged his lean thighs so nicely that heat filled her entire body like someone had turned up her libido thermostat.

His cowboy hat shadowed his eyes. Still, she knew the second he noticed her. He stopped in mid-stride and she could almost feel his soft brown gaze burning a hole right through her. Suddenly, she realized that quitting her assistant's job wasn't going to stop the feelings his kiss had ignited.

Nothing short of leaving Bliss would keep her from making a complete fool out of herself once again for a handsome cowboy.

"Well, I'll be a doggone monkey's uncle. If it isn't Christmas Day Buchanan."

The familiar voice had all the heat draining right out of her body as she slowly turned and stared in complete disbelief at the rodeo cowboy who was climbing out of the passenger's side of Cord's truck. A cowboy she never thought she'd see again.

"Danny Ray?"

"In the flesh." Danny Ray flashed a smile that had melted her like butter at one time. Now she didn't feel anything but confusion. What was he doing here? He strode across the street in a cocky strut she remembered all too well. When he reached her, he gave her a long, thorough once-over. "Woo-whee, honey, you have sure filled out nicely since I last saw you. Have your boobs gotten—?"

Ms. Marble cut in. "You watch your manners, young man. There are children present."

Danny Ray glanced at Ms. Marble and then at Carrie Anne. There was no sign of recognition. Not one. His gaze passed over his daughter as if she were a complete stranger. And that broke Christie's heart in two and completely obliterated any feelings she might still have for the man. It was too bad that her daughter was more observant.

"Danny Ray?" Carrie Anne stepped up, looking confused. "You're my deadbeat daddy?"

Danny Ray shot her an annoyed look. "I ain't a deadbeat. And I certainly ain't your daddy. My daughter is a cute baby. Not some smart-mouthed kid."

It was like blinders were suddenly lifted from her eyes and she saw Danny Ray for what he was: A self-centered man . . . who was a few marbles short of a bag. "She was a baby six years ago when you left, Danny Ray," she said. "She's not a baby anymore."

Danny Ray stared at Carrie Anne. "She's my kid?"

Carrie Anne glared back at him. "I'm not your kid. I'm my mama's kid. You're just a deadbeat who didn't want me."

"I ain't a deadbeat!" Danny Ray hollered.

People walking down the street stopped to see what all the hollering was about, and Christie quickly turned to Ms. Marble. "Could you take Carrie Anne back to your house while I handle this?"

"I don't want to go with Ms. Marble." Carrie Anne crossed her arms and continued to glare at Danny Ray. "I want to know what my deadbeat daddy is doing here."

Before Christie could get after her, Ms. Marble held out a hand. "That will be enough, Carrie Anne. I'm sure you'll find out soon enough why your father is in town. For now, we need to let your parents talk." Carrie Anne started to argue, but all Ms. Marble had to do was lift an eyebrow. She took Ms. Marble's hand and followed her down the street, glancing over her shoulder at Danny Ray until she and Ms. Marble disappeared around the corner.

When they were gone, Danny Ray looked at Christie. "That sassy kid needs a good paddling."

There was a time when she had been so enamored of Danny Ray that anything he'd said she'd agreed with. But those days were gone. "You can't paddle a child for being right. Now what do you want, Danny Ray? If it's money, I don't have any."

He held a hand to his chest. "Why, Christmas Day, you wound me. I would never take money from you. I'm here because I've been offered a job by an honest-to-goodness rodeo legend who needs me to show him how to handle a horse."

She blinked. "What?"

He smiled smugly. "It seems that the great Cord Evans came all the way to Wyoming and offered me ten thousand bucks to saddle break his horse. And if you don't believe me, you can walk right over there and ask him."

Christie slowly turned and looked across the street. Cord was still standing in front of the feed store. But now she didn't notice how sexy his jeans fit or how his gaze melted her insides. Now, she didn't feel melty at all.

She felt pissed.

Just that quickly she got over her rodeo cowboy fever.

CHAPTER TWELVE

CARRIE ANNE WAS USUALLY SO talkative, but she didn't say a word on the walk to Maybelline's house. And Maybelline couldn't really blame the poor child. It had to be a shock to meet your father for the first time in the middle of the street when you had no idea he was coming. Maybelline felt almost as shocked. What was Danny Ray doing here? If not for his surprise, she would've thought that he was there to see his daughter. Or Christie. But it was obvious that he hadn't planned on running into either. And what had he been doing with Cord Evans?

When they reached her house, she led Carrie Anne through the side door and pointed to the hooks on the wall. "Hang your backpack and coat and I'll get you a snack."

After they'd hung their coats, they headed to the kitchen where Maybelline poured Carrie Anne a glass of milk and filled a plate with a variety of cookies. Once Carrie Anne was seated at the table, Maybelline started opening up the Christmas tins on the counter so she could start filling them. When Carrie Anne still didn't start talking, she decided to broach the subject of her father. "So I guess it was quite a surprise to see your daddy."

Carrie Anne stared at the plate of cookies for a few seconds before she lifted her gaze to Maybelline. "Why do you think he's here? Do you think he came to see me?" The hopeful look in her eyes was heartbreaking. Even more so since Maybelline didn't believe for a second that Danny Ray was there to be a father. But she would never tell Carrie Anne that.

"It's certainly a possibility," she said.

"He doesn't like me. He wants me to be a cute baby."

If Danny Ray had been there, Maybelline would've boxed his ears for making his daughter feel so inadequate. "I think he was just surprised how big you've gotten since he last saw you."

Carrie Anne picked up a powder sugar-covered wedding cookie and took a small nibble. "I'm glad I'm not a baby. If I was a baby, Cord wouldn't let me ride Maple."

"That's true. And now that he's back, I'm sure you'll get to ride Maple very soon."

Carrie Anne's face scrunched up in thought. "Do you think Cord went and got my daddy for me?"

The question caused a light bulb to go off in Maybelline's head, and she had to wonder if she was getting senile for not having thought of it before. That's exactly what Cord had done. He'd gone to Wyoming and brought back Danny Ray. And it was all Maybelline's fault. She was the one who had brought up finding a good husband for Christie and a good father for Carrie Anne. She had intended to spark some jealousy in Cord. Instead, she had sparked a plan.

In his mind, he was killing two birds with one stone. He was giving Christie and Carrie Anne a husband and father, and he was giving Danny Ray the second chance that he wished someone had given him. She knew Cord's heart was in the right place. He had spent so many years doing the wrong thing, now he just wanted to do what was right. Maybelline just wasn't sure bringing Danny Ray back was the right thing to do.

Danny didn't seem ready to take on the responsibility of a family. His immature actions today had proven that. And if that were the case, Cord's plan would only bring more heartache for Christie and Carrie Anne. But how could Maybelline fix the mess that Cord had made? How could she keep this precious girl and her mama from getting hurt again?

Before she could come up with an answer to that question, her phone rang.

She excused herself and went to answer it. She was surprised when Bonnie Blue Davidson's voice came through the speaker. Bonnie Blue, or Granny Bon as all her grandchildren called her, was Lucy Arrington's only daughter and the Hadleys' grandmother. In the years since the truth had come out, Bonnie had become like a daughter to Maybelline. But they usually talked in the evenings after Bonnie finished working at the transitional home for foster kids. So Maybelline was instantly concerned.

"Is everything okay, Bonnie?" she asked. "Are you sick?"

"No need to worry, May," Bonnie said. "I'm as

healthy as a horse."

"Then what are you doing home? Don't tell me you finally decided to retire."

There was a pause before Bonnie spoke. "I didn't decide. The new director decided for me. I was let go with a nice going away party and a small severance package."

Maybelline knew Bonnie wasn't happy about being pushed into retirement. The woman was a workaholic. But Maybelline was thrilled. "Congratulations! Now you don't have any excuse for not moving to Bliss. And don't be stubborn, Bonnie Blue. Your entire family lives here. Now that you're officially retired, it's time you lived here too."

Bonnie laughed. "There's no need to browbeat me. The house is already on the market. But I haven't told the family yet. I thought I'd surprise them with the news when I get there on Friday."

"Which will be perfect timing. Autumn and Maverick get in the day before."

"I know. Autumn called and told me all about Maverick deciding to coach instead of play," Bonnie said. "I couldn't be happier. I think it's only a matter of time before those two lovebirds are expecting a little one of their own."

Maybelline smiled at the thought of a bunch of sweet little Hadley babies to cuddle. That only left one Hadley who needed to find a happily ever after. She hadn't mentioned her suspicions to Bonnie about Christie. She had wanted to leave that secret for Christie to share. But that was before Danny Ray had been thrown into mix. Now Maybelline needed an ally if she wanted Christie to find her happiness.

She glanced at Carrie Annie. The little girl was munching on her cookie and staring out the back window, no doubt daydreaming about a daddy who would love her like a daddy should. Maybelline would not rest until she got her that daddy. She moved into the living room where Carrie Anne couldn't overhear her conversation.

"There's something I need to tell you, Bonnie. You know Christie Buchanan, the pretty young woman who helps Summer at the bakery. Well, I think she's—"

Bonnie cut her off. "Holt Hadley's daughter. Yes, I know. After meeting her, I had my suspicions too. She looks a lot like Holt and her daughter looks even more like my grandkids. It's the only explanation for why she showed up in Bliss. So she's finally decided to tell people who she is?"

"No. Christie hasn't told a soul. I think she's a little scared about how the news will be received."

"That's pure foolishness. Although I guess I was as foolish. When I found out I was Lucy Arrington's daughter, I wouldn't have told a soul if not for Dirk falling in love with Gracie. Now I'm glad I did. The bigger the family the better, and I intend to make sure that Christie and Carrie Anne feel the same way. When I get to Bliss, I'll break the news and make sure the Hadleys welcome her with open arms."

Maybelline had never doubted that the Hadleys would welcome Christie into their family with open arms—they had certainly welcomed her already. But with everything else that was going on, she didn't know if now was the right time to drop that bomb.

"Maybe you should hold off on telling the family, Bonnie." She proceeded to tell her the entire story of how she wanted to get Cord and Christie together and the sudden appearance of Danny Ray. When she finished, Bonnie laughed.

"You and your matchmaking, May. You won't be happy until everyone in Bliss has been married off in that little white chapel."

Including you, Maybelline thought with a smile. But she couldn't work on a match for Bonnie until she finished with Cord and Christie.

"But I agree with you," Bonnie continued. "Cord and Christie would make a cute couple. Cord is a good man. I knew that the moment I met him. And this Danny Ray sounds a lot like Holt."

"I agree, but I also think that everyone needs to be given a chance to prove themselves. Maybe I'm wrong. Maybe he'll be a wonderful father to Carrie Anne and a good husband to Christie. But to make sure, we'll need to keep a close eye on him. I can watch him if he's staying in town, but if he's staying at Cord's ranch, I won't be able to keep an eye on him."

"I can," Bonnie said. "I'm staying with Dirk and Gracie. Their ranch is just down the road from Cord's. I'll have no problem popping in to check on Danny Ray. Although I don't know what excuse I'll use for stopping by a single man's ranch."

Luckily, Maybelline did. "Food. Single men don't ever question a woman bringing food. And since Cord eats most his meals at the diner, I'd say he isn't much of a cook."

"And what happens if you discover that Danny Ray's intentions are not honorable?"

"Then we need to get him out of town before two hearts get broken. Or make that three. Cord hasn't accepted it yet, but I think he's more attached to Christie and Carrie Anne then he knows. Which is why he cooked up this harebrained scheme to begin with."

"Talk about scheming," Bonnie said. "People think you're a sweet, harmless old lady. But in reality, you are one devious, manipulating old gal, Ms. Maybelline Marble."

Maybelline smiled and repeated something she'd heard Summer say. "Damn straight."

CHAPTER THIRTEEN

GETTING DANNY RAY CORBETT SETTLED into family life was going to be harder than Cord had thought. He'd hoped that once Danny Ray sobered up, he'd act a little less obnoxious. But as it turned out, Danny Ray was as obnoxious sober as he was drunk.

On the flight to Austin, he'd flirted outrageously with the flight attendants and spent most of the trip bragging to the guy sitting next him about his rodeo skills. And then there was the way he'd handled his first meeting with Christie and Carrie Anne. Cord had been too far away to hear what Danny had said to them, but by Christie's and Ms. Marble's reaction, it hadn't been good. The guy seemed to have no moral compass whatsoever.

But Cord hadn't had a good moral compass either until he'd gotten away from the booze and the bars. Danny Ray just needed a little time to clear his head. As soon as he did, he'd see what he was missing out on. Who wouldn't want a woman as beautiful and kind as Christie and a kid as cute and smart as Carrie Anne?

Feeling pretty good about how his plan was going so far, he finished off the last of his morning coffee and looked in on Danny Ray. The man was sprawled out on the bed in a pair of stars-and-stripes boxer shorts and snoring loudly. Cord should've woken him up and put him to work. Hard work humbled a man. And if anyone needed humbling it was Danny Ray. But after listening to his bragging non-stop on the trip home, Cord needed a morning of peace and quiet. So he left Danny sleeping and headed out to the barn to feed the horses.

Ryker had taken care of them while he was gone, and it looked like his son had done a fine job. The stalls were clean and the water troughs full. Although Raise-a-Ruckus had gotten a little full of himself while Cord had been gone. As soon as Cord leaned over to fill his feed tray, Ruckus tried to nip him.

Cord immediately smacked his muzzle and scowled. "You better watch your p's and q's, mister. And I hope you didn't try that with Ryker while I was gone. He's going to be your new owner as soon as I get you saddle broke." The horse was one of many gifts he planned to give his son.

The sound of a car had him setting down the bag of feed and walking to the open barn door. Christie was just getting out of her Chevy Malibu. He had hoped that the feeling he'd experienced the day before had just been a little indigestion from the airport burgers he and Danny Ray had for lunch. But he hadn't had anything but coffee this morning, and his stomach still felt like he'd swallowed a hive of buzzing bees when he saw her.

She wore an emerald sweater that matched the green in her eyes and tight jeans that hugged her legs and curvy butt. Her hair was in the usual braid, the golden rope hanging over one shoulder. It had glowed like a flame in the flickering light of the fire the night he'd kissed her. Now it glittered like spun gold in the sunlight as she headed for the front porch steps. He should let her go inside. Maybe if she saw Danny Ray in his star-spangled boxers, their old fireworks would re-ignite. But for some reason, he called out to her.

"Good mornin'." He was annoyed by how breathless the greeting sounded.

She whirled on a boot heel. She didn't smile. She didn't lift a hand in greeting. And she didn't say a word. She just stared at him for a few seconds before she walked toward him. Or more like strode. There was definite purpose in her walk. Like she was on a mission. He figured out what that mission was when she hauled off and slapped him hard across the face. And she didn't stop there. After she slapped him silly, she repeatedly poked him in the chest as she backed him into the barn.

"What in the hell do you think you're doing? Have you lost your ever-loving mind? I knew you were an arrogant cowboy, but this goes beyond arrogance. This is you thinking you're God!"

He was scared. Christie might be small, but she was feisty when she was mad. And she was madder than a hornet. He took a deep breath and tried to calm her like he would a horse. "Now hold on there. There's no need to get all riled up. Just take a second and tell me why you're so upset."

Her eyes widened. "You don't know? Are you

kidding?" She threw up her hands and turned away, then started talking to someone who wasn't there. "Are all men idiots? Do they all go through life acting before they think and assuming that's just fine and dandy?" She whirled back to him. "Danny Ray. Why would you bring Danny Ray here?"

He was confused. Wasn't it obvious why he had brought Danny Ray here?

He cleared his throat. "I brought him here to get back together with you." This time, her eyes looked like they were going to bug out of her head. Before she slapped again, he held up his hands. "I can see that you're mad about that. But if you just listen for a second, I think you'll realize what a good idea it is. You told me yourself that you still love Danny Ray. And after seeing Carrie Anne's drawing, I know she would love to have her daddy here for Christmas. Danny Ray might be a little rough around the edges, but he's still her daddy. Besides, I was a little rough around the edges too—maybe not as rough as he is, but pretty rough. And I wish someone had taken me under his wing and shown me the mistake I was making by not being a good husband and father. I wished someone had shown me before I lost out on so many of Ryker's years."

She looked less bug-eyed. Which he took as a good sign so he continued. "That's what I intend to do with Danny Ray. I intend to take him under my wing and teach him everything I wish someone would've taught me. Now I realize I made an error in judgment by bringing him into town without prior warning. I guess I thought it might be like one of those romantic comedies where the hero and heroine see each other again and realize they never should've broken up. I didn't think about Carrie Anne being out of school. Or that Danny Ray still doesn't have control of his unruly tongue." He shook his head. "He needs a little more help than I first thought. But he'll get there. As God is my witness, I'm going to make him the perfect husband and father for you and Carrie Anne."

After his speech, he figured Christie would want to apologize. But she didn't look sorry. She still looked intense and mad. "So that's your plan? To turn Danny Ray into the perfect husband and father? And he agreed to this?"

"Not exactly. He thinks he's here to saddle break Raise-a-Ruckus."

Her eyebrows lifted "But instead you're going to saddle break him."

Cord hadn't really thought about it like that, but now that he did, he couldn't argue the point. He grinned. "I guess you could say that."

She slapped him again. This time even harder. "The first one was for me. That one is for Danny Ray. Because no matter how arrogant and irresponsible that man is, he does not deserve to be a pawn in your little game." She pointed a finger in his face. "And neither do I. And neither does my sweet daughter who is now talking incessantly about her daddy coming back to be a good daddy like Cord Evans. And do you know just what will happen to that sweet thing if your plan doesn't work? She will be heartbroken, that's what. And it will be all your fault."

She poked herself in the chest. "And I'm just as much to blame because I was stupid enough to let another lowdown rodeo cowboy into our lives. I was stupid enough to trust you with my daughter."

That hurt worse than her slaps. "Now hold up there. I think you've got things all wrong. You can trust me. I care about Carrie Anne. That's why I went to Wyoming and brought back Danny Ray."

She crossed her arms. "Bullshit."

He blinked. "Excuse me?"

"Bullshit. You ran off to Wyoming because you got scared after our kiss, and you wanted to make sure that your desire for a woman wouldn't get in the way of you getting back your precious son."

Cord's mouth dropped open, and he squinted at her. "That's just plain crazy. Me going to Wyoming had nothing to do with that kiss. It was just a kiss." That was a lie. It hadn't been just a kiss. But damned if he was going to let Christie know that. Of course, as it turned out, she already did.

"Really?" She stepped closer, her hazel eyes snapping with green fire. "If I kissed you right now, you'd lose it just like you almost lost it the other night. And Cord Evans can't lose hold of the tight reins he keeps on himself. If he doesn't have control, he might do something crazy." She circled her finger next to her head in the age-old sign for crazy.

His temper snapped. "Talk about bullshit. That's a truckload of it. It's you who's worried about losing control. You who wanted to quit working for me because you were scared of what might happen if I ever decided to kiss you again."

Her eyes snapped and her fists clenched. "You are just as arrogant as Danny Ray. But the proof of who is most scared is in the puddin'." Before he could utter a word, she grabbed the front of his shirt, jerked him closer, and laid a kiss on his mouth.

Which proved she wasn't scared of kissing . . . but he sure as hell was.

Because as soon as her lips touched his, he knew she was right. He hadn't just brought Danny Ray back for Christie and Carrie Anne. He'd brought him back to keep this from happening again. To keep him from losing control like he was doing right now. Her soft lips broke down all the walls he'd constructed and released the carnal animal he'd hoped to keep caged.

His hands spanned her waist and he jerked her up to her toes as he devoured her mouth. She accepted his onslaught in a tangle of tongue and hot wet heat that almost brought him to his knees. He pulled her closer, and when that wasn't close enough, he turned and backed her up against the stall, using his hips to pin her. His hand slid under her shirt, and he filled his palm with the satin-covered softness of her breast. She moaned with need, and the sound of her desire speared straight through him. He wanted to fill that need more then he had ever wanted to do anything in his life. He wanted to fall down on his knees and worship her body with his mouth and tongue until she sighed his name over and over again.

He reached for the button of her fly, but froze when he heard the sound of a clearing throat. And still, his body refused to release the woman in his arms. Unfortunately, Christie had no problem pulling away. Or trying to. He still had her pinned against the stall.

"Let me go, Cord," she said in a husky voice. "Please."

It was the "please" that finally penetrated his lust-fogged brain. He released her and stepped back. There was nothing to say. She'd proved her point pretty damned well. The only compensation for his ego was that she looked as shaken as he felt.

"Sorry to interrupt, but I'm here about a horse."

The words had him turning to see Jasper Wheeler standing just inside the opened doorway of the barn. The scruffy old cowboy was a welcome sight. Not only because he'd stopped Cord from making a huge mistake, but also because Cord needed a friend in a bad way.

He sent one apologetic look to Christie before he walked over and gave Jasper a quick hug and slap on the back. "Hey, Jasp. What are you doing here, you ornery cuss?"

"You sounded a little lonely on the phone so I thought I'd come and spend the holidays with you." He glanced at Christie who was blushing profusely. "But it looks like I was wrong."

Cord cleared his throat. "This is Christie Buchanan. She's my . . . office assistant. Christie, this here is Jasper Wheeler, one helluva bull rider and my good friend."

Christie walked over and held out a hand. "It's nice to meet you, Mr. Wheeler. My mother was a big fan of yours. She met you once at the local diner in town and said you were one of the nicest celebrities she'd ever met. You signed a menu for her."

Jasper smiled, showing the wad of chewing tobacco tucked in his lower lip. "I think I remember your mama. I never forget a beautiful woman." His eyes crinkled at the corners. "But that wasn't here in Texas, was it?"

"Wyoming. I just moved here recently."

He winked. "Did your mama happen to move with you?"

A sadness entered Christie's eyes, one Cord had seen before when she'd spoken of her mother. "She passed away last winter. Complications with knee-replacement surgery."

Cord knew Christie's mother had passed, but he hadn't known it was from something as unexpected as knee surgery. No wonder it had blindsided Christie. No wonder she had gone in search of her father. She had been grieving the sudden loss of her mother. She was probably still grieving the loss. And the last thing she needed to worry about was her ex showing up. Which explained why she'd been so pissed.

She had every right to be mad. He shouldn't have run off to Wyoming like some hotshot matchmaker. Hell, he hadn't even been able to keep his own wife. What made him think that he could get Danny Ray and Christie back together? He'd just been so desperate to find a shield to put between him and Christie. And damned if he didn't still need one. The kiss had proven that she was his kryptonite. If he wanted to keep control of his life, he needed protection from her and the emotions she evoked. He would make Danny Ray see the errors of his ways. He had to. He couldn't survive another kiss from Christie.

"Good mornin'." As if on cue, Danny Ray waltzed into the barn in his wrinkled star-spangled boxers.

Cord was instantly annoyed. Not only because he had a younger body with no limp, but also because he was parading it around in front of Christie. He had to remind himself that Christie getting interested in Danny's body was exactly what he wanted. But it sure as hell didn't feel like what he wanted. He felt jealous as hell when Christie gaze landed on her ex.

"Good Lord, Danny Ray," she said. "Would you get some clothes on?"

Danny Ray smiled smugly and ran a hand over his chest. "Don't act like you don't like it, honey. You always loved watching me walk around half-nekked. And if I had known you were gonna come and see me, I would've stayed in bed and let you join me."

"I'm not joining you in bed, Danny Ray." She shot an annoyed look at Cord. "No matter how much it ruins someone's plans. Now if you gentlemen will excuse me, I need to do some social media before I head in to the bakery. In fact, would you mind posing with Cord for a picture, Jasper?"

Before Jasper could answer, Danny Ray started fan-girling. "Jesus H. Christ! You're Jasper Wheeler? I didn't recognize you. You look a lot older than I thought you were. But hey, Cord's old too so you ain't alone." He slung an arm around Jasper and then pulled Cord closer. "Okay, Christie, go ahead and snap some pictures, but make sure you get my good side."

Christie rolled her eyes before she held up her phone and took some pictures. When she was finished, she looked at Jasper. "It was nice meeting you."

Jasper nodded. "Same here, ma'am. Seeing as your Cord's . . . assistant, I'm sure we'll run into each other again."

"I'm sorry, but I'm giving my notice today." She glanced at Cord, and the look she gave him was so mean he braced for another slap. Instead, she slapped him with her words. "Cord will have to find another assistant to put up with his meddling." She held out a hand. "I'm assuming that you haven't paid Danny Ray yet for saddle breaking your horse. I'll take some of that money now."

"Now wait just a doggone minute, Christie Buchanan," Danny Ray said. "You can't take my money."

Christie turned on him. "Shut up, Danny Ray. You haven't paid one dime in child support." She turned back to Cord, and he quickly got his wallet out. He would've given every last dollar he had, but she stopped him after a hundred. "That's enough for now." She folded the money and stuffed it in the front pocket of her jeans before she walked out of the barn with her braid swinging.

When she was gone, Danny Ray whistled through his teeth. "That is one mean-assed woman. And when she was pregnant, she was like a rabid wolverine. Which is why I ran off in the dead of night." He hooked his thumbs in the waistband of his boxers and grinned at Jasper and Cord. "So what do you two old cowboys want to do today?"

CHAPTER FOURTEEN

"YOU'RE NOT COMING TO AUSTIN with me?" Christie glanced down at her cellphone, which was sitting in the cup holder of her car.

"I'm sorry, Christie," Summer's voice came through the speaker. "But Autumn and Maverick got in late last night and Granny Bon gets in today. I just don't want to miss our family reunion."

Christie understood Summer wanting to be with her family, but she still couldn't help feeling disappointed. She had been looking forward to going to Austin with Summer. After they dropped off the gingerbread house at the hotel, they had planned to go Christmas shopping and have lunch. It would've been like a real sister day. And she had never had a real sister day.

She tried to keep the disappointment from her voice. "That's okay. I understand that you want to see your family. I can get the gingerbread house to Austin by myself."

"Don't be silly. You can't get that huge boot there without help. You can't lift it alone and it certainly won't fit in your car. But I have everything under control. You just worry about getting Carrie Anne to school, and I'll worry about getting the gingerbread boot loaded up and ready to go."

"I don't want to go to school!" Carrie Anne whined from the back seat as soon as Christie hung up. "I want to go to Cord's ranch and see Cord, Mr. Jasper, and my deadbeat daddy."

Christie glanced in the rearview mirror and sent her daughter an exasperated look. "How many times do I have to tell you to stop calling Danny Ray your deadbeat daddy?"

"That's what you called him when you and Mimi talked about him." Since it *was* what she and her mother had called Danny Ray, she couldn't exactly argue the point. Thankfully, Carrie Anne continued before Christie had to come up with a reply. "But Cord says we need to be real careful not to call him that to his face 'cause it hurts daddies' feelings. He also says that I need to give Danny Ray a chance to grow up and be a good daddy. But Danny Ray looks pretty growed up to me."

Just the mention of Cord's name made Christie's palm itch. And if he were there, she had little doubt that she'd slap him again. The gall of the man thinking that he could fix her life. Her life might not be perfect, but it was her life and she didn't need a stupid rodeo cowboy sticking his nose into it.

Or his lips.

His hot, unbelievably talented lips.

Of course, he hadn't kissed her. She had kissed him in an attempt to prove that he no longer had any effect on her. But all it had proven was that her mind and body were completely disconnected.

One hated the man and the other craved him.

"Cord Evans has no business talking to you about your daddy," she said. "And he had no business picking you up yesterday after school. Ms. Marble should've called me if she didn't feel well and couldn't tutor you, instead of calling Cord."

Christie had been furious when she'd found out Carrie Anne was at Cord's ranch. She did not want her daughter around an arrogant jackass or a deadbeat daddy. It was too bad that the arrogant jackass had already won over her daughter's heart.

"But I like to be with Cord. He's nice. He put me up on his shoulders to show me the bird nest in a tree. It didn't have no eggs in it 'cause it's winter, but Cord said this spring it will and he'll teach me how to climb up in the tree so I can look at them. And you know who else is nice? Mr. Jasper. He loves horses and can talk to them just like Cord. Maple told him how much she's looking forward to me learning how to ride her. Mr. Jasper also knows how to whit-tel sticks with his pocketknife. And he said he would teach me how to whit-tel too."

"You are not using a pocketknife, Baby Girl. And you're not going to Cord Evan's ranch again. Yesterday was my last day to work for him."

"No!" Carrie Anne yelled so loudly Christie jumped. "I am to going to Cord's house again! He invited me to help decorate his gi-normous Christmas tree and he's even gonna let me put the star on the top."

"We're getting a tree this weekend and you can put the star on top of ours."

Carrie Anne kicked the back of her seat so hard

that Christie bounced forward. "I don't want to decorate a stupid little tree. I want to decorate Cord's gi-normous one."

"Carrie Anne Buchanan, you stop kicking my seat and throwing a tantrum this instant or you won't be getting a tree or that bike you want for Christmas. Santa does not give gifts to naughty little girls."

"I don't care if Santa brings me a bike 'cause Cord Evans is getting me boots and a safety helmet!"

Now Christie didn't just want to slap Cord. She wanted to punch his lights out.

When they got to the elementary school, Carrie Anne was so angry that she didn't even wave when she got out of the car. She just sent Christie a mean glare and stomped into the school with her ponytail swinging. And as far as Christie was concerned it was all Cord Evans fault. She was still fuming when she pulled up in front of the bakery, but her anger dissolved when she unlocked the front door and stepped inside.

Autumn Hadley, or Autumn Murdoch now, was stocking the front display case with baked goods. She was the shyest of the triplets. And yet, Christie felt the closest to her. Autumn had a calm, loving nature that reminded Christie of her mother. As soon as she saw Christie, she closed the display case and hurried over to hug her. She drew back with a soft smile.

"It's so good to be home. I missed you."

"I missed you too. You look great. That Miami sunshine must've agreed with you." Christie winked. "Or is that just newlywed glow?"

Autumn laughed. "I do feel like I'm glowing." She glanced back at the kitchen before she spoke in a low voice. "But it could be more baby glow than newlywed."

"Oh my gosh. You're pregnant?"

Autumn held a finger to her lips. "Shh. Maverick and I are waiting to tell the family until everyone is together."

It meant so much to Christie that Autumn had confided in her first she gave her another hug. "Congratulations. Your sisters are going to be thrilled. Especially Summer. She needs someone to commiserate with about being pregnant. Spring hasn't had one pregnancy complaint."

"That's Spring for you. She doesn't complain about anything . . . except maybe Summer." Autumn studied her. "How are you doing? I heard about your ex showing up. Does he want to get back together?"

"Danny Ray doesn't want to get back with me and I certainly don't want to get back with him."

Autumn looked relieved. "That's good. He seems a little immature to me."

"You met Danny Ray?"

"I met him this morning. He's in the back alleyway helping Cord and Summer load the gingerbread house into Cord's truck."

All the air in Christie's lungs whooshed out. "Cord's truck? Why is my gingerbread house being loaded into Cord's truck?" Before Autumn could answer, Summer walked in from the kitchen.

"There you are, Christie. You need to hurry if you want to get to the hotel before the noon deadline. Austin traffic is brutal."

Christie shook her head. "I'm not going to Austin with Cord Evans."

Summer looked baffled. "Why not?"

It wasn't easy to find an answer without explaining what happened between her and Cord. "I just would rather go alone."

"Don't be silly. It's already loaded and ready to go."

Ms. Marble came out of the kitchen. "Summer is right, dear. Now hurry up. Cord is waiting."

Christie really wanted to throw a Carrie Anne temper tantrum and refuse. But she couldn't let all her hard work on the gingerbread house be for nothing. She needed to get her entry there by noon, and she was going to do it. Even if she had to be stuck in a truck with two arrogant rodeo cowboys.

As soon as she stepped into the alleyway, Danny Ray greeted her with his cocky smile. "Hey there, Christmas Day! You shore are lookin' good this morning."

She ignored him and headed for the truck. Cord hurried over to open the front door for her. She accepted his courtesy, but she didn't acknowledge him. She might have to travel with him, but she didn't have to talk to him.

Cord didn't appear to be in much of a talking mood either. On the way out of town, Danny Ray tried to start up numerous conversations, but Cord only answered with one-word responses. Finally, Danny Ray gave up and sprawled out in the back to take a nap. His loud snoring was hard to ignore.

"Good Lord," she grumbled.

Cord glanced into the backseat. "I guess Danny

Ray is still on Wyoming time." When she didn't reply, he cleared his throat. "The gingerbread house sure turned out nice. Summer and I strapped it down real good so you don't have to worry about it falling out." She hadn't worried about that until now. She glanced over her shoulder. The house was sitting in a big crate, covered in heavy plastic, and strapped tightly against the back window.

"Jasper made the crate when I told him what we needed," Cord said. "That man can make just about anything out of wood." He glanced over at her. "Just like you can make just about anything out of cakes and cookies."

She glared at him and went back to giving him the silent treatment. Finally, he released an exasperated sigh. "Okay, I get it. You're still madder than a hornet at me. And you're right. I shouldn't have butted my nose in your business. I did a lot of thinking after you slapped me silly and I guess I did have a few selfish reasons for going to Wyoming. The main one being my alcoholism."

She couldn't help but turn and stare at him. She shouldn't be surprised. She'd noticed that he always drank soda at town functions and never stopped by the Watering Hole bar unless Ryker was there. Still, it was a bit disconcerting to hear someone state that they had a drinking problem. It was also admirable. Some of her anger faded as he continued.

"Anyway, it hasn't been easy to stay away from the bottle. The urge for a drink is always with me, and it's taken me years to get control over my bodily urges." She watched his cheeks flush a rosy color and his Adam's apple slid up and down his throat as he swallowed. "And lately I've lost some of that control and it's kind of scared me." Was he talking about their kisses? The question was answered when he glanced over at her. "I can't lose control, Christie. Not even for a beautiful woman."

She tried to stay angry, but it was hard when Cord was calling her beautiful and saying that she made him lose control. He made her lose control too. But she wasn't as good at confession as he was.

"I'm not trying to take your control away, Cord," she said. "I'm trying to get control of my life too. And I was starting to feel like I had it, when you up and"—she glanced back at Danny Ray—"pulled your stupid stunt."

"Danny Ray knows. I told him after you left about why I brought him here."

That surprised her. "And he's still here? I would've thought he'd be long gone by now."

Cord glanced over at her. "I know he did you wrong, Christie, but people do change. I'm not the same person I was six years ago and I'm sure you're not either."

It was the truth. She wasn't the same person. She'd thought she would crumble like an over-baked cookie if she ever ran into Danny Ray again. But she hadn't. He no longer cast a spell over her. When she looked at him all she saw a man who had been too weak to be a husband or father. A man who was still too weak.

"I'm not interested in getting back with Danny Ray—or any other man. Carrie Anne and I are just fine and dandy on our own. Which reminds me. I don't want you to pick her up from school any-more. She can come to the bakery with me until

Mrs. Miller gets back from visiting her grandkids in Mississippi."

"Does Carrie Anne know?"

"Yes, and she's not happy about it. But it's for the best."

"The best? For who?" He thumped the steering wheel with his fist. "Damn it, Christie. Can you just think of Carrie Anne instead of your blasted pride?"

Her eyes widened as she stared at him. "I am thinking of my daughter. I don't want her hurt." She glanced back at Danny Ray who was still snoring loudly. "Do you actually think this plan of yours is going to work? Take a good look at him, Cord. Take a real good look. He hasn't grown up at all. He's still the immature boy I fell head over heels for. He can't even take care of himself. What makes you think he can be a father? And when he can't do it, it won't be Danny Ray who pays for it. It will be my daughter. And I won't have it."

He glanced at her, his eyes filled with sadness. "But won't she pay for it anyway?"

"What do you mean?"

"Take a look in the mirror, Christie. You're paying for your daddy leaving you right now. You're paying for it by not being able to trust men. Now, I can't tell you that Danny Ray is going to straighten up and fly right. But what if he does? What if he sees what a great kid Carrie Anne is and ends up falling in love with her? With that kid of yours, it's easy to do. It only took her a second to win me over. And if she can win over a stubborn old cowboy, she can win over anyone. Including her daddy. And are you so mistrusting of men that you're not going to give her that chance? Are you going to keep your daughter from having a father just because you don't have one?"

She had slapped Cord, but he had gotten even with a wallop that knocked all the wind out of her sails. She stared at him with stunned disbelief, terrified that there might be a kernel of truth to his accusations. Did she have underlying motivations that had nothing to do with Carrie Anne getting hurt? Christie knew she mistrusted men. But was she so mistrusting of them that she didn't want her daughter to trust them either? She knew in her heart that Danny Ray was still an irresponsible rodeo bum. But just because he would never make a good husband for Christie didn't mean he couldn't learn to be a good father to his little girl. And if there was even a chance of that happening, shouldn't Christie want that for Carrie Anne? Shouldn't she want her daughter to grow up without all her mama's hang-ups where men were concerned?

The questions rolled around and around in her head like the tires that ate up the highway. She felt confused and wished she could call her mama for advice. But she couldn't. She had to figure this out on her own. While she was sitting there feeling lost and alone, Cord reached out and took her hand in his. Startled, she glanced over at him. His soft brown eyes were compassionate and understanding as he rested their hands on the console and interlocked their fingers.

She was still mad at him. Mad at him for meddling in her life. Mad at him for melting her with his kisses. And mad at him for pointing out things about herself that she didn't want to see. But at the moment, she needed someone to hold on to. They continued to hold hands as the miles rolled past. They only pulled apart when Danny Ray woke and peeked between the seats.

He looked like a little boy waking up from a nap. His hair was mussed and his eyes sleepy.

"Are we there yet?"

CHAPTER FIFTEEN

CHRISTIE DIDN'T TALK MUCH FOR the rest of the trip into Austin. And Cord couldn't blame her. He shouldn't have gotten on her. He should've kept his big mouth shut. What did he know about raising kids? He'd done one helluva job with poor Ryker, and he was trying to tell Christie how to parent? The defeated way she'd looked after he spouted off his careless words had made him feel like a lowdown snake, and he'd been about to take them back when Danny Ray woke up.

Danny Ray had been oblivious to the tension in the truck . . . and to Cord and Christie holding hands. At least that's what Cord thought until they reached the fancy hotel and Christie went inside to find out where they should unload the gingerbread house.

"You got a thing for my ex?" Danny Ray asked.

Cord turned to look at him. "What?"

"You got a thing for Christie? I saw you holding her hand."

Cord gave him the truth. "She was upset and I

was trying to comfort her." He thought Danny Ray would ask more questions about why Christie was upset. Instead, he flopped back in the seat and put his boots up on the console. "Do you think this joint has food? 'Cause I'm starvin'."

The contest entries were set up in the main ballroom. Cord thought he and Danny Ray would have to carry in the gingerbread house, but two of the hotel staff met them at the side entrance to the ballroom and loaded the crate onto a rolling cart and wheeled it inside. Christie walked beside the cart, nervously keeping a hand on the crate all the way to the table with her slot number. After the plastic was cut off, Cord removed one side of the crate with the crowbar he'd brought and they slid the house onto the table.

He was worried when he saw that some of the decorations hadn't survived the trip, but Christie didn't seem upset at all. She opened her purse and pulled out a plastic tube of frosting and set about fixing everything that needed fixing. While she worked, Cord and Danny Ray walked around and took a look at the other entries.

"Damn," Danny Ray said. "There are some awesome gingerbread houses here. Look at that huge mansion with all those decorated trees and pretty windows. Christie's little ole boot doesn't stand a chance in hell against that house."

Cord thumped him on the back of the head, knocking off his cowboy hat.

Danny Ray scowled as he picked up his hat. "What was that for?"

"You say that to Christie and I'll do more than thump you. She's worked hard on that little ole boot and I don't want her losing her confidence."

But Danny Ray didn't have to say anything for Christie to lose her confidence. Once she finished fixing her entry and looked around, she deflated like a helium balloon left out in the sun.

"I told Summer I couldn't compete with professionals. I told her that I wasn't good enough."

"You're good enough," Cord said. "You're a talented baker and twice as creative as anyone here. These other gingerbread houses all look alike. They could be in any contest in the country. But this isn't just any contest." He pointed to the huge banner that hung over the doors of the ballroom. "This is 'The Best Gingerbread House in Texas' contest. And that right there"—he pointed to Christie's gingerbread boot—"is a Texas gingerbread house if ever I saw one. Now let's get out of here and give the judges a chance to figure that out while I take the best gingerbread baker in Texas to lunch."

They ate at one of Cord's favorite barbecue restaurants. Over baby back ribs, tender brisket, and tangy potato salad, Christie finally started to loosen up. On one hand, Cord was happy she was no longer worried about the contest . . . or the things he'd said on the drive up. But, on the other hand, he wasn't real thrilled to have to sit there while she and Danny Ray reminisced.

"Do you remember that little bar we used to hang out at in Cheyenne?" Christie asked.

"Skinny's?" Danny Ray laughed. "Yeah, I remember it. We closed that bar down more than once, didn't we?" He winked at her.

Cord tried to keep a smile on his face and his jealousy at bay. But damned if he could stand the thought of what Christie and Danny Ray had done after they closed down the bar.

"And I always had to drive home because you were too drunk." Christie took a bite of her brisket.

"Now don't be gettin' all self-righteous on me. You drank quite a bit too back then. You were always much nicer after you had a few shots of tequila in you. You were also more willing to dance."

"You were quite a dancer." She smiled at the memory. There was a smudge of barbecue sauce at the corner of her mouth that she'd missed with her napkin and Cord was having a hard time looking away from that smudge. Or not wanting to lick it off. "You were one of the best dancers in the entire state of Wyoming."

"Hell yeah, I was." Danny Ray pointed a rib at her. "And you weren't so bad yourself. It takes quite a woman to keep up with Danny Ray."

It took quite a strong will for Cord not to roll his eyes. He quickly changed the subject. Once Danny Ray started talking about himself, it was hard to get him to stop. "Carrie Anne must've gotten her love of dance from you, Danny Ray," he said. "I caught her dancing more than once in my great room before I got furniture."

Danny Ray stopped eating and stared at him. "The kid likes to dance?"

Cord nodded. "She also got your love of horses. I think once we get her in the saddle, she'll be a natural."

"She hasn't started riding yet? Hell, I was riding by the time I was four." Danny Ray glanced at Christie. "If she had been living with me, I'd already have her jumping fences."

The storm cloud that crossed Christie's face was fair warning of what was about to happen. Before the storm could break, Cord jumped in. "Christie has done a fine job of raising Carrie Anne. Six years of age is plenty soon enough to get into the saddle. Besides, she needs a safety helmet and proper cowboy boots before she can start riding."

Danny Ray's eyes widened. "My kid don't have cowboy boots?"

Cord did roll his eyes. The man just wasn't smart. Christie glared at him and spoke through her teeth. "When it's a choice between feeding my child and boots, I'll choose food every time."

Danny Ray looked like he'd been hit in the face with a cast iron skillet. "You didn't have enough money for food and boots?"

"Good Lord." Christie threw down her napkin and got up. "I'm going to the bathroom."

When she was gone, Danny Ray shook his head and spoke more to himself than Cord. "She was doing just fine living with her mama last time I checked. I didn't know she didn't have enough money to buy my kid boots."

Cord recognized the look in his eyes. It was the look of a man who was just now realizing his mistakes. He gave him a moment to absorb the information before he spoke the truth that he had learned the hard way. "But you should've known. It's a daddy's job to know."

Danny Ray put down his rib and stared at his plate. After a few minutes, he finally spoke. "I know you really didn't bring me here to saddle break your horse. But maybe there are some other odd jobs I could do for you around the ranch to make some money." He paused. "I'd like to buy my daughter some boots."

Cord had wanted to be the one to give Carrie Anne her first pair of cowboy boots. He'd ordered a purple handmade pair from one of his most talented boot makers and the box sat on the top shelf of his closet. But now he wouldn't be the one giving them to her and seeing her eyes light up with delight.

Her daddy would be.

"I happen to know a man who makes boots," Cord said. "I think we can strike up a deal."

After Christie came back from the bathroom, she seemed to notice the difference in the talkative, happy-go-lucky Danny Ray she'd left and the solemn one who now sat there not saying a word. She looked over at Cord in question, but he only shrugged as he got up to pay the check.

On the way out of town, he spotted the Christmas tree lot they'd passed on their way in. He slowed down and pulled into the lot. "I need to get a tree for my tree decorating party. It shouldn't take me long." He thought Danny Ray and Christie would want to stay in the truck, but both hopped out as soon as he parked.

"I'll help you," Danny Ray said. "I'm good at picking out trees." He headed off through the rows of firs and pines.

"I need to get a tree for Carrie Anne," Christie explained. But she didn't head off on her own. Instead, she stayed with Cord. "A decorating party? I thought it was just going to be you, Ryker, and

Summer."

"You're forgetting about Jasper and Danny Ray. I can't leave out my houseguests. And since they were coming, I decided to invite the rest of the Hadleys and Ms. Marble." He glanced over at her. "I was hoping you and Carrie Anne would come too. I promised Carrie Anne she could put on the star." She opened her mouth, no doubt to decline, but he held up a hand. "I get that you don't want anything to do with me, but I need someone to take pictures for my social media. And since you didn't exactly give me two weeks notice before quitting—which is what any conscientious employee would do—I figure you owe me at least one more night."

He expected her to argue. Christie never conceded easily. But she surprised him.

"Fine. I'll give you two weeks notice. And I'll come take pictures tomorrow night." She paused. "But only because Carrie Anne should get to spend time with her daddy." When he lifted his eyebrows, she shrugged. "Don't look so surprised, Cord Evans. I can admit when I'm wrong too." She pointed a finger at him. "But if Danny Ray does one thing to hurt my baby girl, there will be no place that either one of you can hide from my wrath."

He bit back a grin. "Yes, ma'am."

"I found a beaut!" Danny Ray came around the end of the row, dragging a tree behind him.

The tree was huge, but since the great room had a fifteen-foot ceiling, it would work perfectly. The lot guy cut off a couple inches from the trunk before he helped Danny Ray carry it to the truck.

Christie wasn't so easy to please. She had Cord

holding up one tree after another. If she liked the shape of the tree, she didn't like the price tag. Finally, Cord had had enough. When she found a shape she really seemed to like, he hefted the tree onto his shoulder and headed to the side of the sales trailer where they were cutting off the ends of the trunks.

"I'm not sure I can afford that one," Christie caught up with him.

"I'm buying it. Call it payment for all the pictures you're going to be taking tomorrow night."

Once the trees were loaded into the back, they headed home. On the return trip, there was a lot more talking. Too much talking as far as Cord was concerned. Danny Ray and Christie continued to stroll down memory lane until Cord wanted to open his door and jump out on the highway. He finally turned up the radio and tried to drown them out. Christie shot him an annoyed look, but Danny Ray just started singing along. Like his rodeoing, his voice was nothing to brag about. He sounded like a coyote pining for its mate. It was a relief to finally get to Bliss.

"Can you drop me off at the school?" Christie asked. "I need to pick up Carrie Anne."

"Isn't she coming out to the ranch today?" Danny Ray asked. Cord was happy he was finally taking an interest in his daughter. All he needed was a little more time with Carrie Anne, and Cord knew he'd fall head over boots.

Cord sent Christie a beseeching look. "She'd be more than welcome."

Christie only hesitated a second before she nodded. "Okay. Just drop me off at the bakery before you go get her."

When he pulled up to the bakery, Cord hopped out to open Christie's door. But Danny Ray beat him to it, and he was left standing there feeling like a fool as Danny Ray helped her out of the truck. She glanced over at him and he lifted a hand in a lame wave. "I'll drop your tree by your trailer on the way back to the ranch."

She opened her mouth as if she wanted to say something, but then she closed it again and nodded. "Thank you." He watched her walk into the bakery, then stood there staring at the door until Danny Ray spoke.

"Well, what are you waiting for? Let's go get my kid."

Ms. Marble was standing outside the school with all the other parents when Cord and Danny Ray got there. She was dressed all in red again, wisps of her white hair sticking out from the edges of her red knit stocking cap. She smiled at him, but looked intensely at Danny Ray as if she were trying to read him. Cord figured it wouldn't take her long. Danny Ray was like a comic book, a quick glance through and you knew what the story was about.

"I'm assuming you got the gingerbread house there on time," she said.

"We shore did." Danny Ray fielded the question. When Ms. Marble lifted an eyebrow at him, he pulled off his cowboy hat. "Ma'am."

She nodded. "That's good. I was worried you wouldn't be back in time to pick up Carrie Anne from school, but it looks like you're home safe and sound." She looked at Cord. "Which is a little surprising because you two didn't leave on the best of terms. I'm assuming you settled your differences."

They had settled their differences. He felt more than a little relieved that Christie wasn't mad at him any more. He smiled. "Yes, ma'am."

She returned his smile. "Road trips are always good for talking things out. Now if you'll excuse me, my good friend Bonnie Blue has arrived in town and I want to stop by and see her. You know Granny Bon, don't you, Cord?"

"We've met, but I don't know her all that well."

Ms. Marble's smile got even bigger. "You will." She winked before she turned and headed down the street.

When she was gone, Danny Ray spoke. "I know she's just a little old granny, but that woman scares the hell out of me."

Cord released his breath. "Yeah, me too."

CHAPTER SIXTEEN

"YOUR HAIR IS DOWN."

Christie tried not to notice how handsome Cord looked in the forest green button down western shirt as she and Carrie Anne stepped into his house. She self-consciously smoothed a hand over hair, wondering if the wind *had* made it look like Medusa's.

"I probably should've put it in a braid with all this wind," she said lamely.

"No!" His abrupt reply startled her. "I mean, I like it like that. It looks . . . soft."

"My hair is soft too, Cord." Carrie Anne lifted a curl. "You want to feel it? Mama used her curling iron and wound it around and around. And I had to stand real still so I wouldn't get my cheek burnt. And it took forever and a day, but I think I look as pretty as a picture. Do you think I look as pretty as a picture, Cord?"

Cord looked down at her and smiled. "I think you look more than pretty, Half Pint. You look beautiful." His gaze lifted to Christie, and his smile faded. "And so does your mama."

Just like that, Christie got all weak-kneed and breathless. She wished she could blame it on rodeo cowboy fever, but Danny Ray didn't make her breath catch or her pulse race. Only Cord did. And she was terrified that Cord Evans fever might be fatal.

"Your tree *is* gi-normous!" Carrie Anne's loud exclamation interrupted the stare-fest she and Cord were having. "How did you get those twinkly lights all the way to the top? Did you put Mr. Jasper on your shoulders like you did me? And how am I gonna get the star up there? I can't reach that top-pity-top even on your shoulders. Our Christmas tree isn't nearly as big, but it still didn't fit in our trailer and mama had to leave it outside. Mama said once we decorate it, it will be even better because now we'll have a beautiful Christmas tree to share with nature. But I'd rather have a gi-normous tree inside like yours."

"I think having a pretty decorated tree right outside your front door is much better than having one inside," Cord said. "And I have a ladder for you to use to put the star on. But you'll need to be careful climbing up and down it. I'm sure your daddy will be happy to help you."

Carrie Anne didn't look thrilled with that suggestion. "Can't you help me? I mean Danny Ray is good at dancing—he taught me how to two-step in the barn yesterday—but I don't think he knows how to help kids get on ladders."

Her daughter's reply spoke volumes. She liked Danny Ray, but she didn't trust him. She trusted Cord. By the softening of Cord's eyes, Christie knew he cherished that trust. But he also knew how it felt to be on Danny Ray's side of the fence.

"But don't you think your daddy will get his feelings hurt if you don't want his help?" Cord asked. Christie's heart squeezed. She knew that was exactly how he felt every time Ryker declined his help with anything.

Carrie Anne thought for a moment before she nodded. "Okay. He can help me as long as you're right there to catch me if he gets to talking and forgets about me." It showed how smart her daughter was that she had a back-up plan where her father was concerned.

Cord placed a hand on her shoulder. "I promise. I'll be right there to catch you, Half Pint. Now let's get your coats off so you can join the party."

While Cord was helping them off with their coats, Spring, Summer, and Autumn came over. Each woman carried one of Dirk and Gracie's triplet girls. The toddlers were adorable and looked so similar that Christie always had trouble figuring out who was who. Although she recognized Lucinda as soon as she opened her mouth. The little girl spoke as loudly as Carrie Anne.

"Kiki! Kiki!" It was the name she used for Christie. Her sisters parroted her, and Christie gave them each tummy tickles until they chortled.

"It's about time you two showed up." Summer ruffled Carrie Anne's hair. "Hey, Squirt."

"Don't mess up her hair," Autumn said. "Can't you see that it's been beautifully styled?"

Carrie Anne beamed. "Mama did it with a curling iron. I even got a spray of par-fume." She held up her wrist. "Wanna smell me?"

Summer leaned closer and took a dramatic whiff.

"Why you smell better than a bouquet of flowers." She held the baby closer to Carrie Anne's wrist. "Doesn't she smell good, Luana?" The baby instantly held out her arms to Carrie Anne.

"Can I hold her?" Carrie Anne begged.

"She's a little too big for you to hold," Summer said. "But you can hold her hand." She set the toddler on her feet and Luana immediately took off for the tree with Summer and Carrie Anne chasing after her.

Cord laughed. "If you ladies will excuse me. I better go check on Ms. Marble and Ms. Davidson and see if they are finding everything okay in my kitchen. Those two women brought enough food to feed an army."

"Who is Ms. Davidson?" Christie asked.

"Our ornery grandmother." Spring tried to keep Luella from pulling out her dangly earring. "But you don't have to call her Ms. Davidson, Cord. Everyone calls her Granny Bon."

"I think I'm a little too old to be her grandchild." His gaze wandered to Christie. "Something I need to remember." He turned and walked away.

Once he was gone, Spring exchanged looks with Autumn. "That man is so hot," they said in unison before they laughed.

Her sisters were right. Cord *was* hot. And what made him even hotter was that he didn't even know it. While Danny Ray was arrogant and obnoxious about his looks, Cord was humble and unpretentious.

"And speaking of hot guys," Spring said. "I think I'll go join my hot sheriff who is no doubt comparing notes with Ryker about their pregnant wives."

Hearing Ryker's name, Lucinda almost jumped right out of Autumn's arms. "Wy-ka! Wy-ka!"

Spring shifted Luella to her other side and took Lucinda from Autumn. "Come on, Sweetie. Auntie Spring will take you to your Wyka."

When they were gone, Autumn turned to Christie. "I noticed you didn't say much about Cord being hot."

Christie shrugged and lied through her teeth. "I don't really pay much attention to his appearance. He's just my boss. I appreciate him giving me a job when I needed it and being so good to Carrie Anne, but that's all."

Autumn studied her with blue eyes almost as piercing as Ms. Marble's. "That's what I thought before I left, but something has changed between you two while I've been gone. First, you got all bent out of shape about him taking you to Austin, and then there was the scene I witnessed when you got back."

"What scene?"

"When Cord dropped you off yesterday. Danny Ray might've opened your door, but you only had eyes for Cord. And Cord only had eyes for you. It was like watching two love-struck characters in a romantic comedy. The same thing happened tonight when you walked in that door. You couldn't stop looking at each other. You like Cord as more than just a boss, Christie, and he likes you as more than just an employee."

She should've kept up the charade, but she was tired of running from the truth. Tired of not being able to confide in anyone about what had been happening with Cord. She glanced around to make sure no one was listening before she leaned in and spoke in a low voice. "We kissed. Twice. And they were the best kisses I've ever had in my life."

Autumn didn't look surprised. In fact, she looked ecstatic. "I knew it." She gave her a hug. "This is so great."

Christie shook her head. "No, it's not. I can't get all loopy for a man again. I can't do it, Autumn. I just started to get my life back together. I just started to give my daughter a mama she can be proud of."

"I'm sure you've always been a mama that Carrie Anne can be proud of."

"No, I haven't. I spent the first five years of her life pining over a rodeo cowboy that I didn't even love. Then once Mama passed away, I became a crazy person who dragged Carrie Anne across the country looking for—" She cut off before she mentioned Holt. "For no good reason."

"It wasn't for no good reason. You were looking for a home." Autumn glanced over at Cord who had come out of the kitchen carrying a big tray of cheese and crackers. "And maybe you found more than that."

"I don't want more," Christie said. "Things are perfect just the way they are. I don't need another man messing that up."

"You don't want another man? Or you don't want another Danny Ray?" Autumn placed a hand on her shoulder. "I get that you're scared. Like you, I didn't trust men. Because of my daddy, I thought that one bad apple ruined the entire bushel. So I fought against giving my heart. I looked for any reason not to fall completely in love with Maverick. As it turned out, I had already fallen completely in love with him. I just hadn't accepted it."

Christie held up a hand. "I'm not in love with Cord. And I have no plans of falling in love with him. We are attracted to each other—physically attracted. But that's all it is. I made the mistake with Danny Ray of confusing physical lust with love. I refuse to make the same mistake again."

Autumn studied her. "But how will you know the difference?"

"What do you mean?"

"I mean how will you know it's just physical lust unless you give whatever is going on between you two a chance?"

"Are you saying what I think you're saying? You think I should have sex with Cord? I can't do that. I'm a mother."

"And mothers don't need sexual release?"

"Of course mothers need sexual release." Maverick walked up and slipped an arm around Autumn's waist. "I intend to make sure the mother of my child gets plenty. And if we didn't have an announcement to make, I'd take you back to our little apartment over Ms. Marble's garage and—"

Autumn placed a finger on his lips. "Would you hush? You're embarrassing Christie."

Maverick winked at Christie. "My apologies. I'm just a newlywed husband whose wife has him tied around her little finger." He lifted Autumn's hand and kissed her pinkie.

Autumn rolled her eyes. "Right. You weren't tied around my little finger last night when you, Waylon, Stuart, and Race were going over this past season's game film. You didn't even answer my text."

"Now, honey, just because I get distracted with football, doesn't mean you're not the most important thing in my life. And the only reason I was watching the game film with the boys was because you were at the new library with Joanna Daily."

"How is that going?" Christie asked, hoping to keep Autumn from going back to the subject of Cord with Maverick standing there.

The excited look that entered Autumn's eyes said it all. "It's going great. The library is completely finished and we have most of the books cataloged. I was worried about being able to work there after the baby's born, but Maverick says he can watch the baby in the mornings and Joanna has another librarian lined up in the afternoons."

"Baby?" Dirk stepped up behind Maverick and Autumn. "You're pregnant, Audie?"

Autumn looked at Maverick and smiled. "I think it's time to make that announcement. But first we need to get everyone in the kitchen into the great room."

"I'll do it," Christie said. She hesitated, not wanting to leave until she could ask Autumn not to repeat what they'd talked about. But she couldn't do that with Dirk and Maverick there. Luckily, Autumn read her hesitation and leaned in to give her a hug.

"I won't say a word," she whispered.

When Christie got to the kitchen, she found Ms. Marble slicing loaves of pumpkin bread and Granny Bon holding out a spoonful of whatever she was cooking on the stove for Cord to taste. It must've been good because he closed his long-lashed eyes and made a yummy sound that had

Christie heating up like a convection oven. And she couldn't help thinking about her conversation with Autumn.

She couldn't have sex with Cord. She wasn't the type of person who slept around. Danny Ray had been her one and only, and she had to wonder if sex had only confused her feelings for him. She refused to let her feelings for Cord get any more confused. Which was why it was best if she continued to ignore their attraction. As long as she didn't touch him and he didn't touch her, everything would be fine. Once she quit working for him, hopefully her libido would stop rearing its ugly head.

"That green chile stew has to be the best thing I've ever tasted in my life, Ms. Davidson," Cord said.

"Then you haven't tasted my chicken enchiladas." Granny Bon set down the spoon. "I got the recipe from my friend, Rosa Martinez, who got it from her grandmother who lives in Mexico. I'm telling you, it will knock your socks right off and have steam coming out of your ears. And call me Granny Bon. Ms. Davidson was my mother-in-law and she was one mean-natured woman."

"Well, if your chicken enchiladas are as good as this, Granny Bon, then I can't wait to taste them."

Granny Bon glanced over at Ms. Marble and the two women shared a look before Granny Bon spoke. "I'll be happy to bring you a casserole dish of enchiladas."

"It certainly would be appreciated. Jasper has been trying his hand at cooking, but he's as bad as I am in the kitchen."

"Sounds like you need to hire a cook." Ms.

Marble looked at Granny Bon. "What do you say, Bonnie? Do you want to come out of retirement to cook for Cord?"

Granny Bon went back to stirring the pot of stew, a smile quivering around her lips. "Well, I certainly can't let three good-lookin' cowboys go hungry, now, can I? But I have to have my mornings off so I can spend time with my sweet great-granddaughters."

Cord looked a little confused about suddenly having a cook when all he'd wanted was enchiladas, but he didn't say anything as Ms. Marble handed him a plate of pumpkin bread.

"Just set that on the dining room table with the other desserts, dear."

Cord turned and finally noticed her standing in the doorway. He froze, and his gaze immediately went to her hair. It was a struggle for Christie not to self-consciously smooth it again.

"I'm sorry to interrupt," she said, "but Maverick and Autumn want everyone to come into the living room for an announcement."

"An announcement?" Ms. Marble exchanged looks with Granny Bon once again and smiled conspiratorially. "Now I wonder what that could be."

Once Maverick and Autumn made their baby announcement, there were hugs all around followed by toasts with the cranberry juice and ginger ale punch Ms. Marble had made. Then Cord turned up the Christmas music and everyone started hanging decorations on the tree.

Christie couldn't help feeling a little out of place. She was fine when it was just she and the triplets at the bakery, but the entire family was a little intimidating. She had to wonder if Cord didn't feel the same way. While everyone else was gathered around the tree, he stood by the fire that crackled in the fireplace. She expected him to be watching Ryker with the same look of longing he always had when his son was around. But instead, every time she glanced up, he was watching her. It made her feel even more uncomfortable, and she was relieved when Carrie Anne started distracting him with her non-stop chatter.

"Cord! Look at this ornament. Isn't it pretty?"

"Cord! Is this supposed to be Santa Claus 'cause he looks more like the street guy in Cheyenne who used to ask for quarters for coffee."

"Cord! Should we go check on Maple and Ruckus? It's pretty cold outside and they might need a warm blanket."

"Cord! Can I put on the star now? Can I? Can I?"

Christie would've intervened if Cord had seemed annoyed by her daughter. But he didn't. He laughed at her funny comments, patiently answered her questions, and set up the ladder for her to put on the star before calling Danny Ray over to help. Danny Ray didn't look as thrilled as Carrie Anne by the prospect. The look of fear on his face made Christie remember that he had always been afraid of heights. She started to volunteer when Cord handed Carrie Anne the star and followed her up the ladder.

Christie couldn't help feeling a little nervous when her daughter leaned over the tall tree to place the star on top, but Cord was standing right behind her with a protective arm around her waist. Christie lifted her phone and clicked off numerous pictures. Once the glittering star was on and Carrie Anne was safely on the floor, she reviewed the shots she'd taken. What she saw brought tears to her eyes. Not only because of Carrie Anne's happy, smiling face, but also because of the look on Cord's as he watched her.

It was a look of complete and utter love. A look that Christie had hoped and prayed would come from Danny Ray. Instead, it came from a man who didn't have her blood, but who had still made room for Carrie Anne in his heart.

CHAPTER SEVENTEEN

JASPER SNORTED. "THAT BOY AIN'T dealin' with a full deck."

Cord watched Danny Ray struggling to maneuver the forks of the front loader under the bales of hay. He should probably go over and help him, but he was hoping he would eventually figure it out on his own. "He'll get it. He just needs some time."

"Yeah, maybe he'll have that hay stacked by Christmas . . . of next year. Damn, it's cold out here." Jasper flipped up the collar of his sheepskin jacket.

If ever a man looked like a cowboy, it was Jasper. His body was bent from all the horses and bulls he'd been thrown off of. His face was weathered from all the heat waves and windstorms he'd driven cattle through. And his blue eyes held a wealth of knowledge that only time and experience could give you. Cord could only hope that time and experience would teach Danny Ray.

"Give Danny Ray a chance," he said. "It took me a long time to figure out what I was doing wrong,"

"Because you were swimming in a bottle of

tequila. That boy"—Jasper nodded his head at Danny Ray who had just toppled the two rows of hay bales he'd stacked—"is stone cold sober."

"Okay, so he's a slow learner. But I don't give a damn if he can stack hay. I care if he can learn to be a good daddy." He'd given up on the good husband idea. Christie had made it perfectly clear that she didn't want Danny Ray back. Part of him was pretty upset about that. He had hoped that her getting back with her ex would get rid of all the emotions that consumed him every time she was anywhere near. But the other part of him, the emotional part, was damned happy that she was no longer in love with Danny Ray.

Jasper leaned his arms on the top rail of the fence. "I hope Danny Ray can be a good daddy too. It sure would be nice for that sweet little Carrie Anne." He glanced over at Cord. "Of course, you don't have to be a blood relative to be a good daddy."

Cord leaned on the fence next to him. "I hope you're not thinking what I think you're thinking. Because I can't be a good daddy to Carrie Anne when I couldn't even be a good daddy to my own son. You were there. You saw what a deadbeat father I was. Which is why you didn't like me to begin with."

"I didn't just dislike you. I pretty much hated you. You were one arrogant, screwed up, sorry SOB."

Cord shot him a glance. "Gee, thanks."

Jasper grinned. "It's the truth. And if I hadn't run into those old boys from the Double Diamond Boys' Ranch, I would've never learned why."

"Lucas and Chester had no business telling you

about my past."

"If they hadn't, I might not have looked beneath the asshole to the hurt man beneath." Jasper's eyes filled with concern. He might be a crusty old cowboy on the outside, but on the inside, he was a big ol' marshmallow. "It had to be tough losing your daddy at an early age and being left with a mama who couldn't recover from her grief long enough to raise her son proper."

"It wasn't that bad. I loved being at the Double Diamond Ranch."

"From the sounds of it, those two old cowboys did right by you. But they couldn't heal everything that was wrong. Which is why you tried to heal it in a bottle." Since Cord couldn't argue with that, he kept his mouth shut. "But you've climbed out of that bottle," Jasper continued. "And I'm damned proud of the man you've become. It's time that you become proud of that man too."

He buttoned up his coat. Jasper was right. It was damned cold outside. "I can't be proud of causing my son the same pain and hurt that my mother caused me when she sent me away. I can't be proud of that."

The punch came out of nowhere and knocked him on his ass. Jasper had always had one helluva punch. Cord sat in the dust, holding his jaw and staring up at his friend.

"What the hell was that for?"

Jasper spit a stream of tobacco onto the ground. "Because I'm damned tired of you bellyaching about how you did your son wrong. Hell yeah, you did Ryker wrong. No one can argue that point. But you also did him right by coming here and spending the last few months trying your damnedest to gain your son's forgiveness and respect. And from what I can tell, Ryker has given you both."

Cord got to his feet and dusted off his jeans. "I'm not so sure about that."

"Then you're a damned fool. A son who hasn't forgiven you is not coming to your house for no tree-trimming party. He's not spending hours a day helping your business be successful. And he's not watching you just like a proud son watches his daddy."

Cord stared at him. "Ryker looks at me with pride?"

"He does. And if you weren't so wrapped up in your self-pity, you'd realize it."

"Then why won't he hug me back or call me Daddy?"

"Maybe he's as stubborn as his father. Maybe he's hanging onto the past and fighting against his feelings." Jasper squinted at him. "Sorta like you're fighting against the feelings you have for that pretty little Christie Buchanan."

"I don't have feelings for Christie Buchanan," he said a little too quickly. "We're just friends."

Jasper laughed. "Yes sirree. Those looks you were giving her the other night looked real friendly to me. You almost set your entire house on fire with those friendly looks." He picked up Cord's hat and dusted it off on his leg before he handed it to him. "But go ahead and stick your head in the sand if you want to, boy. It's no skin off my nose."

There was nothing to say to that. Cord was working damn hard to keep his head buried in the sand where Christie was concerned.

The sound of tires on gravel had both men turning to the dirt road that led to the ranch. Cord recognized the blue Ford Fiesta immediately. Since the tree trimming party, Granny Bon had showed up every afternoon to cook supper for the three men. She was a nice woman and a great cook, but she was also a little bossy. Something that Jasper didn't seem to mind at all.

"Yeehaw! Bonnie's here."

"Get a grip on your hormones, Jasper. She's Summer's grandmother. Not to mention that she's older than you."

Jasper shrugged. "So what? If you want to ignore the pretty young thing who only has eyes for you, you go right ahead. But I'm not going to ignore a beautiful woman just because we weren't born in the same year." He took off his hat and hurried over to open Bonnie's door.

"Good mornin', Miss Bonnie. You're lookin' awfully beautiful today."

Granny Bon got out. "Why, thank you, Jasper. Now get the groceries out of the back. And if you dribble any of that tobacco juice out of your mouth onto the groceries, I'll have your hide."

Jasper grinned from ear to ear. "You can have all of me, sweetheart. All you have to do is ask."

"Mind your manners, you ornery cowboy," Granny Bon said, but there was a twinkle in her gray eyes that said she didn't mind Jasper's flirting all that much. Cord had to admit that the two made a cute couple. Granny Bon was just feisty enough to handle a crusty old cowboy like Jasper.

After Cord helped Jasper and Granny Bon bring in all the groceries, he went back out to see if

Danny Ray had made any progress with the hay. He hadn't. In fact, he'd made a real mess of things. He looked more than relieved when Cord took over the job and sent him inside to warm up. The temperature had dropped considerably, and if the clouds were any indication, they were in for more sleet and ice.

Cord hurried to get the hay stacked beneath the shelter before that happened. As he worked, his mind wandered back to what Jasper had said. Was his friend right? Had Ryker forgiven him and Cord was just too wrapped up in his own self-pity to notice? Ryker did help him out a lot with his business. And he had shown up to the tree decorating party and seemed to have a good time. He had even stayed for lunch the day before and then watched Cord work with Raise-a-Ruckus. Now that Cord thought about it, he had seen a little sparkle of pride in Ryker's eyes. Of course, he could've just been looking at the horse.

His cellphone buzzed in his pocket. He finished stacking the last bale of hay before he shut off the engine of the front loader and answered it. He was instantly concerned when Christie's frazzled voice came through the speaker.

"I'm sorry to bother you, Cord, but I didn't know who else to call. I took a day off from the bakery to go Christmas shopping for Carrie Anne at the Walmart in Fredericksburg and my car broke down in the parking lot. I can call a tow truck so that's not the problem. The problem is that I'm not going to make it back in time for Carrie Anne's school Christmas party." Her voice quavered. "And this is her first Christmas party at her new school and I wanted to be there for it, which is one of the reasons I took the day off. Now the other kids will have their parents there, but she won't have anyone." A heart-wrenching sob came through the speaker. "Not anyone."

Her tears almost brought Cord to his knees, and he wished like hell he could reach through the phone and pull her into his arms. Instead, he tried to convey his comfort through his voice. "It's going to be okay. Now you stay put. I'll call a tow truck to come get your car. And I'm coming to get you."

"Didn't you hear me? I'm fine. I want you to be with Carrie Anne."

"I'll take care of Carrie Anne. I give you my word. Now stay put." He hung up the phone and called a tow service before he headed into the house. He found Jasper and Danny Ray sitting at the center island watching Granny Bon cut up vegetables.

When Granny Bon saw him, she set down her knife. "What happened?"

"Christie's car broke down in Fredericksburg and I need to go get her. But Carrie Anne's holiday party is today and she needs family to be there with her." He looked at Danny Ray. "You're up, Daddy."

"What?" Danny Ray shook his head. "I don't want to go to no kids' party. One kid is fine, but multiple kids scare the hell out of me."

This time, Cord wasn't willing to wait while Danny Ray figured things out on his own. He grabbed him by the front of the shirt and lifted him off the barstool. "You don't need be afraid of kids. You need to be afraid of me. If you don't show up at that party and make your daughter happy, I'm going to kick your ass from one end of Bliss to the other. Do you understand me?"

Danny Ray swallowed hard and nodded. "Yes, sir."

He released his shirt. "Good. Now I'll be back as soon as I can with Christie."

"You want me to go with you?" Jasper asked. Before he could answer, Granny Bon cut in.

"I'm sure Cord can handle it just fine without you." She followed him to the door. "There's no need to hurry. I'll make sure Danny Ray gets to the school." She paused. "Along with the rest of Carrie Anne's family."

He glanced at her in surprise. "You know?"

"Yes, but I wish Christie had trusted us enough to tell us." She smiled. "You must be special if you were the first one she shared her secret with." She gave him a quick hug and a kiss on the cheek. "Something I knew the moment I met you. Now go get our Christie and bring her home."

Cord pulled on his cowboy hat. "Yes, ma'am."

He went over the speed limit all the way to Fredericksburg. He planned on calling Christie when he got to the Walmart to find out where she was. But as soon as he pulled into the parking lot, he saw her standing next to the tow truck. He pulled up next to her and hopped out. She did not look happy to see him.

"I told you I wanted you to stay with Carrie Anne," she said. "Now she won't have any family with her."

"Trust me. Carrie Anne will have plenty of family at the party." He came around the front of the truck. "Now finish yelling at me in the truck. It's freezing out here." He opened the passenger side door, but when she started to climb in, he noticed the tears in her eyes. "Hey." He placed a hand on her shoulder.

That was all it took for her to fall into his arms. She pressed her face between the open lapels of his sheepskin coat. "I can't do it," she said in a muffled voice that heated right through the cotton of his western shirt. "I can't give Carrie Anne her perfect Christmas. The tree I picked out doesn't fit in the trailer and I had to leave it outside in a big bucket and act like that was so much better than having it inside. But it's not better, and she knows it. And I'm not going to win the gingerbread house contest, so I won't have money to buy her the bike she has her heart set on. I couldn't even buy the decorations I wanted for the stupid tree because my credit card got rejected. And now, I'm missing her Christmas party. I'm the biggest failure in the history of mothers."

She burst into tears, her shoulders shaking with big racking sobs. The people walking by with their full carts slowed down to stare, but Cord didn't care. All he cared about was comforting Christie. He opened his coat and pulled her closer, wrapping it and his arms tightly around her. In her high-heeled boots, her head still only reached the center of his chest. He pressed a kiss to her sweet smelling hair and tried to come up with something to say that would make her feel better. What he finally came up with was a truth he'd just now realized.

"I guess all parents feel like they're the worst parent in the world at one time or another. It's just part of being a parent. But I figure if you're worried about it, then you aren't bad at all. You're just like all the rest of us that are struggling to do right by our kids."

The tow guy finished hitching up her car and glanced at Christie's head peeking out of Cord's coat. "Is she okay?"

"She's fine. She just needs a minute." He took note of the name and address printed on the door of the tow truck. "Go ahead. We'll meet you at the garage."

A few minutes after the tow truck left, Christie finally stopped crying and drew back. Her cheeks were wet with tears and her eyes were red-rimmed, but she still looked beautiful to him. "I'm okay now," she said. "You can let me go."

"You sure? Because I don't mind standing here holding you for a little while longer." Like for days. Or maybe years. It was another truth he'd just realized. He liked holding Christie. He liked kissing her. Hell, he just flat out liked her. And he couldn't hide from it anymore.

But she stepped out of his arms. "No, I'm fine." She glanced around. "Besides being completely humiliated."

He pulled out the bandanna from his back pocket and handed it to her. "I bet you aren't the first person to cry in a Walmart parking lot. And you won't be the last."

They didn't say much on the drive to the garage to check on her car. He cranked up the heater and then turned on the radio. It was a country Christmas station that Jasper had programmed in, and he quickly changed it to something that wouldn't remind Christie of missing Carrie Anne's party.

Although she had more to worry about than missing her daughter's party when the mechanic gave her the list of what he thought was wrong with her Chevy Malibu.

"If I was you," the guy said. "I'd sell it for scrap metal and be done with it."

When Christie looked like she was going to burst into tears again, Cord stepped in. "Can you keep it for a day until she decides what she wants to do?"

"Sure. Just call me tomorrow. Even if you decide to fix it, it will take two weeks to order the parts and fit it into the schedule."

"Thanks." Cord looked at Christie. "Is there anything you need to get out of your car before we leave it?"

She nodded, and he could tell she was struggling to hold back her tears. "Carrie Anne's booster seat."

He handed her the keys to his truck. "I'll get it. You go get warm." He figured she needed a few moments alone so he took his time getting the booster chair and calling Granny Bon.

"Did Danny Ray get to the party?" he asked.

"Not only is Danny Ray at the party, but so are Autumn, Spring, and Summer," Granny Bon said. "Ms. Marble is covering for Summer at the bakery. And I'm covering for Spring at the sheriff's office."

"Did you tell them?"

"No. I figure that Christie's job. They went because she's their friend and they care for her and Carrie Anne. Now how is everything going there?"

"Not good. Christie's had a helluva day and feels pretty bad about her mothering skills."

"We all have those moments, moments when

we're so consumed with everything that goes along with parenthood that we can't think straight. What she needs is a little time off. After school, I'll take Carrie Anne back to Gracie and Dirk's with me. She can spend the night. She loves playing with the triplets. You think of something to do with Christie that has nothing to do with kids." Granny Bon paused. "I'm talking adult fun."

Cord almost choked on his spit. "Excuse me?"

"You heard me. Now I need to go and answer the sheriff's phone." The call ended, but Cord stood there for a while holding his cellphone to his ear.

Oh, he could think of something fun for two adults to do.

It was something he'd been thinking about for a long time.

CHAPTER EIGHTEEN

THE RESTAURANT CORD TOOK CHRISTIE to in Fredericksburg was called a grill, but it was fancier than any grill she'd ever been to. The tables were covered in white tablecloths and candles flickered in pretty glass holders that were surrounded by sprigs of holly. She had wanted to go back to Bliss, but Cord had insisted that Carrie Anne was having the time of her life at Dirk and Gracie's. Too exhausted from all her tears to argue, she had finally given in.

But she felt completely underdressed in her sweater and jeans as the hostess took their coats and Cord's cowboy hat. The hostess led them to a circular booth across from a big Austin stone fireplace that was decorated with swags of greenery and pretty gold stockings. Stockings. Christie needed to buy Carrie Anne a stocking for Santa to fill along with everything else she needed to buy.

"Stop worrying about Carrie Anne," Cord said as they slid into either side of the booth. "She's fine."

"Dirk and Gracie shouldn't have to babysit my

daughter. They have enough with their three girls." She unfolded her utensils and placed the cloth napkin on her lap. "We need to eat quickly and get back to Bliss so I can pick her up." She sighed. "Although I can't pick her up because I don't have a car."

"I'll pick her up tomorrow morning and get her back to you. But for now, she's fine right where she is. She's not going to cause Dirk and Gracie any more work. In fact, she'll be a big help entertaining the triplets. Besides, Granny Bon is there. Now open your menu and relax."

Everything on the menu cost a fortune. At least, it seemed like a fortune to a woman who had just had her credit card denied. She picked out the cheapest salad, and when the waitress arrived to take their drink orders, she just ordered water. Unfortunately, Cord butted in.

"And she'll take a glass of your best wine. I'll have a Dr Pepper. And bring us the stuffed jalapeños to start."

When the waitress left, Christie turned to him. "I don't want a glass of wine."

"Then don't drink it. Of course, if you don't drink it, I might be tempted to. And you wouldn't want that on your conscience along with being a bad mom."

"I'm not a bad mom," she snapped.

He smiled at her. "That's what I've been trying to tell you. Now what are you going to get to eat? And if you say you're not hungry or order something puny, I'll just order for you."

He ordered for her. He ordered them both a wedge salad with bacon crumbles and blue cheese dressing and a lobster-topped, chicken fried Angus rib eye with tarragon baby potatoes and steamed buttery asparagus.

"I'll never eat all that," she said.

"That's what to-go containers are for."

By the time she'd finished her glass of wine and Cord had ordered her another, she finally relaxed enough to enjoy the beautiful setting. The fire crackled in the fireplace and the pianist at the piano in the corner played soft Christmas music. She ended up eating three jalapeño poppers, her entire salad, and putting a pretty big dent in the delicious rib eye steak. As she ate, Cord regaled her with funny stories about his rodeoing days. She laughed until she cried when he told her about wearing jeans so tight that they split right up the center seam when he got tossed off a brahma bull.

"I learned that tight jeans didn't always impress the ladies," he said. "They weren't impressed at all by my holey underwear."

"Is that before Ryker's mom?" she asked.

He shook his head. "Sadly, I was still trying to impress the ladies after I was married to Jenn. Which is one of the reasons she left me."

"What were the other reasons?"

"Too many to name. But I think the straw that broke the camel's back was that I was never there for her."

She just couldn't imagine Cord not being there for his wife. "You certainly seem to be there for me," she said as she cut into her steak. "You'll probably be glad when I'm no longer your employee, and you no longer feel responsible for me."

He stopped eating and looked at her. The golden

flames of the fire danced in his dark eyes. "Actually, I've kind of gotten used to having you and Carrie Anne around."

"You love her, don't you?" The words just popped out. She glanced down at her half-full glass of wine sitting on the table and wondered if she was drunk.

Cord didn't seem upset by the question. He calmly set down his fork and wiped his mouth with his napkin. "She's hard not to love."

She should shut up. The warm glow inside her was a pretty good indication that she was, if not drunk, slightly buzzed. But her mouth refused to listen to her brain and she continued. "Danny Ray doesn't love her. He's starting to like her, but he doesn't love her. And I doubt that he ever will."

"He will. He just needs a little more time."

She set down her fork and knife. "I know you think that Danny Ray is a lot like you. And at one time, I thought all rodeo cowboys were the same too." She studied him. "But you proved me wrong, Cord Evans. You're nothing like Danny Ray. He acts before he thinks, and you think before you act. He can't seem to do anything right, and you seem to do everything right."

He snorted. "I think Ryker would disagree."

"Not now he wouldn't. He admires the man you are as much as I do."

Surprise flickered in his eyes for a second before he glanced at her wine. "I think you're a little tipsy, Christmas Day Buchanan."

She had always hated her name. She didn't mind being born on a holiday, but she wished her mother had been a little more inventive with her name. Noelle or Holly would've sounded much less silly.

But when Cord said her name, it didn't sound silly. It sounded beautiful.

"I guess I am a little tipsy," she said. "And maybe that's why I'm being so truthful. You are a man to admire, Cord. You might've been a no-good rodeo bum at one time, but you're not anymore. You're a father any child should be proud of and a man any woman would love to call her own."

Okay, she was drunk.

Her face heated, and she looked down at her napkin. "Not me, of course. But any other woman."

"Because you don't need or want a man."

It wasn't a question. It was a statement. And it was partially true. She didn't need a man, but she certainly wanted one. Not a boy like Danny Ray. But a man like the one who looked back at her with soft, brown eyes. She couldn't keep the truth from spilling out of her mouth.

"I want a man."

Surprise flicked in his eyes for only a second before it was doused by steamy heat. The waitress came up to ask if they would like dessert menus. Without taking his hot gaze off Christie, Cord shook his head. "Thank you, but we'll just take the check."

Her knees were so wobbly, she didn't know how she made it to Cord's truck. The temperature outside had risen while they were eating. Or maybe her inside temperature was what had risen. She seemed to be radiating heat as he held the truck door open for her. Some of it had to do with the wine she'd consumed, but most of it had to do with acknowledging her desire for Cord.

When they were in the truck on the way back

to Bliss, she couldn't help glancing over at him. He seemed to have the same problem. More than once, their eyes collided and held for a heart-stopping second before he returned his gaze to the highway.

They didn't talk. There was too much underlying sexual tension in the cab of the truck to squeeze in words. So they just exchanged quick, heated glances that made Christie grow warmer and warmer. When they reached her trailer, she should've bid him a hasty goodnight and gotten inside as quickly as possible. Instead, she just sat there.

He turned the engine off and a stillness settled around them, the only sound their soft, uneven breaths. After what felt like forever, she turned. Their gazes caught and held once again. But this time, no one looked away. This time, they moved together like two magnets flipped to the right side. Their lips met in a kiss that was slightly off center. They readjusted, and their lips parted to share the addictive heat of mouths and rough strokes of tongues.

They shifted in their seats to get closer, but their seatbelts and the console kept them from achieving that goal. Cord unhooked his seatbelt, then reached for hers. Once it snapped back against the door, he lifted her over the console and onto his lap. She was cocooned by his steely arms and chest . . . and an even steelier bulge beneath her bottom. As the kiss grew deeper and more consuming, his hand shifted from her waist and slid inside her coat to cover her breast. He cupped it gently, brushing his thumb back and forth over the hardened nipple beneath her sweater and bra. The rush of wet heat that accumulated between her legs caused her to shift restlessly against his hardness.

He groaned low and deep in his chest and pulled back from the kiss, resting his forehead against hers. "Can I come inside?" His breathing was as rapid and heavy as hers.

Her answer was more of a croak. "Please."

He opened the door and helped her out. As soon as her feet hit the ground, she hurried to the trailer on wobbly legs. Once inside, she flipped on the light and searched for anything embarrassing that might be lying around. She picked up a pair of panties, then grabbed all Carrie Anne's stuffed animals off the bed and shoved them into the tiny closet. She slammed the door closed and saw Cord standing there. He must've left his sheepskin coat in the truck because he was no longer wearing it or his hat.

He glanced around and his gaze landed on the small bed. It was easy to read his skepticism.

She laughed. "Are you thinking you won't fit?"

He looked back at her and smiled. It was a sensual smile that made her insides turn to mush. "Oh, I'll fit. I'll fit just fine."

He stepped closer and slipped her coat off her shoulders. After he placed it on the table, she thought he would reach for her sweater. Instead, he reached for her braid. He wound it around and around his hand, pulling her closer to him. "I've had a lot of fantasies about your hair. A lot of fantasies." He bent his head and rubbed his cheek against the thick coil of her braid, his eyes closing and his lungs filling as if breathing the scent of her hair in. He opened his eyes and allowed her braid to slip through his fingers. He caught it on the end and slid off the elastic band. Then slowly, and extremely sensuously, he started to unbraid her hair. "And one of those fantasies was seeing you completely naked surrounded by all this gorgeousness."

She couldn't help the tremble that ran through her body at his words and the feel of his hands as they loosened each strand. When he finished, he slipped off her sweater, then unclasped her bra with one twist of his fingers. Once he slid it off her shoulders, she felt a twinge of self-consciousness. She stood in front of him, one breast covered by her unbraided hair and the other completely exposed to his gaze. He studied her for one uncomfortable moment before his breath rushed out.

"Damn. You're so beautiful, I'm afraid to touch you. I'm afraid you'll disappear."

His sweet compliment dissolved her self-consciousness, and she reached out and took his hand, pressing his open palm to her breast. The feel of his warm callused hand cradling her had her breath hitching. "I'm real. And I'm not going anywhere. For tonight, I'm all yours." She left his hand where it was and slowly unsnapped his shirt to reveal the muscled chest beneath. She ran her hand down the very center, enjoying the feel of his hair against her fingertips. "And you're all mine."

His eyes slid closed as if savoring her touch. He pressed his hand against her breast and the beating heart beneath. "Christmas," he said her name like a prayer before he lowered his mouth to hers and set her already spinning world upside down.

Somehow, between the small space and the

heated kisses, they managed to get their clothes off. When they were naked, they stood back and looked their fill. The rest of Cord's body was as lean and muscled as his chest. It was also covered with scars. Scars that were heartbreaking and intriguing at the same time.

She traced the one on his shoulder, and he answered her question before she could ask it. "Oklahoma City. A bull named Ornery."

She caressed the scar along his ribcage.

"Amarillo. A horse called Demon Fire."

She touched the scar under his chin.

He blushed. "Vegas. I don't remember the name of the bar."

She looked down and studied the scar on his knee.

"Albuquerque. A bull named Redemption. He was the one that gave me my limp and almost killed me. The one that made me give up rodeo and tequila and change my ways." He tipped her chin up. His eyes were solemn. "I have a lot of scars, Christie. Some you can see, and some you can't. Are you sure you want this beat-up old cowboy?"

His kisses had left her slightly dizzy and off-kilter. But her mind was clear, and she knew exactly what she wanted. "Take me to bed, Cord Evans."

He closed his eyes for a second and took a deep breath, before he opened them and smiled. "Yes, ma'am."

Cord was right. They fit in the bed just fine. Even in the small space, he had no trouble finding every one of her erogenous zones with his talented fingers and even more talented tongue. When he had her completely mindless with want, he positioned himself above her and slid deep inside.

The fit was perfect, and they both took a moment to savor it before their desire grew hot and restless. The first thrust was like a match to a fuse, there was no stopping the sizzling heat that raced toward detonation.

"More," she moaned.

Cord thrust faster and deeper, but there was still an underlying tenderness in the way he cradled her head between his arms and the way his soft brown gaze held hers. It was this tenderness that had her melting like sugar to a flame. Her body liquefied and turned into caramelized heat that bubbled and popped . . . and finally boiled over. As her orgasm hit and her body tightened around him, he found his own release—which sent after-tingles cascading through her.

When it was all over, she felt like she had been drained of every last ounce of energy. She also felt happy. Extremely happy.

Cord rolled off her and flopped an arm over his eyes. "Damn."

She smiled up at the low ceiling of the trailer.

Damn.

CHAPTER NINETEEN

CHRISTIE DIDN'T KNOW WHAT WOKE her from the sound sleep. But after she sat up and looked around, she figured it had been Cord leaving. She felt hurt and surprised. She hadn't taken him for the type of man to slink off in the middle of the night. But it was probably for the best. Waking up with him would've been awkward. Especially when her emotions were such a jumbled mess.

Autumn had been wrong. Having sex with Cord hadn't cleared anything up. In fact, it had left Christie feeling even more confused. She had hoped that her attraction to him was just physical. But last night had proven otherwise. She felt a connection to him that went beyond the physical. He touched something deep inside her. Something that had needed to be touched for a long time.

And it scared the hell out of her.

She couldn't fall for another cowboy with commitment issues. And the fact that she was in her bed all alone was a pretty good indication that Cord had commitment issues. He was still struggling to deal with his past mistakes, and she couldn't fault him for wanting to focus his attention on his son. That's exactly what she needed to do. She needed to stop thinking about Cord and focus on her daughter and making this a Christmas Carrie Anne would remember. But how could she do that without credit or a car?

She could come up with only one answer.

It was time to tell her family the truth and ask for help.

She was trying to figure out how to break the news to the Hadleys when a scraping noise had her glancing at the ceiling of the trailer. She would've thought it was a tree branch if there had been trees growing by the trailer, but there weren't any. And the noise was too high to be a bush. It sounded like something was being dragged across the top edge of the trailer.

Her first thought was to call Cord, but she immediately vetoed the idea. If it turned out to be something stupid like a tumbleweed caught on the top of the trailer, he'd think she'd made up the lame excuse to get him back out there. She refused to become the clingy, desperate woman she'd been with Danny Ray.

She got out of bed and grabbed her robe off the hook by the bathroom. As she was pulling it on, a thump followed by a muffled cuss word made her freeze. Tumbleweeds did not cuss. She quickly locked the door, then crouched low and peeked out the kitchen window over the sink.

It was dark outside, but not so dark that she couldn't see the outline of a man as he moved in front of the window. She ducked down and searched for her phone to call Cord. She didn't care if he thought she was desperate and needy. She *was* desperate and needy. Thankfully, he answered on the first ring.

"Hey." He didn't sound like she'd woken him up. He sounded wide-awake and . . . happy. Suddenly, she was annoyed. She didn't expect him to stay the night with her, but he didn't have to sound so happy that he hadn't.

"Christie?" he said, making her realize that she was sitting there glaring at the phone.

She put it back to her ear and snapped. "What?"

There was a pause. "I don't know, darlin'. You were the one who called me."

"Believe me, if this wasn't an emergency, I wouldn't be calling you at all. I don't want you thinking that I'm some clingy woman who can't live without you now that we've had sex. I realize that last night was just us letting off a little steam. Nothing more and nothing—"

The door rattled like the man outside was trying to get in. When he couldn't, he pounded on the door. Christie's heart pounded right along with it.

"Unlock the damned door!" Cord yelled. She started to ask him why he would want her answering the door for some mass murderer when she realized that his voice wasn't coming through the phone. It was coming through her door. She got up and pulled it open to see Cord standing there looking extremely sexy in his Stetson and sheepskin coat. He also looked extremely ticked.

"Letting off a little steam?" he said.

"What are you doing here?" She looked down at the string of Christmas lights in his hand.

"Just answer the question," he said. "Is that what

you thought last night was? Just the two of us letting off some steam? Because it was much more than that for me, Christie. A helluva lot more. I agree that we have a lot going on in our lives right now. You have Carrie Anne and your work, and I have the ranch and Ryker, but just because we have a lot going on that doesn't mean we can't continue to see each other. Especially when being with you makes all the other stresses in my life fade away. And I thought you might feel the same way too. But obviously I was wrong." He held out the string of lights. "Here, you can finish the job I started." He turned and headed toward his truck.

She looked down at the lights in her hands and then glanced around the yard. It was too dark to see much of anything so she flipped on the outside light. When she did, her entire yard lit up with Christmas lights. Every bush and weed was covered in colorful twinkle lights. And smack dab in the middle, was the tree she'd bought. Cord had planted it in the ground and covered its branches with so many lights it glittered like the tree at New York City's Rockefeller Center.

Christie covered her mouth and blinked back the tears that welled in her eyes. He hadn't run off and left her. He'd given her and her daughter a Christmas Wonderland.

Dropping the string of lights, she leapt down from the trailer and raced across the yard. "Cord!" He turned and she jumped right into his arms, hooking her bare legs around his waist and cupping his sweet, endearing face in her hands. "I'm sorry. I thought you'd left and I got a little hurt that you had. And I tried to hide that hurt by acting like what happened wasn't a big deal. But it was a big deal. It was a big, amazing deal."

He stared back at her, his brown eyes reflecting the multi-colored lights. "It was a big deal for me too. And I'm sorry I left you without saying goodbye. I just wanted to surprise you."

She glanced over her shoulder at the light display. "It's beautiful. Carrie Anne is going to love it. You turned her home into a dreamland."

"It is a dreamland. My dreams sure came true here." He bent his head and kissed her. It wasn't as hungry as the kisses the night before. It was much slower and sweeter, but just as melty. She kissed him back for all she was worth. His hands moved from her waist to her butt and she sucked in a startled breath when his cold fingers brushed her naked skin. He drew back. "Are you naked under that robe, Christie Buchanan?"

"Yep."

The sound he made in the back of his throat could only be described as a feral growl. With long strides, he carried her straight back to the trailer where he made love to her against the bathroom door without removing one article of clothing. When they'd both reached orgasm, he dropped down to the bed with her still straddling him.

"A six-time champion rodeo star and I can't even last eight seconds."

She reached for the snaps of his shirt and smiled seductively. "Now I'm sure you can beat that time." She jerked open his shirt.

They made love until the sky started to brighten, then they fell into an exhausted sleep. When Christie woke, late morning sun was pouring through the windows.

"Carrie Anne!" She sprung out of bed and would've started getting dressed if Cord hadn't calmed her.

"No need to panic, darlin'." He reached for her phone and handed it to her. "Why don't you give her a call and see how she's doing? If she's ready to come home, we'll go and get her. If not," his gaze ran over her naked body, "we can take our time."

"But I have to post on your social media and work on your 'Christmas on the Ranch' contest before I head into the bakery."

"My followers can follow someone else today, the contest doesn't go up until Monday, and I'm sure Ms. Marble or Autumn won't mind helping out at the bakery until you get there."

She looked back at the sex-mussed man in her bed and couldn't argue with his good logic.

Carrie Anne wasn't upset at all that her mother hadn't come to get her. As soon as Dirk put her on the phone, she started enthusiastically chattering about her overnight stay.

"It was soooo much fun, Mama. Granny Bon and Gracie let me and the triplets make little gingerbread houses—except they weren't made out of gingerbread cookies like your house. They were made out of graham crackers. But once we glued all the candy on with frosting they looked just like real gingerbread houses. And Granny Bon said I can bring mine home once it dries. And guess what, this morning it was dry. And you know who cooked dinner and breakfast for me? Mayor Dirk! 'Cause he's not only good at mayoring, he's good at cooking. He asked me what I loved to eat and when I told him pepperoni pizza that's exactly what he made for dinner. And he put loads of pepperoni and plenty of stringy cheese. And he also made a salad, but he didn't make me eat it like you do. And he didn't make me eat all my waffle this morning either, but I did. And Ms. Marble came to have waffles with us. But she can't eat them 'cause she has sugar died-and-beat-us."

Christie stifled her laughter, but she had the phone on speaker, and Cord didn't stifle his.

"Is that Cord?" Carrie Anne asked. Before Christie could come up with a good lie of why she was with Cord, her daughter continued. "Hey, Cord!"

Cord winked at Christie. "Hey, Half Pint. Sounds like you're having fun."

"I am. You're not coming to get me yet, are you, Mama? Because Gracie's gonna take me out to the corral and show me how she barrel races. Did you know she won lots of ribbons barrel racing? And she said once I learn how to ride, she'll teach me how. But I don't want to be a barrel racer. I want to ride bulls and wild broncos like you, Cord."

Cord's face registered fear and Christie intervened. "We'll talk about that later. Remember your manners and I'll pick you up in a few hours, Baby Girl."

"Are you coming to get me too, Cord?"

"Yes, ma'am. Your mama's car broke down so until she can get it fixed, I'll be driving you around. Is that okay with you?"

The squeal of excitement pretty much said it all.

After Christie said goodbye and hung up the phone, she crossed her arms over her chest. "And just who said that I'm going to let you drive me around, Cord Evans?"

His eyebrow lifted. "Is there someone else you'd rather let drive you around?"

She pretended like she was thinking for a second before she shrugged. "I guess I'm stuck with an arrogant rodeo cowboy."

"Damn right, you are." He reached out and pulled her back to bed.

They didn't get up until close to noon. After they got dressed, she fixed him a lunch of peanut butter and jelly sandwiches and Cheetos. The orange dust that got on their lips resulted in a make-out session that left them both wishing that they hadn't gotten dressed.

On the way to pick up Carrie Anne, Cord swung by his house to change clothes. When they pulled up to the porch, she noticed all the lights that were missing from his front shrubs. "So that's where you got the lights," she said.

He laughed. "And almost a butt full of buckshot when Jasper heard me slipping around in the dark and came out with his shotgun."

"Did you tell him where you were taking them?"

"No, but I think he figured it out."

She heaved a sigh. "Great. The way news travels in a small town, I won't be surprised if some kid on the playground doesn't tell Carrie Anne that her mama had S-E-X with Cord Evans."

He cringed. "I didn't think about that. From now on, we'll need to be a little more discreet. Which is too bad because I was hoping that you'd come in and take a hot shower with me."

After showering in the small shower in the trailer for the last few months, a regular shower with plenty of hot water sounded like heaven. But she shook her head. "I'm not stepping foot in your house. If I do, we'll never get my daughter. Now get!"

He laughed as he got out. "Bossy woman."

Once he was gone, Christie went through the pictures on her phone looking for something to post on Cord's social media. When she didn't find any pictures she liked, she got out of the truck and headed to the barn. People loved the pictures she'd posted of the horses.

Inside the barn, she was surprised to find Danny Ray mucking out a stall. She couldn't remember ever seeing him work so hard, and she had to wonder if Cord was right. Maybe Danny Ray could change.

"Hey, Danny Ray," she said.

He startled and whirled around. "Jesus H. Christ, Christie! You scared the shit out of me." He glanced down at the horse poop covering his boots. "Pardon the pun."

She laughed. "I didn't think the day would come when Danny Ray shoveled poop."

He leaned on the shovel and scowled. "Yeah, well, I didn't think I'd ever go to a kids' Christmas party and have a good time, but I did. Kids are kinda cute—as long as you only have to deal with them for an hour. That constant chatter of Carrie Anne's can drive you to drink in a hurry."

"She does talk a lot. And there are days I've wished for a stiff drink."

"But I bet you never drank one." He studied her, then surprised her once again. "You're a good mama, Christmas Buchanan. You're a damn good mama."

She squinted at him. "Speaking of drinking, are you drunk, Danny Ray?"

"Sober as a preacher on Sunday. Cord doesn't keep a drop in the house. Believe me, last night when he was gone I searched it from top to bottom looking for a bottle." His gaze narrowed. "Did he spend the night with you?"

She stumbled over her reply. "Umm . . . why would you think that?"

"Because he left to get you and then you both show up here this morning looking as happy as two bugs in a rug." He shrugged. "And I don't blame you for sleeping with him. Why settle for a rodeo bum when you can have a rodeo star? Damn, I should've asked you to marry me when I had the chance."

There was a time when she had wished with all her heart that Danny Ray had asked her to marry him. But now she realized that marriage to him would've been a huge mistake.

"No, you shouldn't have," she said. "You didn't love me, Danny Ray, and I didn't love you. We were just two immature kids in lust."

"Nothing wrong with lust." He flashed his cocky smile, but it quickly faded. "Is it just lust with Cord?"

The question left her feeling stunned, and she scrambled around for an answer only to discover that she didn't have one. She wanted to say it was just lust, but she'd had lust with Danny Ray and what she had with Cord wasn't anything like that. It was more intense. More consuming. More . . . beautiful.

When she didn't answer, he sighed. "That's what I thought. But if you're smart, you'll be real careful. His record with women is as bad as mine. And a leopard can't change his spots."

She'd once believed that, but she didn't believe it anymore. Cord had taught her that people can change. He had changed. And she had too. She was no longer the mistrustful woman who had first come to Bliss. In the last few months, she had learned to trust. She trusted the Hadleys. She trusted Cord.

And more importantly, she trusted herself.

"You're wrong, Danny Ray. You can change your spots. You just have to want to." She smiled. "Now if you'll excuse me, I need to go get our daughter."

CHAPTER TWENTY

CORD *WAS* HAPPY. IT HAD been a while since he'd felt completely happy, so it took him a few days to identify the buoyant feeling bubbling around inside him. He woke up smiling and went to sleep smiling. And smiled like an idiot all through the day.

At first, he tried to tell himself that it was the sex. Good sex could make you happy. And sex with Christie had been more than good. It had been spectacular. But with Carrie Anne on holiday break, he and Christie hadn't been able to even share a kiss since their night in the trailer and his sexual glow still hadn't worn off. Which made him wonder if it was the woman more than the physical satisfaction she'd given him. When she was around, he didn't feel like a failure. He felt like a man who could do anything.

"What's that song you're whistlin'?"

He stopped whistling and grooming Raise-a-Ruckus and glanced over to see Jasper leaning on the stall door. He had his cowboy hat tipped back and was studying Cord with an intense look.

"I don't know," Cord said. "I was just whistling."

Jasper cocked an eyebrow. "Hmm? I don't think I've ever heard you whistle before."

"So?"

"Nothin'." He pointed over his shoulder. "There's a man out front asking for you."

"What does he want?"

"I'm not one to stick my nose in other people's business, which is exactly why I'm not going to say why I think you're so happy."

The man was too much of a know-it-all for his own good. "Ornery cuss," Cord grumbled as he put away the currycomb. Once outside, he recognized the pot-bellied cowboy instantly. It was the metal artist he'd commissioned to make the entrance sign for his ranch.

"Hey, Marty. Good to see you." He walked over and shook his hand. "You got something for me?"

"I sure do," Marty said. "I put a rush order on it because I'm such a fan." He walked around to the bed of his truck and pulled back the tarp. C & R Ranch had been laser cut into a large piece of steel with two bucking broncos on either side. It looked better than Cord had imagined it would and he could only hope that Ryker loved it as much as he did.

"It looks great, Marty. Thanks for doing it so quickly." He glanced back at Jasper. "Can you help him get it into the barn, while I run into the house and write him a check?"

Jasper squinted at the sign and then at Cord before he nodded.

Inside, Cord found Danny Ray snoring on the couch and Carrie Anne shaking one of the presents under the tree. He couldn't help but smile. He'd done the same thing when he was little. Which is why his father had put his gifts in bigger boxes and added rocks and marbles to trick him.

"I think that's called cheating, Half Pint," he said.

Carrie Anne startled and dropped the present. "I was just lookin' to see whose name was on it, is all."

"Uh-huh. And I guess you had to shake it to read it." Her cheeks turned pink just like her mama. He laughed. "So did you figure out what it was?"

She visibly relaxed and grinned. "My riding helmet."

Damn, it looked like he'd have to use marbles and rocks next year. Since he couldn't lie to her, he changed the subject. "I thought you and Danny Ray were going to play a game."

"He tried to teach me poker, but it wasn't any fun so I taught him Old Maid using one of the jokers. And when I was organizing my pairs, he fell asleep. I was gonna wake him, but then Jasper said it's best to let sleeping dogs lie. And I asked him what that meant and before he could tell me somebody rung the doorbell asking for you. So what does that mean? Do dogs lie? And why is it best to not wake them? And why does Jasper think my daddy is a dog?"

Cord knew why Jasper thought Danny Ray was a dog. He didn't trust him. Cord had to admit that Danny Ray still wasn't the kind of devoted daddy he had hoped he would be. But his work ethic had improved. Once he'd paid off Carrie Anne's boots, he'd continued to volunteer for odd jobs. And that was something.

"It's just an expression, Half Pint. Let me finish

taking care of some business outside and I'll come in and play Old Maid with you." He pointed a finger at her. "And leave those presents alone."

She smiled sassily. "It's a helmet, isn't it?"

He bit back a grin before he headed to his office to get a check.

Once he'd paid Marty and the man had left, Cord went to the barn. He wanted to make sure the sign had been placed out of sight just in case Ryker happened to stop by. He didn't want the surprise ruined like Carrie Anne's riding helmet. Now he'd have to get Carrie Anne another surprise. Maybe he'd get her a dog. Every kid should have a dog. Of course, she'd have to leave it here because a new puppy wouldn't fit in the trailer. Christie and Carrie Anne barely fit there. They needed a bigger place to live and not some small apartment or house. Carrie Anne needed space to run and be a kid.

He was still mulling over Christie and Carrie Anne's living arrangements when he stepped into the barn. It was a good thing he checked to see where Jasper had put the sign because it was leaning up against a stack of hay in full view.

"We need to get that out of sight," Cord said to Jasper who was standing there staring at the sign. "It's a surprise for Ryker."

Jasper continued to study the sign. "I figured as much. So you're going to surprise him by using his initial on the entry sign?"

"That's not the surprise. The surprise is the ranch. I built it for Ryker."

Jasper turned to him, looking thoroughly confused. "For Ryker? But where are you going to live?"

"Right here with him. That's why I built the house so big. There's plenty of room for everyone."

Jasper gaped at him for only a second before he burst out laughing. He laughed so hard that he had to lean against the stalls to keep from falling over.

Cord watched him with growing annoyance. "What's so funny, you ornery old cowboy?"

After a little more side-grabbing laughter, Jasper sobered and wiped at his eyes. "That has to be the stupidest plan I've ever heard in my life. And believe me when I tell you that I've heard some pretty damned stupid plans. But this one takes the cake."

Now more pissed than annoyed, he glared at his friend. "What's so stupid about wanting my son to live with me?"

"Nothing if he was ten years old. But Ryker is a grown man, Cord. He has his own life with a wife and a new baby on the way. He has a nice house in town and a place in this community that doesn't include ranching. From what I hear, he doesn't even enjoy riding horses that much."

"He will once I give him Ruckus."

"You're training that horse for Ryker?" Jasper looked at Cord like he was the dumbest man alive. "You do realize that even when Ruckus gets saddle broke, he's still not going to be a mild-mannered mount. He's going to need an experienced rider to handle him."

"I'll teach Ryker to be an expert horseman. Once he moves here, I'll teach him everything I know. I'll teach him how to ride and rope. This spring, I'll stock the pond and I'll teach him how to fish and skip rocks and—"

Jasper cut him off. "And maybe he'll sit on your lap and let you read him a bedtime story every night before you tuck him into bed."

"Don't be a wiseass," Cord snapped.

"Then pull your head out of your ass!" Jasper snapped back. His eyes turned sad. "I get that you're having a hard time forgiving yourself for not being a good daddy. I get that you want to go back and do it over. But there are no re-dos in life, Cord. Just like you can't re-do a bull ride and get a few more seconds on the clock, you can't go back and be the father you weren't to Ryker. You just can't do it. He's a grown man. You can't expect him to give up being an adult and move back in with his dad. He has a wife and soon he will have his own son or daughter. And yes, if you're lucky, he'll want to share a portion of that life with you, but he won't want to share all of it." His eyes grew even sadder. "This is his chance to be a father. And you don't want him to miss out like you did. You want him to spend every second he can with his family."

All Cord could do was stare at him as the truth of his words sank in. And still he couldn't accept it. If he accepted it, that meant there was no fixing the mistake he'd made. There was no way to recover what he'd lost. There was no redemption.

"I'm not asking him to give up being a father," he said much louder than he intended. But he was hanging by a thin thread and if he let go of this dream—a dream that had gotten him through the hellacious years of recovery from alcoholism—he feared he'd go plummeting back into oblivion. "But he can be a father here." He waved a hand around. "Who wouldn't want to raise their child on a place like this with horses and plenty of space to run around?"

Jasper studied him. "And what if Ryker says yes? What if he wants to come live here and play out your foolish dream? What about Christie and Carrie Anne? Where do they fit into this plan?"

The question broadsided him. "What do you mean? They'll fit in just like they're fitting in now. Christie will continue to work for me and Carrie Anne will continue to hang out here after school."

"Work for you? That's what Christie is to you? An employee? And Carrie Anne is just a kid who shows up occasionally and hangs out?"

Cord didn't know why his heart started racing and his palms started to sweat like he was getting ready to climb on the scariest bull he'd ever ridden. "Well, no. Christie and Carrie Anne are more than that, but what we have doesn't have to interfere with what I'm going to have with Ryker. They're two different things. Ryker is my family—my son. He comes first. He has to come first. And Christie and Carrie Anne are only my . . ." He struggled to find the right words to describe what they were to him. When he couldn't, he chose a word that didn't even come close. "Friends."

"But I don't want to just be your friend."

He turned to see Carrie Anne standing in the open doorway. Her big, tear-filled hazel eyes cut right through his heart.

"I thought you were gonna marry me," she said in a quivery voice. "I thought you loved me. But you don't love me. All you love is your stupid son." She whirled and ran out of the barn.

Cord felt like he'd been in the worst bar fight ever. He stood there stunned, not knowing what to do. He turned on Jasper. "This is all your damned fault! If you hadn't butted your nose into my business, Carrie Anne wouldn't have gotten her feelings hurt and everything would've worked out just fine."

"Everything wouldn't have worked out just fine, boy. And you're off your rocker if you think it would've. Eventually, that sweet little girl's feelings were going to be hurt. Eventually, she was going to figure out that you're still too screwed up to accept a gift when it's offered to you. And that's what she is, Cord Evans. A gift. You can't turn back time and make Ryker six years old again. But God gave you a precious six-year-old who you can teach to ride and fish and skip rocks. You're just too stubborn to see it. Just like you're too stubborn to see that you're in love with her mama. Now if you'll excuse me, I'm gonna go check on Carrie Anne, and after that, I'm gonna pack. I refuse to spend Christmas with an idiot."

"Good!" Cord called after him. "I don't need a friend like you, anyway. You're just a crazy old cowboy who doesn't know the first thing about being a daddy. And you certainly don't know anything about sons. Ryker will want to come live with me. He damn well will!"

His yelled words echoed in the rafters of the barn and came right back at him. He wanted to believe them. He wanted to believe that there were re-dos in life. That people could go back and fix their mistakes. But deep down he knew that Jasper was right. Deep down, he knew that there was no going back.

The craving for a drink fisted his gut, and his hands started to shake uncontrollably. He needed a shot of tequila. He needed it in a bad way. And why couldn't he have one? No one would have to know. He could go to a bar outside of Bliss. Or better yet, to a liquor store and get a bottle. He wouldn't drink the entire thing. He just needed a shot.

Just one shot.

He headed out of the barn, but before he could reach his truck, Jasper came out of the house with Danny Ray right behind him. "We can't find Carrie Anne," Jasper said. "She's not in the house."

His urge for a drink was quick replaced by concern. "What do you mean she's not in the house? Did you look—?" A horse's nervous squeal cut him off. He turned and ran toward the back paddock where the horses were grazing. He spotted Carrie Anne immediately. She had somehow gotten a lead rope on Maple and was standing on the fence trying to mount the horse. Unfortunately, when Maple saw Cord, she headed toward him. Carrie Anne fell off the fence and landed hard on the ground.

"Carrie Anne!" Cord stepped up to the bottom rail of the fence and vaulted over. The horse moved out of his way as he ran to Carrie Anne. By the time he got there, she was sitting up, holding her arm, and screaming loudly. He knelt next to her and tried to calm her. But it was hard when he wasn't calm.

"It's okay. I'm here. Let me see your arm."

"Don't touch me," she wailed. "It hurts!"

"I know it does, sweetheart. Does anything else hurt? Did you bump your head when you fell?"

She sucked in quivery gulps of air, and he worried that she would have another asthma attack if he couldn't calm her down. "No. I-I-It's just my arm."

He studied the place on her arm she was clutching. It was already swelling, and with the tumble she'd taken, he was pretty sure she'd broken it.

"Is she okay?" Danny Ray came running up with Jasper close on his heels.

Not wanting to upset Carrie Anne, he didn't voice his concerns. "She's going to be just fine, but we'll need to take her to the doctor's to get her checked out." He pulled his truck keys from his pocket and tossed them to Danny Ray. "Start up my truck." He looked at Jasper. "Run in and get a bag of ice and her inhaler. It's in her backpack."

When they both left to do his bidding, he turned back to Carrie Anne. Her crying had softened. Now she just whimpered pathetically. It broke his heart in two. "Hold your arm tightly to your chest, Half Pint," he said. "I'm going to pick you up." She did what he asked, and he carefully lifted her. Her swift intake of breath told him how badly she hurt, and damned if her pain didn't make him hurt too. "I got you, baby," he said once he was standing. "And it's going to be okay. Everything is going to be okay."

But everything wasn't okay. He'd screwed up again. This time, he didn't know if he could forgive himself.

CHAPTER TWENTY-ONE

"YOU HAD SEX WITH CORD, didn't you?"

Christie dropped the cake pan she'd just taken out of the oven and stared at Summer with surprise.

"Good grief, Summer? Do you always have to be so blunt?" Autumn grabbed an oven mitt and hurried over to pick up the pan. The red velvet cake in the shape of a candy cane remained on the floor. Summer walked over with a broom and dustpan to clean it up.

"Why beat around the bush? It's pretty obvious by the sappy smile on her face that something has happened, and since Cord has the same sappy smile, I think it's a fair question."

Spring, who was sitting at the counter having her morning cup of coffee, chimed in. "Summer does have a point. I ran into Cord yesterday at the diner and he was acting pretty darned giddy. He was laughing and talking with everyone. And somehow I don't think it was Christmas cheer as much as Christie cheer."

Christie couldn't help feeling hopeful that Cord's

happiness was connected to her. Hers was certainly connected to him. She had been walking around for the last few days in a bubble of sheer Cord Evans contentment.

"Would you two stop?" Autumn took the filled dustpan from Summer and tossed the cake in the trash. "If she doesn't want to talk about her personal life, she doesn't have to."

"Of course she has to," Spring said. "We tell her everything about our boring married lives. It's only fair that she shares a little information about the steamy, torrid affair she's having with the hottest rodeo cowboy ever."

Cord *was* the hottest rodeo cowboy ever, but Christie wasn't exactly having a steamy, torrid affair with him. After the night at her trailer, they hadn't been able to share more than heated glances with Carrie Anne on holiday break and always underfoot. But what she had with Cord wasn't about the physical. What she had with him was a deeper connection. Something she felt every time she saw him. Or heard his voice over the phone. Or looked into his soft brown eyes.

After Danny Ray, Christie had convinced herself that she didn't need another man in her life. But her mistake was thinking that Danny Ray had been a man. Cord had taught her the difference.

A real man prefers to listen intently rather than talk continuously. He respects others' opinions, but isn't afraid to argue his points. He's kind to animals, loving to children, and respectful to women. He's comfortable in his own skin, but never boastful. He's a true friend who is willing to offer whatever is needed, whether it's refuge from the storm or just a shoulder to cry on. He makes mistakes, but he learns from his mistakes and works hard to fix them.

Cord Evans was a real man.

At the moment, he was her man. And damned if Christie could keep the secret a second longer.

"I slept with Cord Evans." The words rushed out of her mouth so quickly they sounded like one long word.

Her sisters exchanged knowing smiles before Spring patted the seat of the stool next to her. "I only have a few minutes before my morning break is over, but that should be plenty of time for you to give us the highlights."

Once Autumn and Summer joined them at the counter, Christie started talking and couldn't seem to stop. She told them about her and Cord's first kiss by the fire and about their second one in the barn. She told them about Cord taking her to dinner and how they couldn't stop looking at each other on the drive back to the trailer. She condensed what happened once they got to the trailer, but shared every detail of him decorating her tree and yard with a thousand lights. Occasionally, the front bell would ring and Autumn or Summer would make her stop while they hurried to wait on a customer. Once they got back, she'd start up again.

When she was finished, Autumn smiled. "So it's not just lust. It's love."

"I don't know," she said. "My heart says yes, but my mind refuses to let me make the same mistake I made with Danny Ray. I thought I loved him, but it turned out that it was only lust mixed with my childhood hang-ups about my father. And what if this is the same thing? What if I'm still looking for a man to be the father I never had?"

Summer, Autumn, and Spring exchanged looks and she knew they understood exactly how she felt. The understanding and compassion she saw in their eyes gave her the strength to finally share the truth.

"There's something you need to know about me," she said. "Something that I should've told you as soon as I got to Bliss. I didn't just go see Holt in jail to tell him about my mom passing away. I went there looking for my father." She tried to swallow the lump of fear in her throat, but it seemed to be getting bigger. "You see, Holt Hadley is my—"

"Daddy," Summer cut in. "Yeah, we know."

Christie stared at her. "You know?"

Autumn smiled. "We've known you were our sister for a week, Christie. We were just waiting for you to trust us enough to tell us."

"But how did you find out?" She couldn't believe that Cord had shared her secret.

"Our Daddy," Spring said. "I called to tell him that Autumn, Summer, and I had sent him a Christmas care package that included pumpkin pie baked by Summer's new assistant Christie Buchanan. He started laughing hysterically. He thought it was pretty funny that all four of his daughters were now living in the same town. He calls us his four seasons: Spring, Summer, Autumn, and Christmas. After I got over my shock, I asked why he'd never mentioned the fact that we had a half-sister. In typical Holt fashion, he said that it had never come up." She shook her head. "The man is a lost cause."

Christie looked at her sisters. "So you're not mad at me for not telling you sooner?"

"I was a little miffed," Summer said. "But Autumn and Spring reminded me that the Hadleys can be pretty intimidating."

"We didn't say the Hadleys," Spring said. "We said *you* were intimidating."

Before an argument could start, Christie jumped in. "I was a little intimidated at first. I was worried that you would think that your father didn't love your mother. But he did. My mama was just a fling. He proved that by never once coming back to see her . . . or me." The triplets exchanged looks before they burst out laughing. Christie didn't get the joke. "What's so funny?"

"Holt didn't love our mama," Summer said. "He doesn't love anyone but himself. The only reason he came back to see our mother was to beg for money. And if your mama had lived closer, I'm sure he would've dropped by to get money from her too."

Her father being a selfish jerk shouldn't have made Christie feel better, but somehow it did. Holt didn't love his other children more than he loved her. He didn't love anyone.

Autumn smiled at Christie as if reading her mind. "Holt doesn't know how to love, but thankfully our mamas taught us how to." She reached over the counter and took Christie's hand and squeezed it. "Welcome to the family, Christmas Day."

Summer placed her hand over Autumn's and Christie's. "Ditto."

"Daddy was right. All four seasons *are* finally together." Spring used both her hands to cover her sisters.

Before Christie's eyes could finish welling with tears of joy, the phone rang and the sisters released hands so Summer could hurry over to answer it. "Blissful Bakery. Can I help you?" She glanced at Christie. "Yes, she is. Hold on." She held out the phone. "It's for you, sis."

Christie's heart swelled at the endearment, and she couldn't help giving Summer a quick hug before she took the phone from her. "This is Christie Buchanan."

"Hello, Ms. Buchanan. This is Debra Schemer. I'm the event coordinator for the Regal Hotel. I'm calling to let you know that your entry 'A Big Boot-iful Texas Christmas' won our gingerbread contest."

Christie wasn't sure she heard right. "Excuse me?"

"Your entry won the grand prize. You won five thousand dollars. And as soon as you can, we'd like you to come to Austin and receive your trophy and check. Ms. Buchanan? Are you there?"

Christie snapped out of her shock. "Yes, ma'am, I'm here. Thank you. Thank you so much. I'll be there as soon as I can." After she hung up, she turned to her three sisters who were all staring at her.

"Well?" Summer said. "Did you win or not?"

Still in a daze, she slowly nodded her head. Summer released a whoop and Autumn and Spring squeals before they all hurried over to hug her. That was all it took for Christie to start crying like a baby. Not because she'd won a silly gingerbread contest, but because she'd been accepted by her sisters.

When they finally drew apart, she searched for a way to thank them for welcoming her with open arms. But before she could find the words, Spring smiled smugly and pointed a finger at Summer. "You don't get to boss us around anymore. You're no longer the oldest."

As it turned out, Summer cared nothing about birth order. "Sorry, but the die has already been cast. Audie, go place those cooled pumpkin pies in the display case. Spring, get back to the sheriff's office, your break is over. And Christie, call my niece and tell her that her mama is the best gingerbread house baker in all of Texas."

Everyone followed her orders with smiles on their faces. When Christie pulled her phone from her purse, she was surprised to find five messages from Cord. She wondered why she hadn't heard her phone ring, and then remembered that she had turned off the sound that morning when Carrie Anne had been playing a noisy game during breakfast. She flipped the side button to turn the volume back on and called Cord. He answered on the first ring. Just the sound of his voice made her heart beat faster.

"Where have you been?" he said. "I've been trying to get ahold of you for the last hour." He sounded extremely worried, and she couldn't help but smile.

"I'm sorry, Mr. Evans, but you need to know that I'm not the type of woman to be at a man's beck and call." She thought her teasing would make him laugh. Instead his voice remained serious.

"I don't want you to get upset, Christie. Carrie

Anne is fine. She's just had a little accident out at the ranch."

Christie's heart had been thumping with joy. Now, it raced with fear. "What kind of accident? Is Carrie Anne hurt?" Summer stopped pouring red velvet cake batter into a pan and turned to her.

"The doctor thinks she broke her arm. We're at the emergency room of the county hospital."

"I'll be right there." As soon as she hung up, Summer walked over to her.

"What happened?"

"Carrie Anne broke her arm. She's at the county hospital."

"I'll drive you." Summer called into the store. "Autumn, lock the front door and put up the closed sign. Carrie Anne had an accident."

The trip to the hospital felt like it took forever. Once there, she didn't even wait for Summer to park before she jumped out and ran into the emergency room entrance. She was going to ask the woman behind the information desk where Carrie Anne was when she saw Cord and Jasper sitting in the waiting room. She hurried over to them.

"How is my baby? And why aren't you with her?"

Cord quickly got to his feet. He looked as upset as she felt. "She's fine. She wanted Danny Ray to stay with her." That didn't sound right. Carrie Anne had gotten closer to Danny Ray, but she still didn't trust him as much as she trusted Cord.

"Where is she?"

"This way." Cord led her through two automatic doors to a room with multiple beds. He pulled back the second curtain to reveal Carrie Anne propped up in bed with her casted arm resting on a pillow.

"Mama!" she yelled as soon as she saw Christie.

Christie hurried over and hugged her close, careful not to touch her arm. She continued to hold her until she'd gotten her tears under control, then she sat down on the edge of the bed and smiled. "Are you okay, Baby Girl?"

"Yeah, Mama. And you know what? Hospitals are fun. They took pictures of my bones with this machine and then the doctor looked at the pictures and showed me where my bone was fracchaired. Then they put this cast on my arm so the bone wouldn't move and covered it in this pretty pink tape. And Cord said I can get all my friends at school to sign it once I go back after holiday break, but I didn't answer him 'cause I'm not talking to Cord. And he also said that it wasn't Maple's fault that she moved and I fell off her. It was his fault 'cause he had hurt my feelings. And he did. He hurt my feelings real bad."

Christie was completely confused. She glanced back to see if Cord was still standing there. When he wasn't, she looked at Danny Ray. "Cord let Carrie Anne ride Maple?"

Danny Ray got up. "That's not how it happened. Carrie Anne decided to go riding all by herself. And before the mama yelling starts, I'm going to go get me a breath of fresh air. Hospitals give me the willies." Surprisingly, he placed a kiss on Carrie Anne's head before he disappeared through the crack in the curtain. When he was gone, Christie turned to her daughter.

"You got on Maple without Cord being there?" Carrie Anne's eyes went wide, and she looked like she was about to burst into tears. That was enough of an answer for Christie. "What were you thinking, Carrie Anne? Why would you do that?"

Her bottom lip trembled. "Because I wanted to prove to Cord that I was better at riding than Ryker. And then maybe he'd love me more than Ryker. And then maybe he'd ask me to come live with him on his ranch instead." A tear dripped down her cheek. "But he's not gonna do that. He doesn't love me and he never will."

Christie took Carrie Anne's hand. "That's not true, honey. Cord does love you. He's shown it time and time again."

Another tear dropped and another. "Then why doesn't he want us? Danny Ray doesn't want us either. He told me he's leaving right after Christmas is over and heading back to Wyoming."

Christie smoothed her daughter's hair out of her eyes. "I'm sorry, Baby Girl. I know you've started to love Danny Ray, but he lives in Wyoming. And just because Danny Ray is leaving that doesn't mean Cord is."

Carrie Anne shook her head. "But he still doesn't want us. He only wants Ryker. I heard him talking to Jasper in the barn about how he was going to invite Ryker to come live with him so that he could teach him fun things like fishing and being a cowboy, and Jasper said what about Christie and Carrie Anne, and Cord said that you could still work for him and I could still come see him, but that we couldn't live with him because Ryker was his family and we were just his friends."

Just friends? While she had been talking to her sisters about possibly being in love with Cord, he had been talking to Jasper about them being just friends? Of course, maybe Carrie Anne had misunderstood. It wouldn't be the first time.

But before she could question her daughter more, the curtain was pulled back and a doctor with a clipboard appeared. For the next few minutes, Christie's mind was focused on the details of her daughter's injury. Then the doctor gave her a prescription for pain medicine, a pamphlet on home care, and instructions to make an appointment for Carrie Anne after Christmas so they could see how her arm was healing. After the doctor left, an orderly arrived with a wheelchair and rolled Carrie Anne out to the waiting room. It was filled to the brim with Hadleys. Not only Summer, Spring, and Autumn, but also Dirk, Gracie, Waylon, Ryker, Maverick, Granny Bon, and Ms. Marble.

Christie was touched. "You didn't have to all come," she said.

"Of course we did." Granny Bon winked at her. "That's what family does."

It was obvious that the triplets had spread the word about her being Holt's daughter, and it looked like no one was upset about it. In fact, everyone circled around Carrie Anne and showered her with attention and concern. It was a scene she had hoped for: her daughter surrounded by a loving family.

The only person missing in the circle was Cord. He stood in the far corner of the waiting room, holding his cowboy hat. When she'd arrived at the hospital, she'd thought the look on his face had been concern. Now she realized that it was more regret.

A lump of foreboding settled in her stomach. Or maybe it wasn't foreboding as much as acceptance of the truth. She didn't need him to confirm Carrie Anne's story. Cord had never promised her more than friendship, and she had always known that Ryker came first with him. It was only her heart that had started believing she'd found the man who would finally put her first.

Foolish heart.

Still, if it was just her heart she had to worry about, she might accept friendship. But it wasn't just her heart. It was her daughter's. And she couldn't let Carrie Anne be hurt any more than she already was.

She walked over to him. They stood there looking at each other for only a moment before he spoke.

"I'm so sorry, Christie." She knew he wasn't only talking about Carrie Anne breaking her arm.

She glanced away. "It's not just your fault. I shouldn't have let things go as far as they did. I should've learned my lesson with Danny Ray."

"Don't say that, Christie. It's not the same thing."

She looked back at him. "Then what is it, Cord?"

He frantically rolled the plastic beads of his hatband between his fingers. "I just need some time to fit all the pieces together."

She clenched her fists to keep from slapping him. "All the pieces? That's what Carrie Anne and I are to you? Just pieces of a puzzle that you can't figure out how to squeeze into the beautiful picture you have of you and Ryker? Sorry, but my daughter and I aren't just misplaced pieces that you need to try to fit into your life. Carrie Anne deserves better than that." She thumped her chest. "I deserve better than that."

Before Cord could answer, Autumn walked up. Her eyes held concern. "Everything okay?"

Christie nodded. "Cord and I were just clearing some things up. But they're perfectly clear now." She looked at him and tried to keep her voice from showing the emotions that squeezed her heart. "Goodbye, Cord."

"No!" He took her arm. "Please don't go like this, Christie. Please let me take you and Carrie Anne home so we can talk this through."

She pulled away before the tears in her eyes could fall. "There's nothing more to say." She glanced back at the Hadleys who were still fussing over Carrie Anne and smiled. "And my family will take us home."

CHAPTER TWENTY-TWO

"ARE YOU SURE RUCKUS IS ready for a rider?" Danny Ray stood on the other side of the corral fence and held onto the horse's bridle. "He don't look ready to me."

Ruckus wasn't ready. His eyes were wild and his ears slicked back as Cord tightened the cinch on the saddle. But Cord needed an outlet for the frustration that had consumed him the last few days and being tossed around on the back of a horse was better than drowning in a bottle of tequila.

Or at least that's what he thought until he settled into the saddle and Ruckus started to raise a ruckus. Cord had forgotten how bone-jarring riding a bucking horse could be, and it took all his concentration to stay on as Ruckus kicked up his heels. When the horse couldn't shake Cord with bucking, he tried to shake him by running. Which was exactly what Cord wanted.

"Open the gate," he called to Danny Ray. Once outside the corral, he gave Ruckus free rein and the horse took flight. As they flew across the pasture, Cord leaned low over the horse's neck and yelled into the cold wind that hit his face. "Give me your worst! I can handle it."

He didn't know if he was yelling at the horse or God. More than likely God.

Cord had worked so hard to get his life on the right track. He hadn't had a drop of alcohol. He hadn't caroused. He'd built a ranch for his son and tried to be the best father he could be. But regardless of all his hard work, his life was still in shambles.

His best friend had moved out—Jasper had gotten a job on Dirk and Gracie's ranch working with Gracie's barrel horses and no doubt chasing after Granny Bon. Ryker still wouldn't call him Dad or spend time with him. And Christie had quit and refused to take his calls.

He'd lost her. He'd known it the moment she turned to him in the waiting room. She'd had the same look Carrie Anne had given him when she'd overheard him talking with Jasper. A look that had ripped his heart right out of his chest. And no matter how fast Ruckus ran, Cord couldn't seem to outrun the pain.

He finally reined the horse in near a familiar corpse of trees. After the hard ride, Ruckus was more manageable and allowed Cord to guide him down the path that led to a wide-open meadow. In the spring, the meadow was filled with bluebonnets. Now there was nothing but brown winter grass surrounding the pristine little white chapel.

The chapel had been built over a hundred years earlier for the mail-order brides and their cowboys to be married in. Recently, all the Arringtons and Hadleys had been wed here, including Ryker to Summer. It was a quaint little church with its tall steeple and pretty stained-glass windows. It looked even quainter with the two holly wreaths hanging on the double doors.

Cord dismounted and led the horse to a nearby pine tree. He wrapped the reins around a lower branch and left him to cool down and graze while he headed to the double doors. Once inside, he took off his hat and moved down the center aisle. A lit Christmas tree filled one corner of the altar and swags of greenery were draped above the windows.

He took a seat in the front pew. During his recovery, he'd done a lot of praying. But he didn't pray now. He didn't know what to pray for. So he just sat there and stared at the large wooden cross hanging on the wall. He didn't know how long he'd been sitting there when the door opened and Ryker rushed in.

"Dad!" He stopped short when Cord turned to him with surprise. "What the hell, Cord? You scared the crap out of me." He pointed a finger at one of the stained-glass windows. "When I saw Ruckus grazing by himself, I thought he'd thrown you and you were lying dead somewhere. I searched the entire area before I thought to look in the church."

Cord wanted to jump up and hug the hell out of Ryker for calling him Dad. Ryker did think of him as his father. And he did care. It showed in his eyes, which still held concern. But rather than force himself on his son like he'd done in the past, Cord kept his seat.

"I'm sorry. I didn't mean to scare you."

Ryker moved down the aisle. "You should be

sorry. You shouldn't ride off without telling people where you're going. And what are you doing riding Ruckus when he's not saddle broke yet? You're not a spring chicken anymore, you know."

Cord's eyebrows popped up. "Thanks for pointing that out."

"That's what kids are supposed to do for their parents." Ryker sat down next to him. "So what are you doing here?"

"I was just thinking."

"About Christie?" When Cord glanced at him, Ryker shrugged. "Summer told me the entire story about you two getting together."

"The entire story?"

"Pretty much." Ryker grinned. "Something you should know about sisters is that they don't keep secrets from each other."

He wasn't surprised that Christie had finally shared her secret. He'd gathered as much at the hospital. "I'm glad the Hadleys welcomed Christie and Carrie Anne into their family."

"They're good people. Unless you're on their shit list, which you are. Summer wants to kick your butt. And Spring and Autumn want Waylon and Dirk to run you out of town on a rail."

"And what does Granny Bon want to do to me?"

"She and Ms. Marble think that you just need to figure things out. In order to do that, they think we need to have a good father-son talk."

Smart women. It was past time that he and Ryker had a talk.

He nodded. "They're right. We do need to talk. I should've told you my plans a long time ago. Deep down, I guess I knew they were pretty crazy." He cleared his throat. "I built the ranch house for you. I was hoping that you and Summer would come live there with me and we could somehow turn back the hands of time—that we could recapture all the moments I missed when you were growing up. But it's been brought to my attention recently that there are no re-dos in life. Some mistakes we make we just have to live with."

He waited for Ryker to either laugh or stare at him with shock. He did neither. He just sat there looking down at his boots before he finally spoke. "You built an entire ranch for me? That *is* pretty crazy." He glanced over and grinned. "You could've just bought me a pony like other dads."

"I did that too—not a pony but a horse. Raise-a-Ruckus is yours."

Ryker's eyebrows lifted. "That ornery horse? Are you trying to kill me?"

Since Cord had just had the ride of his life, he couldn't disagree. "You do have a point. Maybe I better give you Maple instead."

Ryker's smile faded. "You don't have to give me presents to get my love, Cord. You already have it. I know I've been acting a little like a belligerent teenager. I guess I was still holding a grudge and wanted to punish you. But it turns out that I was just punishing myself because I really did need your help fixing my toilet. And I really could use some fishing time to unwind after dealing with a pregnant woman who changes her mind at the drop of a hat. And I'd like to meet for breakfast some time just so I can talk about how scared shitless I am about becoming a father. The best person to do all these things with is a dad." He smiled. "My dad."

Cord had been taught by his father that tears were for women, but he wasn't going to teach his son that. He was going to teach his son that sometimes tears were the only way to express intense pain or overwhelming happiness. So he let his tears fall as he pulled Ryker into his arms. This time, his son hugged him back and held on tight as if he never wanted to let go. They stayed that way for a long time until Cord finally pulled back and grinned.

"Are you sure you don't want to come live with me?"

"I'm sure, but I know a couple people who should." Ryker gave him a knowing look. "You want to talk about it?"

Cord sighed and ran a hand through his hair. "I screwed up again. I opened my big mouth and broke a little girl's heart . . . and her mama's trust. And I'm not sure how to fix it."

"I guess the first question is do you want to fix it?"

"Of course I do. I love Carrie Anne and I love—" He cut off and hesitated for only a second before he accepted the truth. "I love Christie too. I love them both. But it's too late. Jasper was right. God gave me a second chance at being a good husband and father and I blew it."

Ryker shrugged. "Maybe not. They are still right here in Bliss and so are you."

"But they hate me."

"I hated you too, but you won me over. And I'm pretty sure I hated you much more than they do."

Cord rolled his eyes. "Gee, thanks."

Ryker laughed. "All I'm saying is that if you got

me to forgive you, you can get anyone to forgive you. I'd start with Carrie Anne. Christie won't stand a chance against the two of you."

Cord had to admit that was a pretty good idea. "But how will I get Carrie Anne alone to talk with her when Christie has been taking her to the bakery with her every day?"

Ryker thought for only a moment before his eyes lit up. "Tonight is the dress rehearsal for the church Christmas Pageant and they don't want parents to see it before Sunday night so Christie won't be there. I bet you can get Carrie Anne away for a few minutes. Especially when Savannah Arrington is the director."

Cord smiled. "Thanks, son."

Ryker grinned back. "Anytime, Old Man."

It wasn't Daddy, but it was close enough.

Not wanting to run into Christie, Cord waited to arrive at the church until the dress rehearsal had already started. He slipped into the back row and watched as Savannah tried to corral the stage full of kids in nativity costumes. She did a pretty good job. Of course, she had some help from her husband. Raff sat in the front row holding Dax, and whenever the kids got too out of hand, all he had to do was stand up to get them to stop.

Carrie Anne didn't get out of hand. She stood so still and silent on the top riser behind the stable that Cord began to grow concerned. Did she have stage fright? Or did her broken arm hurt? Her arm was in a glittery gold sling that matched her wings and halo, the cast's bright pink tape peeking out from the edge.

Worried that she was scared or in pain, he started to get to his feet. But then it was her turn and she delivered her lines in a clear, booming voice that made Cord proud as hell. The rehearsal continued with only a few hitches. The first wise man dropped his frankincense container and the M&M's he'd stashed inside spilled out and sent the surrounding kids scrambling for a piece of candy. Dax, who was Baby Jesus, didn't like lying in the manger and screamed every time Savannah placed him in it. And the donkey lost his tail, which resulted in Savannah calling for a short break so she could look for it.

Cord got up and made his way through the herd of kids heading to the bathroom or to get a drink. He found Carrie Anne sitting on the risers behind the stable. He climbed up and sat down next to her. She might be dressed like a precious little angel in the white dress and glittery wings, but her expression was as mean as sin.

"I'm mad at you, Cord Evans," she grumbled.

"I know, and you have every right to be. I said some things in the barn that day that weren't very nice. But have you ever said some things you didn't really mean?"

She scrunched up her cute little nose in thought. "Sometimes I get real mad at Mama and say things I don't mean."

Cord nodded. "Well, I was mad at Jasper for pointing out the truth."

The grumpy expression faded slightly. "About Ryker not wanting to live with you?"

Obviously, Carrie Anne had been listening to more of the conversation than Cord had thought. "Yes, and about you and your mama being a gift."

"I'm a gift?"

"You certainly are. You are one of the best gifts I've ever gotten in my life. You're my ray of sunshine. You've brightened my life with your laughter and chatter. And I've missed you something fierce."

She smiled, and it *did* brighten his world. "I've missed you too, Cord. And I've missed the ranch and Maple. But I'm not gonna try to ride her no more 'cause it really hurt and I cried a lot. And if I broke my other arm, I wouldn't be able to open presents on Christmas or eat two donuts at the same time or hug you."

He put an arm around her and pulled her close. "I would sure miss those hugs. And I understand how you feel. When something hurts you, you don't want to do it again. But sometimes you have to get back in the saddle and get over your fear."

"You mean you want me to get back on Maple?"

"Yes, but with the proper equipment and with me right there with you making sure you don't fall. It's time for me to face my fears too."

"What are you scared of?"

"Becoming a husband and a daddy again. I'm scared I won't do a good job."

She stared at him with big, hopeful eyes. "Maybe you could practice on me and Mama."

His heart filled with love for this smart, amazing little angel that God had given him. "That's exactly what I was thinking. Because I love your mama. And I love you. While Danny Ray will always be your daddy, I hope to be your second daddy."

She fell against his chest, her cast pressing into his stomach and her halo bumping against his chin. "I love you too, and if it's okay, I'm gonna call you Daddy because Danny Ray has already said that he wants me to call him Danny Ray." She drew back and smiled up at him. "So yes, Daddy, me and Mama will marry you."

CHAPTER TWENTY-THREE

"I'M SORRY, CHRISTIE, BUT I can't go with you to Austin after all. I have too much baking to do."

Christie looked up from the cupcake tins she was filling. "But I thought we were all caught up on the holiday orders."

Summer busied herself with wiping off the prep counter. "Umm . . . we are. I just need to do some baking for the big family dinner we're having at Waylon and Spring's house on Christmas afternoon."

As disappointed as she was, Christie understood. Not only were all the Hadleys coming to Christmas dinner, but all of the Arringtons were too. That was a lot of people to feed.

"That's okay," she said. "I'll find someone else to drive me." If her car hadn't still been in the shop, she would've driven herself. But the mechanic at the garage had said that her car wouldn't be finished for another week. So she was stuck bumming rides.

After putting the cupcakes in the oven, she

walked into the front of the bakery where Autumn, Maverick, and Carrie Anne were sitting at a table eating donuts. When Maverick saw Christie, he waved her closer.

"Would you stop your sister from tempting me with sweets? I swear she's trying to fatten me up."

Autumn placed a hand on her stomach. "I refuse to be the only one gaining weight. I'm getting as fat as a tick while Spring and Summer don't look like they've gained a pound."

Maverick grinned proudly. "When you're growing the greatest quarterback in the world, you're bound to gain a little extra weight, honey."

"And what makes you so sure our baby is going to be a son?"

"Did I say son? Who says a girl can't be the best quarterback in the world?"

"That's right," Carrie Anne piped up. "When I get in high school, Coach Maverick's gonna let me try out for the team."

Christie shot Maverick an annoyed look, and he held up his hands. "She asked, and I have a hard time telling her no. If I have a daughter, I'm in big trouble."

"Daddies have to tell kids no." Carrie Anne continued to munch on her donut. "It's their job. Cord tells me no all the time."

Just the name got Christie's hackles up. "Cord is not your daddy, Carrie Anne. Danny Ray is."

Carrie Anne shrugged. "I know. I was just saying that Cord acts like a good daddy 'cause he won't let me do things that will get me hurt or eat things that will make me throw up."

Christie studied her daughter suspiciously. Carrie

Anne hadn't had anything good to say about Cord for the last few days, and now suddenly she was thinking of him as a good daddy? Something was up. But before she could interrogate her daughter, Autumn cut in.

"Did you need some help in the kitchen, Christie?"

Christie turned from her daughter. "Actually, I need a favor. I need someone to drive me to Austin to pick up my grand prize check."

"I can do it," Maverick said. "I need to do some Christmas shopping anyway."

Autumn put a hand on his arm. "Sorry, but you can't take Christie to Austin. I need you to help me at the library."

"But I thought Ryker was helping you with the library computer system today. And you know that I'm not good at that techy stuff."

"I need you to help me unload boxes of books."

"But all the books have already—"

Autumn cut him off. "And before we go to the library, could you run to the diner and get me one of Carly's blueberry shakes? I'm having a craving for blueberries."

Maverick looked down at the half-eaten blueberry donut on his wife's plate with confusion before he leaned over and gave her a kiss. "Okay, honey, I'll get you whatever you want." He got up and glanced at Carrie Anne. "You coming, Squirt?"

Carrie Anne quickly jumped to her feet. "Beat you there!" She raced out of the bakery, and Maverick had to hustle to catch up with her. When they were gone, Christie turned to Autumn.

"Okay, what's going on? Why doesn't anyone

want to take me to Austin?"

Autumn looked like a deer caught in the headlights. Just as she started to answer, the door opened and Ms. Marble and Granny Bon stepped in. They resembled Christmas elves. Ms. Marble wore a red knit cap and coat and Granny Bon wore green ones.

"Good mornin'," Granny Bon said. "Summer just called and said you needed a ride to Austin, Christie. Maybelline and I would be more than happy to drive you. We want to see all the gingerbread houses."

The drive to Austin was hair-raising. Granny Bon drove like an Indie racecar driver. Christie sat in the back and kept checking her seatbelt as she listened to Granny Bon and Ms. Marble talk about why people hated fruitcake, how much they were looking forward to the Tender Heart final book release in January, and how wonderful the church Christmas pageant had been this year.

"Dax was the perfect baby Jesus," Granny Bon said. "I'm sure Jesus wasn't too happy about being placed in itchy hay either."

"It was a good thing that the Angel of the Lord's voice had plenty of volume so it could be heard over Dax's screaming," Ms. Marble said.

A little bit too much volume. Carrie Anne's booming voice had not only scared baby Jesus into silence, but it had also made the baby lambs start to cry. Still, Christie agreed that Carrie Anne had done a great job.

"I was very proud of her," she said.

Granny Bon zipped around a semi truck. "As was the entire family. Of course, we weren't the only ones proud." She glanced in the rearview mirror at Christie. "Did you happen to notice Cord Evans sitting in the back row?"

Christie kept her face expressionless. "No. I didn't notice him." It was an out-and-out lie. As soon as Cord had stepped into the church, her heart had felt like it was being squeezed in a cookie press. It had taken a strong will to keep her gaze on the stage.

"Well, I noticed him," Ms. Marble said. "And he couldn't have looked prouder when Carrie Anne said her lines. It's quite obvious how much he loves your daughter."

Christie knew he loved Carrie Anne, but it wasn't enough. Carrie Anne deserved a daddy who wasn't struggling with his own demons. And Cord was still struggling with his. As much as that truth hurt, she had accepted the fact that she and Cord weren't going to live happily ever after.

"Sometimes love isn't enough," she said.

Ms. Marble and Granny Bon glanced at each other, but neither said a word.

When they reached the hotel, Granny Bon parked in the underground parking garage and they took the elevator up to the main floor. Before they reached their floor, Ms. Marble took Christie's hand and pinned her with her piercing eyes.

"You're wrong, Christie. Love is always enough. And with love comes forgiveness. Remember that."

Before Christie could think of a reply to that, the elevator doors opened.

Her gingerbread house had been moved from the original spot to a table in the center of the ballroom with the three runners-up. A huge blue ribbon had been attached to the top corner of the boot. The sight made Christie's bruised ego feel a little better. While Ms. Marble and Granny Bon went to look at her house, she asked one of the hotel staff where she could find Ms. Schemer.

The young teenager made a call on his radio and Ms. Schemer arrived only moments later with a huge check. With Granny Bon, Ms. Marble, and a group of onlookers watching, Christie stood in front of her gingerbread boot as Ms. Schemer formally presented her with the check and another hotel staffer snapped pictures. When they were finished, Ms. Schemer congratulated her again.

"You won hands down," she said. "You captured the spirit of Texas and the warm coziness of the holidays in gingerbread. And the cute little family epitomizes—" She cut off when she glanced down at the house. "What in the world happened to your gingerbread man?"

Christie followed her gaze. The cowboy gingerbread man was no longer standing by the corral and horses. Someone had eaten off his legs and stuck him in a wad of chewing gum in front of the gingerbread woman.

Ms. Schemer was as shocked as Christie. "Who would do something like this? And where did that ring come from?"

Christie had been so appalled to see her precious gingerbread man defiled that she hadn't even noticed the ring hanging on his arm where a licorice lasso had once been. She removed the ring and studied it. She wasn't an expert on diamonds, but the three stones that sparkled in the lights of the ballroom looked real. But who would leave a real diamond engagement on her gingerbread—? Before her mind could even finish the thought, her heart began to race.

Clutching the ring in her hand, she glanced around the ballroom until her gaze landed on a cowboy sitting in the far corner with his hat pulled low. She recognized the hatband. She recognized the shirt. And she recognized the broad shoulders that filled out that shirt.

"Cord," the name came out on a whispered breath of disbelief . . . and hope.

As if he had heard her clear across the room, he rolled to his feet and walked toward her. With each step, she tried to steel herself. She tried to remind herself of all the reasons why she shouldn't let this man back into her life. But when he was standing right in front of her, with his soft brown eyes looking right through her, all those reasons didn't seem to matter.

"Hey," he said in a voice that caused her tummy to flutter with a thousand butterflies.

She tried to answer, but she couldn't get a word out.

"I take full responsibility for what happened to your gingerbread house, Ms. Buchanan," Ms. Schemer said. "And I promise we'll find the culprit once I get a chance to look at the surveillance videos."

"Let's not worry about the culprit," Granny Bon said. "I think my granddaughter will be quite happy with how things turn out." She took Ms. Schemer's arm. "Now why don't you show me and Ms. Marble some of your favorite gingerbread houses? She is quite the baker herself, you know."

After Ms. Marble and Granny Bon led a confused Ms. Schemer away, the other onlookers dispersed, leaving Christie and Cord standing there staring at one another. Cord was the first one to find his voice.

"I'm sorry. I'm sorry I was too stupid to realize what I had until I lost it."

She swallowed her emotion. "That seems to be a reoccurring problem of yours."

He nodded. "You're right, but it's one I'm trying to fix."

"By breaking my gingerbread man and placing a diamond ring on his arm? Are you crazy? Someone could've stolen it."

"That did cross my mind, but you don't worry about those things when you're trying to win a woman's heart." He looked at the gingerbread man. "Although now that I look closer, it was a pretty pathetic attempt at romance."

The winning her heart part pretty much dissolved the last of her anger. She glanced at her kneeling gingerbread man, then back at Cord. "I don't know about that."

His eyes lit up. "Are you saying you accept?"

"What happened to you being scared of marriage?"

"I'm still scared. I'm terrified of screwing things up. But I'm more terrified of losing you and Carrie Anne." He swallowed hard. "I've made a lot of mistakes in my life. And I figure I'll make a lot more before it's over. I'm stubborn and bullheaded and a damned slow learner. But once I learn something, I learn it well. What I've learned in the last few days, is that I love you, Christmas Day Buchanan.

And I love Carrie Anne. I don't want to live without either one of you."

Her heart melted at his words, but she couldn't give in that easily. This wasn't just about her. It was about her daughter. And she wasn't going to let Carrie Anne get hurt again.

"What about Ryker? I can't marry a man who is consumed with his son and fixing his past mistakes. I want a man who can forgive himself and live in the present moment. I want a man who not only loves his son, but also has room in his heart for me and my daughter. And if you can't be that man, then you're not the man for me."

He took off his cowboy hat and held it over his chest. "I'm that man, Christie. You and Carrie Anne are already in my heart. Ryker is my son and I want a relationship with him. But I've realized that he doesn't have to live with me for us to have that relationship. Which works out good because it looks like my house is going to be crowded enough for the holidays."

"No one said I was going to move in with you for the holidays, Cord Evans." She held up the engagement ring. "This is a beautiful ring, but I won't be moving in without a wedding band on my finger. I made that mistake once, I won't do it again."

She realized she had just accepted his proposal when he let out a whoop and lifted her off her feet and swung her around.

After she was dizzy and giggling, he stopped spinning and smiled down at her with twinkling eyes. "Then I guess we better plan our marriage soon because I have a dream of my entire family gathered around a gi-normous tree on Christmas morning." He hugged her close, and she melted into the strength and love of his embrace.

Over his arm, she could see her gingerbread boot, the butterscotch windows glowing warmly. The gingerbread girl was happily petting the horses in the corral and the little gingerbread boy was playing in the yard. And the gingerbread man was kneeling and promising to love his gingerbread family forever.

Christie heart overflowed as she drew back to accept that love. "Let's get married, Cord Evans, so we can have a Big Boot-iful Texas Christmas."

CHAPTER TWENTY-FOUR

"YOU LOOK JUST LIKE A fairy princess, Mama," Carrie Anne said.

Christie smiled at her daughter before she looked back in the full-length mirror. The wedding gown Summer had insisted on buying her did look like a princess's dress. The bodice was strapless and fitted and the skirt was full with numerous petticoats beneath. The only thing that didn't look like a princess's were the red cowboy boots she wore. But she loved the handmade boots with hers and Cord's initials engraved in the leather more than any glass slippers. Cord had given them to her as an early birthday present.

"I figure a woman named Christmas should own a pair of red boots," he'd said. "Happy birthday, my love." The fact that he'd remembered her birthday in all the excitement of the holidays and planning a Christmas Eve wedding had made her cry. Even now, her eyes misted at the thought of the kind, considerate man she was about to wed.

"Don't you dare start crying, Christie," Summer said. "I refuse to walk down the aisle with a bunch of blubbering sisters." But even as she said the words, she pulled a tissue from the box on the table next to her and blotted her eyes. "Damn pregnancy."

"Auntie Summer said damn, Mama. And you said that damn was a cuss word and people shouldn't say it." Carrie Anne spun around in a circle, causing the full skirt of her own princess-style dress to bell out. Beneath she wore the purple cowboy boots Danny Ray had given her. Although Christie knew who the boots were really from.

"You are exactly right, Sweet Pea," Autumn said as she smoothed out a curl in Christie's hair. "Summer has no business cussing. Especially in a church."

Christie expected Summer to argue the point, but instead she winked at Carrie Anne. "That's my girl. You keep your Auntie Summer in line." It seemed that Carrie Anne was the only one who could keep Summer in line. The two had formed quite a bond. Probably because they were two peas in a pod. Of course, Carrie Anne had formed a bond with all the Hadleys and was thrilled when she found out that they were her relatives. And they weren't her only new relatives.

Carrie Anne stopped spinning. "Uncle Jasper made me a swear jar for the ranch. And every time somebody cusses they have to put a dollar in the jar for my college education. But I don't make Danny Ray put in as many dollars as he should 'cause he'd be flat broke if he did."

Danny Ray still wasn't the best daddy in the world, but he *had* become a better daddy. He'd stopped by the trailer the other night to give Christie all the money he'd made working for Cord the last few weeks. He was planning on leaving once the holidays were over, but he claimed that he would call and come back to see Carrie Anne often. He also wanted Christie to send him videos and pictures of their daughter. "She's a chip off the old block," he'd said with a proud smile on his face. Christie now believed that Cord was right. Sometimes you just needed to look for the best in people to find it.

"Speaking of Uncle Jasper," Spring said. "I think there's something going on between him and Granny Bon."

Christie knew for a fact that there was something going on between Jasper and Granny Bon. She had caught them passionately kissing in Cord's kitchen the other morning, and she wouldn't be too surprised if the Hadley family didn't have another wedding in the New Year.

But right now it was her turn.

Autumn finished fixing her hair and stepped up next to her, smiling at her in the reflection of the mirror. "You look perfect. Are you ready to get married to the man of your dreams?"

Cord *was* the man of her dreams. Christie had always dreamed about marrying a man who was a great rodeo cowboy. But she had learned that it was better to marry a rodeo cowboy who was a great man.

She smiled back at her sister in the mirror. "I'm ready, but first I wanted to thank you for befriending me when I first came to Bliss." She glanced at Summer. "For giving me a job that I love." She turned her smile on Spring. "And for giving me and Carrie Anne a place to live. I don't know what

I would've done without y'all."

Summer and Spring got up and joined her and Autumn at the mirror. "We're glad you came looking for us," Spring said.

"Amen." Summer slung an arm around her sisters and tugged them close.

As Christie looked at their reflections, she had to agree. She was glad she'd come looking for her family. And she had found them. She had found a bigger, more loving family than she'd ever thought possible. She couldn't help wondering if her mama hadn't worked a little heavenly magic to make sure her daughter and granddaughter would be well loved and taken care of. And Mama wasn't the only one who had helped her find bliss.

"Holt could've kept his family a secret from me," she said. "He didn't have to tell me about his other children, but for some reason he did. Maybe he named you after the other seasons on purpose. Maybe he hoped that one day all his children would be together and live happily ever after."

Summer started to say something, but Spring cut her off. "You could be right, Christie. But it doesn't matter how we came together. Just that we did."

They smiled at each other as someone knocked on the door.

"Come on in," Summer called.

Dirk peeked his head in. He had volunteered to walk Christie down the aisle, and she expected him to say it was time. Instead, he said something else entirely. "We seem to have lost the groom."

All of Christie's happiness drained right out of her. "Cord is gone?" Before he could answer, Carrie Anne piped up.

"He's not gone. He's standing right outside."

Christie hurried to the window where her daughter was standing and looked out. Sure enough, there was a silhouette of a tall cowboy standing in the meadow in front of the chapel.

"I'll go get him," Dirk said, but Christie shook her head.

"I will."

"But the groom isn't supposed to see the bride before the wedding," Spring said. "It's bad luck."

Bad luck would be if Cord had changed his mind, and if that were the case, Christie wanted to be the first to know. She headed for the door. Once outside, she wished she had brought a coat. It was freezing, and she shivered as she picked up the hem of her dress and walked down the path toward Cord. Right before she reached him, he turned.

"Christie? What are you doing out here?"

"I was going to ask you the same question." She stopped in front of him. "Have you gotten cold feet? Because I'm going to tell you right now, Cord Evans, if you leave me at the altar, there will be no place you can hide from my wrath."

His eyes widened for a fraction of a second before he tipped back his head and laughed. "You'll hunt me down, will you?"

"You better believe it."

His gaze ran over her. "Damn, you are beautiful. A man would have to be plumb crazy to leave a woman like you at the altar. And I'm not crazy."

Relief flooded her, and she released her breath. "Then what are you doing out here?"

"I just needed a moment alone to thank the

good Lord for giving me a second chance."

Tears filled her eyes, and she took his hands in hers. "Mind if I say a prayer of thanks with you? The Lord gave me a second chance too."

"Your hands are like ice. Come here." He turned her and pulled her back into his arms so they were both facing the little white chapel. It had no Christmas lights, but it didn't need any. The multi-colored stained-glass windows glowed like a cluster of lights, and directly above the white spire a bright star twinkled in the night sky.

"The Christmas star," Cord whispered close to her ear.

They stood there looking at the star and counting their blessings for a few moments before the chapel doors opened and Carrie Anne came racing out, her blond ringlets and red ribbons flying. She halted in front of Cord and Christie.

"Hey, what's goin' on? You're still gonna marry us, ain't you, Daddy?"

Cord released Christie and scooped Carrie Anne into his arms. "Yes, ma'am. I sure am, Half Pint." He slipped an arm around Christie's shoulders and smiled. "Now let's go get our second chance."

As they headed into the little white chapel, Carrie Anne glanced over at Christie and grinned. "I told you that catching that bouquet would work, Mama."

It was a glorious Christmas Day. One of the most glorious days Maybelline Marble had ever witnessed. And it had nothing to do with the bright, shining sun outside the window. It had to do with the bright, shining faces inside the house.

Spring and Waylon's rambling house was filled to bursting with Hadleys and Arringtons who had arrived in the late afternoon to celebrate the Lord's birth with their family.

Cute toddlers who carried the name of their great-great aunt and great-great grandmother sat on the floor beneath the huge glittering Christmas tree amid a pile of wrapping paper and toys. As in the way of children, Lucy, Lucinda, Luella, and Luana seemed more interested in the bright bows and crinkly paper than the expensive toys. Which had Cole, Emery, Dirk, and Gracie laughing as the couples watched their children with love and pride in their eyes.

And speaking of love and pride, Raff and Zane were as loving and proud as two daddies could be. They sat on opposite couches with one arm tucked around their sleeping sons and the other tucked around their beautiful wives. Carly glanced over at Savannah and the two friends exchanged a look of contentment before they went back to admiring their babies and husbands.

In the New Year, there were going to be more babies. Not only were the Hadley triplets pregnant, but Becky Arrington-Granger had announced only moments before that she and Mason were expecting. That brought the total up to four, and Maybelline wondered if there wouldn't be more. She glanced over at Cord and Christie who were cuddled up in a big chair by the fire whispering sweet nothings to each other. It would certainly be nice if Carrie Anne got a little brother or sister.

Carrie Anne was standing in the middle of her three aunts, regaling them with the story of how she had gotten to ride Maple that morning with Cord and how she was "gonna play football and ride wild broncos in the rodeo." Spring and Autumn looked concerned. Summer just looked proud.

"Those two are peas in a pod." Bonnie walked up with a present in one hand and a cup of tea in the other. She held out the cup of tea. "Peppermint, no sugar."

"Thank you, Bonnie." Maybelline took the cup before she glanced around. "Where's Jasper?" Jasper had been following Bonnie around like an adoring puppy, which fit perfectly with Maybelline's plans.

Bonnie took the chair next to her. "He fell asleep on the porch swing so I left him to nap."

"I hope after you got in a few kisses."

Bonnie blushed. "Maybe a few. But don't get any ideas about another wedding in that little white chapel. Jasper and I enjoy each other's company, but I'm not in any hurry to tie the knot. Although dating has made me realize that I need a place of my own. I was thinking about renting that room over your garage once Autumn and Maverick move into the new house they bought. That's if you wouldn't mind living with a stubborn old woman who's set in her ways."

Maybelline smiled. "You coming to live with me would be the best New Year's present I could ask for."

"Then it's a deal." Bonnie held out the beautifully wrapped present. "And here's your Christmas present."

Maybelline took the gift. "You're spoiling me, Bonnie. You already knitted me that beautiful red scarf."

"This isn't exactly from me."

Curious, Maybelline set down her teacup and carefully unwrapped the book. Her eyes filled with tears when she saw the cover. "The final Tender Heart novel."

Bonnie nodded with a poignant smile. "The publishers sent me advance copies. I plan to give one to all my grandkids, nieces, and nephews, but I thought you should get the first being that you were my mama's closest friend."

It was an honor, and Maybelline couldn't help running her fingers over Lucy's name on the cover. "She would be so proud."

"Yes. It certainly is a great ending to her series and the perfect happily-ever-after for her fans."

Maybelline glanced up in surprise. "Oh, I wasn't talking about the book. Lucy didn't write her books for her fans. She wrote them to get over the loss of her child." She smiled. "You. She would be proud of the woman you've become and the wonderful family you raised. Her books were about her heritage." She looked around the room, her aged eyes taking in the beloved people who filled it. "This is about her legacy. While books fade from people's minds, this love will live on long after she's gone. Lucy knew this. Which is exactly why she ended the book the way she did."

Maybelline didn't need to open the novel to recite the last lines. The last words Lucy had ever written were engraved in her heart.

"This is not the end of Tender Heart. It's only the beginning."

~ THE BEGINNING ~

DO YOU WANT TO KNOW HOW **TENDER HEART TEXAS** AND THE **BRIDES OF BLISS TEXAS** ALL STARTED?

Here's a sneak peek of the very first book,

FALLING FOR TENDER HEART,

and for a limited time you can get it absolutely **FREE** at

www.katielanebooks.com/tender-heart

"EXCUSE ME, MA'AM."

Emery Wakefield looked up from the book she was reading—more like rereading for the hundredth time—and was disappointed that the man speaking wasn't a handsome cowboy with a sexy smile. He was just the businessman sitting next to her on the plane.

He was nice-looking, but not nearly as nice-looking as Rory Earhart. Although few men could compare to her favorite fictional hero—the key word being *fictional*.

Emery had a wee bit of a problem keeping fiction separate from reality. As an editor and avid reader, she loved to get lost in the fantasy worlds of her characters, which sometimes caused her to lose sight of her own life. Her two older brothers teased her about having her head in the clouds. And her close friends Carly and Savannah were always reminding her to live in the real world. In the real world, there were no perfect heroes. Just regular guys like this businessman who had ignored her the entire trip to play video games on his phone. But if she ever wanted to be in a relationship again, she needed to lower her standards and make an effort.

She smiled. "Yes?"

He nodded at the aisle. "The plane's landed."

She finally noticed that people were out of their seats and collecting their luggage from the overhead compartments. "Oh! I didn't even realize." She pulled her laptop bag from beneath the seat in front of her and placed the tattered paperback in the side pocket.

"So you like those naughty romance novels?" When she glanced over, the businessman winked.

Emery felt her spine stiffen, but she quickly reminded herself that few men understood romance—books or otherwise. Romance to them was all about the sex. It wasn't about the first prolonged glance. The first heated touch. The first breathless kiss.

She blinked. *Reality, Emery, reality.*

"Yes," she said. "I like those 'naughty' romances. What genre do you read?"

"I don't do a lot of reading. I usually just wait for the movie."

Okay, she was willing to lower her standards, but not that much.

Since the conversation was pretty much dead, she busied herself by straightening the pages of the manuscript she'd been reading earlier. While most of the other editors at Randall Publishing did their reading and editing electronically, Emery preferred to have a hard copy. There was something about holding the pages in her hands that made the reading experience so much better. Although it hadn't made this particular manuscript any better.

After talking to the writer's agent and reading the first few chapters, she'd had high hopes for this book. The author had a fresh voice and a great ear for dialogue. Unfortunately, the entire plot had crumbled midway through, and there was little hope of salvaging it. Which meant that this wasn't the book that was going to give Emery job security and make her boss overlook the other books that had flopped. But hopefully, she had the key to the one novel that would. She looked at the zippered pocket where she'd carefully tucked the envelope she had received a month ago.

She was a firm believer in fate, and there was no other explanation for her having received the envelope. When she'd first opened it, she felt like Harry Potter getting his invitation to Hogwarts. And even if her boss was convinced it was a hoax, there was no way Emery could ignore it. That would be like ignoring destiny.

The Tender Heart novels were her favorite books of all time. The ten-book series about mail-order brides in the old West had gotten her through her horrific puberty years. The pimples and braces wouldn't have been so bad if she'd been a genius like her brothers and could've fit in with the geeks. But she wasn't a genius. She was horrible at math, couldn't have cared less about science, and hadn't gotten through one *Star Wars* movie without falling asleep. In school she'd been labeled the homely, weird girl who walked around with her nose in a book.

It was in those books that she'd found refuge from school bullies and the fact that she didn't fit in with the rest of her family of geniuses. And she was still struggling to fit in. She had yet to find her place in New York City and was only months away from losing her job.

Unless what was in the envelope turned out to be authentic.

"So what brings you to Austin?" The businessman pulled his briefcase out from under the seat.

She got to her feet. "I'm meeting my two best friends for spring break." It wasn't a lie. She had roped her two unsuspecting friends into joining her on this trip. They thought they were checking out the setting of their favorite series. They knew nothing about the letter Emery had received . . . or the chapter.

Something about her reply made the businessman's eyes light up. Probably the prospect of spring break with three naughty romance readers who were only interested in sex. "Really? I live here so I'd be happy to show you and your friends around if you'd like. Austin is an exciting town."

"I'm sure it is, but we're not staying in Austin. We're staying in Bliss."

He looked confused. "Bliss? Why would you want to go there? It's practically a ghost town."

She glanced at her laptop case, and a smile bloomed on her face. "In a way, that's exactly what I'm looking for. Ghosts." She didn't wait for him to ask any more questions before she moved into the aisle.

Since Carly and Savannah's flights didn't get in until much later, Emery planned to meet them in Bliss. Excited to get to the small town, she wasted no time picking up her luggage and renting a car. The entire drive from Austin, she couldn't help feeling like she was on the Hogwarts Express headed to a place that had only existed in her dreams.

Unfortunately, that excitement fizzled when she drove into Bliss and reality hit. She knew a modern town wasn't going to be like an old western town—especially a fictional western town—but she had expected to find something that reminded her of Tender Heart. A quaint knick-knack shop that sold souvenirs. A bookstore with the entire series displayed in the window. The 1950s diner where the author Lucy Arrington had plotted her famous stories. The pretty little chapel where all the mail-order brides had found their happily-ever-afters.

Instead, the two-lane highway Emery drove into town on was lined with vacant brick buildings that had fading signs and cracked windows. Rusty grain silos stood like aged sentinels, and weeds filled every empty lot.

The businessman had been right. It did look like a ghost town.

There were few cars on the road. So when a muddy pickup truck passed her going the opposite direction, Emery couldn't help but stare. The old guy behind the wheel stared back with a suspicious look. Or maybe it was her clean Hyundai that he found suspicious. The few vehicles parked along the street looked as dirty as his truck. It was hard not to feel disappointed. She had arrived at Cinderella's castle to find a hovel nothing like her fantasies.

She glanced at her laptop bag on the front seat next to her. The town might not look like what she expected, but there was still hope that her fantasies would be realized—if not in the town, then on paper.

Pushing her disappointment down, Emery searched for the Bliss Motor Lodge where she'd made reservations. It was the only place to stay in town, and she hoped she hadn't booked the Bates Motel. If she walked into the lobby and spotted a bunch of stuffed birds, she was out of there.

Since Main Street was only a couple of blocks long, she easily found the motor lodge. But before she pulled in, she couldn't help driving a little further to see if she could find a little white chapel with beautiful stained-glass windows. She didn't, but what she did find was a gas station that wasn't boarded up. In fact, two men sat at a table in front. And she couldn't help pulling in to see if she could get some information.

The old guy with the balding head looked at her just as suspiciously as the man who had driven past her on the street. She couldn't tell how the other man looked. He wore a brown felt cowboy hat that was tugged low on his forehead and shaded his face. But the hat turned in her direction when she got out.

Since she couldn't just start asking questions without adding to their suspicions, she decided to get gas. The pump didn't have a credit card slot, so she topped off her tank, then leaned into the car to get her purse from the front seat. That's when she heard one of the men speak.

"You gonna gawk? Or are you gonna play?"

She straightened and peeked around the pump in time to see the cowboy hat turn away. She had assumed he was the same age as the old guy. But on closer examination, she realized her mistake. The hard chest and broad shoulders that filled out the western shirt belonged to a much younger man. As did the dark hair curling on the back of his strong, corded neck.

She watched the muscles in that neck tighten as the old guy continued, "I thought you just got finished telling me that you didn't have time for women."

"Would you keep it down, Emmett?" the cowboy hissed as he picked up a domino. His hands were big, but agile enough to manipulate the small white tile into place on the table. Something about those long fingers made Emery's heart skip and her stomach feel all light and airy. The empty stomach she could blame on being hungry. She'd only had a bagel at the airport and a Cranapple and peanuts on the plane. The skipping heart was a little harder to explain.

"Now that was stupid." Emmett positioned a domino on the table, then picked up the pencil next to the notepad to put down his score. "Almost as stupid as wasting your time gawking at a woman who's just passing through. That's a rental car if ever I saw one, and no woman from around here wears heels that high unless it's Easter Sunday." He glanced over at Emery and noticed her watching. He smiled, revealing a chipped front tooth. "Howdy, ma'am."

Emery stepped around the gas pump, and both men stood up from their chairs. But it was the cowboy she couldn't look away from. If she'd thought his body was nice sitting down, it was nothing compared to how he looked fully stretched out. He had to be well over six feet tall with long, muscled legs that were emphasized by the fit of his well-worn blue jeans.

And his legs weren't the only things they emphasized.

Her gaze zeroed in on the bulge beneath the zipper. Not a small bulge, but a long, hard one. Before she could blink, his cowboy hat blocked her view. She lifted her gaze. Everything inside Emery went very still as reality collided with fantasy.

She had been searching for some sign of Tender Heart. Some small piece of the series she loved so dearly. And she'd finally found it. From the lock of raven black hair that curled over his forehead to the intense eyes as blue as a Texas sky at twilight, the man standing in front of her looked exactly like her favorite book boyfriend.

Her hero Rory Earhart had come to life.

DEAR READER,

Thank you so much for reading *Christmas Texas Bride*. I hope you enjoyed Cord and Christie's love story. If you did, please help other readers find this book by telling a friend or writing a review. Your support is greatly appreciated.

Love,

Katie

Be sure to check out all the books in Katie Lane's

The Brides of Bliss Texas

series!

Spring Texas Bride
Summer Texas Bride
Autumn Texas Bride
Coming soon…
Christmas Texas Bride

OTHER SERIES BY KATIE LANE

Tender Heart Texas:

Falling for Tender Heart
Falling Head Over Boots
Falling for a Texas Hellion
Falling for a Cowboy's Smile
Falling for a Christmas Cowboy

Deep in the Heart of Texas:

Going Cowboy Crazy
Make Mine a Bad Boy
Catch Me a Cowboy
Trouble in Texas
Flirting with Texas
A Match Made in Texas
The Last Cowboy in Texas
My Big Fat Texas Wedding (novella)

Overnight Billionaires:

A Billionaire Between the Sheets
A Billionaire After Dark
Waking up with a Billionaire

Hunk for the Holidays:

Hunk for the Holidays
Ring in the Holidays
Unwrapped

Anthologies:

Small Town Christmas (Jill Shalvis, Hope Ramsay, Katie Lane)
All I Want for Christmas is a Cowboy (Jennifer Ryan, Emma Cane, Katie Lane)

About the Author

Katie Lane is a USA Today Bestselling author of the *Deep in the Heart of Texas*, *Hunk for the Holidays*, *Overnight Billionaires*, *Tender Heart Texas*, and *The Brides of Bliss Texas* series. She lives in Albuquerque, New Mexico, with her cute cairn terrier Roo and her even cuter husband Jimmy.

For more on her writing life or just to chat, check out Katie here:

Facebook www.facebook.com/katielaneauthor
Instagram www.instagram.com/katielanebooks

And for information on upcoming releases and great giveaways, be sure to sign up for her mailing list at www.katielanebooks.com!

Made in United States
Troutdale, OR
09/15/2024

22825278R00153